Bound by Honor

Mafia's Children, Volume 2

Amara Holt

Published by Amara Holt, 2024.

Copyright © 2024 by Amara Holt

All rights reserved.

No part of this book may be reproduced, distributed, or transmitted in any form or by any means, including photocopying, recording, or other electronic or mechanical methods, without the prior written permission of the author, except in the case of brief quotations in book reviews.

This is a work of fiction. Names, characters, places, and incidents are the product of the author's imagination or are used fictitiously. Any resemblance to actual events, organizations, locales, or persons, living or dead is coincidental and is not intended by the authors.

PROLOGUE

Cinzia

Pietra was taking a long time, so I took off my sandal, sitting on the edge of the pool, gently kicking the water with my feet that emerged from the water.

It was summer in Sicily, the weather was mild, sometimes a bit stuffy, but nothing that the sea breeze from nearby couldn't fix, bringing a bit of the freshness it emanated.

I let out a long sigh, lifting my eyes to see the two brothers in the distance. They were coming from the back of the house, passing over the rocks that separated the beach house from the house at a long distance. I remembered that Mrs. Verena was always scolding the twins for always coming through there, as it was dangerous, but it was useless to tell those two blockheads anything.

My friend's brothers were fourteen years old, considered the future of *Cosa Nostra*. What worried me was what that future would be, since everyone knew their nickname was the Terror Twins, all because their father gave them a knife for their first birthday, and they killed their sister's pet together, concluding that they couldn't have anything else, as nothing survived the Terror Twins.

The two were pushing each other, laughing about something they were saying to each other. Valentino and Santino were identical, not even their personalities set them apart; they were mocking, always thinking they owned the world, but who judged them? Their father had emphasized this to them since they came into the world.

I saw one of them approaching me.

"A week lying to mom to manage this," the brother who stayed behind declared as the other came in my direction.

I raised my eyes trying to figure out which one was there, but it was almost in vain; they had nothing physically to differentiate them, except when they spoke long sentences. Santino spoke faster, Valentino had pauses when he spoke, as if he was thinking about what to say, unlike Santino, who tended to be impulsive.

Until he started speaking or told me his name, I wouldn't know which twin it was, and even then, I would have a small doubt, as those two had a terrible habit of switching places, just to confuse people, like two little devils who loved to cause trouble.

Maybe they were...

"Cinzia," his white teeth appeared with the smile he gave, kneeling beside me, "what are you doing here?"

I lowered my eyes, analyzing his combat boots, the worn jeans, ripped at the knee, a cut visible on his knee, showing clearly that he fell on the rocks or just scraped his knee.

"What do I always do here? Seeing you is not one of them." I rolled my eyes, turning my gaze back to his face, noticing his smile growing wider. It was a big waste of time being sarcastic with a Vacchiano, as they had a tendency to be ten times worse.

"My presence is almost as good as Pietra's." He shrugged. "Actually, she's annoying and spoiled."

"It's a good thing you said 'almost,' because you will never be better than her. Pietra is my friend; you're just her annoying brother," I said, noticing that the smile didn't leave his lips.

"The annoying brother you're in love with..."

"But you're so full of yourself. I don't even know who you are; how can I fall for someone I can't distinguish?" I turned my attention back to the pool.

"You're in love with the appearance, the stereotype of a Vacchiano, for representing the high status of *Cosa Nostra*."

"Did you have your dose of arrogance today? Because your self-esteem could resurrect a corpse with how high it is." I turned my face back to look into the green eyes of the arrogant Italian.

"Every morning on an empty stomach, you should try it." The twin continued with the sarcasm.

"No, thanks." I made a move to get up, but his hand held me on the shoulder, stopping me. "Let go, I'm going inside to find out why Pietra is taking so long..."

"She must be sleeping; she needs to recharge her energy to play the daddy's little princess, when we all know that girl is all wrong." He mocked his sister again.

"Maybe that's a Vacchiano curse, all wrong." I rolled my eyes, wanting to get out of there.

The twin didn't let me leave, holding firmly onto my shoulder, preventing me from standing up. *What the hell did he want?*

"I made a bet with Valen." He spoke again.

I hated their bets. *Oh, what a family to live off bets...*

"As far as I remember, your mother forbade you from doing that." I squinted my eyes, knowing that the one there was Santino, since he mentioned Valentino in the second person.

"There are so many things Verena forbade that I don't remember most of them." He shrugged, unconcerned.

"Maybe if you started obeying, there would be fewer of them."

"I hate following rules." I turned my face to see the hand holding my shoulder. "I want to kiss you, Cinzia..."

"Are you crazy?" I cut him off, widening my eyes, wanting to get up, managing to do so, but seeing him stand up as well.

We were only a few months apart in age, but he was older; Santino was already fourteen, and I was still thirteen, and he was much taller than me. Maybe he would end up being as tall as his father, unlike me, who couldn't see myself growing much taller, given my short mother.

"Come on, just one kiss. I know you've never kissed anyone, so I'm doing you a favor, and in return, you help me win the bet with Valentino..."

"I'm not desperate to give my first kiss, especially not to someone as arrogant as you." I shook my head.

I turned my body, about to head towards the house's door, but his hand grabbed my wrist, pulling me closer to him, making me hold onto his shirt, his hands holding my face. My eyes widened as I realized he was going to kiss me without my consent; it was so typical of Santino, if he couldn't get what he wanted, he would take it his way.

"If you dare..." My sentence died out, actually, my mouth was muffled by his, pressed against mine.

His lips weren't aggressive, fitting against mine. This was definitely not in my plans, kissing a Vacchiano. They were the epitome of everything I hated most, extremely handsome but arrogant.

I didn't move, didn't even hold onto him, his tongue touching mine, which I didn't move, not knowing what to do. And even though it was a kiss against my will, it was harmless; Santino didn't force it, he was gentle, or maybe it was madness.

His face pulled away from mine, his scent still lingering in my nose, the taste of nicotine in his mouth, making it clear that he and his brother had been secretly smoking on the beach.

"You're actually quite cute." His voice was hoarse from the brief kiss.

"Did you just call me cute?" I pushed him, catching him off guard.

"Are you crazy? That was a compliment, *ragazza*!" Santino's eyes widened in my direction.

"You called me chubby! How can that be a compliment?" I moved towards him, acting on impulse.

Who did he think he was to kiss me and then call me cute? *Cute?* Santino didn't even have time to escape when I pushed him towards the pool, making him fall into it.

"Fuck! You're crazy!" he roared as he emerged from the water.

"Never call me cute again, got it?" I pointed my finger at him while standing at the edge of the pool.

"I never want to touch you again, in case your madness rubs off on me."

"Good, then we're even." I turned my body to see my friend finally appear at the door, running with wide eyes at the sight of my brief confrontation with her brother, while the other twin appeared behind her, laughing loudly.

No one needed to know about that kiss, the most humiliating kiss a girl could have as her first kiss.

CHAPTER ONE

Cinzia

Eleven years later...

"It's time, Cinzia..." Dad said, making me let out a long sigh.

"It's been seven years since that agreement was made, all because you thought it would be better for me to marry a Vacchiano, Dad!" I emphasized the madness Aldo Bianchi had imposed.

"I still think it's the best decision. You'll marry Santino, become a Vacchiano, and continue our bloodline in our clan," Dad said confidently.

"How can that be? He's a jerk. He'll marry me but will keep warming the beds of various women, and I don't even fit his type—those long legs." I curled my lip, remembering the last woman who posed next to Santino Vacchiano at a famous brand event, a tall, dark-skinned model, as tall as he was, with a sculpted body.

Unlike me, I'm short, with many curves, not that it's a problem for me because I love my body. I love how I look extremely sexy wearing a cropped top with a high-waisted skirt, my ample breasts always making daring décolletages. Being midsize has never been an obstacle for me.

But the issue was that I hated those Vacchiano twins. They thought they were the center of the universe, incredibly good-looking, not just good-looking, but hot, toned, tattooed, desirable...

It took several blinks to shake off my thoughts. Santino, like his twin brother, was hot but worthless. He didn't love, he was a bastard.

From the first moment he inserted himself into a woman, he never stopped, and for God's sake, I didn't want to be one of those women.

We were different, we didn't match in any way, our tastes were different. How could I marry someone as arrogant as him?

"Those are details," Dad interrupted my thoughts.

"Details? Dad, being cheated on is a detail? Everyone knows Tommaso cheated on Aunt Verena in their early days of marriage..."

"Yes, but he changed, he never cheated on her again." Dad continued defending his friend and father of the twins.

"Even if he changed, I would never forgive him. Cheating is cheating, there's no forgiveness," I declared firmly.

"That's beside the point. You're getting married, Cinzia. An agreement was made, and you will honor it for being born into the heart of the Cosa Nostra," Dad exploded, running his hand through his hair, exasperated.

Of course, as the daughter of an active Cosa Nostra member, I had to follow everything to the letter. That's why Dad sent me to another country for college. In his eyes, I was losing my way, a path I never had. Being born and raised in the mafia made me bored, which is why I was always a little rebel. I got caught with fake IDs when I was seventeen, which complicated my situation because my father sent me away. I spent five years living in New York, studying at Columbia. I graduated in business administration, took an accounting course because the plan was to take over my mother's place as the Cosa Nostra accountant, but the truth was I didn't want to be part of the clan.

Sometimes I just wanted to be a normal person, date, fall in love, and give myself to the man I loved, as I almost did several times with Marco. He was different, calm, unlike me, who was always agitated. He graduated with me, we connected because we both came from Sicily. He knew everything about me, knew about my engagement to a mafia member. In fact, Marco shouldn't have known, but during one of my drunk moments, I told him everything, exposing him to my chaotic life.

Marco Lombardo was from a family with many assets in Sicily but had nothing to do with the mafia. He always did everything for me. Of course, he didn't match a Vacchiano's beauty, but he was honest, not a player, and remained faithful to me, even when I said I wasn't ready for our first time.

Which was a big waste, as I had been involved with so many men before Marco, though I never reached the final step, as I had the belief that I would only give myself to my husband, whether he was Santino or not, on my honeymoon.

It was silly, but I had been holding onto it for so long that I didn't even realize I had kept myself for 23 years and was still a virgin. Maybe just a virgin in terms of my intimacy, but in reality, I was so experienced that I knew everything about men. They had given me pleasure, made me orgasm, I had given pleasure to men, but giving away my intimacy? No.

Which was crazy, since my future husband had been spreading his penis around so much that it should be worn out by now.

Maybe I should commit my final act of madness and run away. Marco was willing to do that, willing to marry me in secret, even bought a ticket to Vegas. By the time my parents found out, I'd already be married to someone else.

It would be a good thing for both me and Santino, after all, neither of us could stand each other, and we hadn't seen each other for so many years that it wouldn't make any difference.

I didn't know if I loved Marco, but he was good, made me feel good. His calmness balanced my agitation. It was somewhat monotonous, but better than being cheated on to the point of a headache from all the horns I'd receive.

"Cinzia? Cinzia?" I shook my head, realizing Dad was calling me, and I hadn't even noticed.

"What is it, Dad?" I asked impatiently.

"I just ask that you marry Santino Vacchiano, honor this agreement," Dad said, letting out a long sigh. "I am the advisor to Cosa Nostra, think of me, not just yourself."

I rolled my eyes. Dad was the Advisor to Don Tommaso Vacchiano. This was Tommaso's last year in charge of the clan. He had decided it was time to step down and make his son Valentino Vacchiano his successor. I knew Santino never wanted to be the boss; there were rumors that Santino would be Valentino's underboss because if he were the advisor, he'd sink the clan.

There were two agreements: the son who wasn't the Don would marry me, and the son who was the Don would marry Yulia Aragón, the sister of the Cartel boss. Valentino would marry the Latina girl, but only after she graduated from college, in about two years.

That's what my friend Pietra said because they were always arguing. The fact that one of them had to marry me was the most discussed topic since neither of them wanted to marry me. How humiliating! And only my father didn't see it!

"Alright, Dad," I muttered, getting up from the sofa. After all, he didn't know about Marco. If he did, he would force me to get married at that moment.

Dad's desperation to see his only daughter marry a Vacchiano was almost palpable, but the truth was I didn't want that marriage. A Vacchiano wasn't made for marriage. They were devils in designer suits, not even hiding their boldness and debauchery.

"I'm going to Pietra's house. I miss her and Tommie," I declared with a spontaneous smile, thinking of my friend's son.

And like the good fool I was, I thought my father would welcome me with joy. Of course, the first topic was the wedding, and Mom stayed silent, observing everything.

CHAPTER TWO

Cinzia

"Come in, friend." Pietra opened the door to her house, smiling. "I've missed you so much..."

She hadn't even finished speaking before we embraced in a tight hug. We've always been very close, even though Pietra Vacchiano is almost three years older than me, it never hindered our friendship. We shared everything, including the same frustrations of girls who grew up confined by the mafia's grip.

Unlike me, she bore the emotional burden of being the daughter of the Don of the Cosa Nostra, and had always been in love with her father's right-hand man, a man old enough to be her father, but quite the opposite. Pietra and Enrico loved each other, which caused a small war, since Tommaso, her father, refused to accept their love until he discovered that his daughter was pregnant by the underboss.

Pietra was her father's little princess. She fell for his right-hand man, and everything could have gone off the rails, but I wasn't there to witness it. However, Tommaso had no choice but to accept, which made things easier. Back then, I was already studying abroad, but Pietra kept me updated on everything. It took a long time for Tommaso and Enrico to become friends again as they were before.

Perhaps the influence of little Tommie, Pietra and Enrico's son, helped, as they named him after his grandfather, Tommaso.

"Come on, let's go to the living room." Pietra took my hand and guided me to the living room of her house.

We all lived in the same condo. My parents lived at the start of the street, Verena's parents in the middle, and she and her husband further down. There were several members of the Cosa Nostra living there.

"Ready to officially become my sister-in-law?" Pietra sat on the sofa, crossing her leg and making her delicate dress ride up slightly over her knee.

"Actually, I just wish he'd back out of this marriage," I murmured discontentedly, sitting next to her.

"Santino won't back out of a decision made by my father." My friend looked at me with sympathy. "You always liked him, what's the problem?"

"Everyone?!" I raised an eyebrow questioningly. "Your brother is going to cheat on me, and I'll want to kill him for doing it. I don't even fit his type..."

"Don't talk about type. We both know my brother has no type," Pietra interrupted.

"Seriously, Pipi? Are you defending him? How many plus-size girls have you seen him with?" My friend seemed to think about it, which made me smile at the sarcasm. "See, you're thinking. Santino does have a type; he only dates tall, slender models, just like Valentino. They're both jerks, plain and simple."

"Where's the woman who considered herself hot? Are you going to lower yourself to this, my friend?"

"And I am. What you don't understand is that I'm not his type, and he's not mine. I'm too good for any Vacchiano. Do you really think he'd find someone as hot as me? He only hangs out with those models because he doesn't have the balls to get someone like me, beautiful and perfect." I shrugged, confident, seeing my friend smile.

"I missed that self-esteem of yours." Pietra took my hand, looking deeply into my eyes. "You're thinking of something, what's on your mind? I can see the smoke coming out of your head."

"You know me so well, Pipi. It's like we haven't been apart for five years." My smile was a bit melancholic.

"What happened?"

"I met someone. Marco is nice, maybe it's not love, more like the right choice, you know? He's good to me, understands me, and loves how I'm always hyper, and he bought tickets for us to go to Vegas..."

"Cinzia Bianchi, no!" My friend cut me off abruptly.

Her eyes were wide, the green orbs almost popping out of her face, but we were interrupted when the door to the house made a noise as it opened. A boy's voice echoed in the room.

"Honey, is that you and Tommie?" Pietra called out loudly, but from the footsteps, there were more than one man.

"Yes, Santino is with us."

My body froze. I hadn't intended to see my fiancé that day. It was my first day back, and I didn't even want to see him.

Soon, a little whirlwind of green eyes and black hair ran into the room, it was Tommie, with a smile on his lips.

"Mommy, Uncle San and I are going out today." The little boy jumped in his happiness.

"Oh, no you're not!" Pietra was emphatic. "Remember your absent-minded godmother?"

The little copy of Pietra and Enrico looked at me, that boy was a typical Vacchiano, with a sly smile and features that strongly resembled his mother's family.

"Don't pay attention to your mother. Not everything she says is true. I'm a gem of innocence," I teased, seeing that the five-year-old didn't understand what I was saying.

I opened my arms to receive the little one's hug. I was his godmother along with her brother.

The sound of male footsteps became evident in the room. I didn't want to look in that direction, but it was inevitable. And there was my future husband, dressed in his typical mafioso attire with an air of self-importance.

The black dress pants molded to his legs, paired with dress shoes. The button-down shirt was untucked with the top buttons open, revealing a tattoo on his chest. His hair was slightly tousled, and his green eyes were fixed on me. Santino had tanned skin, as he always did, perhaps from spending time in the sun.

"Look who's back," Pietra's husband said, the man who was standing next to Santino.

"Yeah, maybe not for long." I shrugged, turning my gaze back to my arrogant fiancé, who narrowed his eyes in my direction and pressed his lips into a straight line.

"I don't think you're going anywhere, as this marriage needs to happen as soon as possible." His tone echoed in the room, his voice slightly rough, his eyes always seeming to be assessing me.

"A marriage neither of us wants. I'm sure if you talk to your father, he'll figure something out..."

"My father has great regard for yours. The marriage will happen!" Santino was firm in his decision.

"I don't even want him, let alone desire him..."

"Good then, I see we still share the same opinion because I don't desire you either, but I have a commitment to my clan."

I stood up from the sofa, growing increasingly sure of my decision to escape and marry Marco.

As I stood, Santino's eyes traveled down my body. It wasn't a look of disgust, but that typical male gaze of desire, assessing what he thought would be his, but only in his dreams.

"I'll do you a favor then: I'll run away and marry someone else," I declared, hearing a growl echo through the house.

"If you do that, do it well, because when I find out, I'll kill you and your lover!" Santino moved towards me so quickly it made me widen my eyes.

His hand moved like a blur towards my neck, gripping it tightly, his green eyes coming closer to mine. I grabbed his wrist, trying to get that bastard to let me go.

"No one escapes from me, no one makes a decision that I've already decided. It's been five years since you were promised to me, and I don't waste anything. You're mine, Cinzia Bianchi, whether you like it or not!" The mafioso growled, trying to intimidate me, but all he managed to do was increase my disgust.

"I will never be yours," I roared, feeling his grip tighten around my neck.

"Let her go now, Santino!" Pietra tried to push her brother, but was unsuccessful.

It was Enrico who managed to pull him away. Santino never took his eyes off me, maintaining that look of hostility, making clear the war that was starting to brew.

"Never touch me again. I loathe the day my father thought it was best for me to marry someone as arrogant as you!" I declared, rubbing my neck, feeling the sting from his grip.

"*Ragazza* fool, don't you know you shouldn't provoke the devil, as he loves to pull your foot while you're sleeping." He gave that frightening smile.

"Know that not even the devil scares me, let alone you!" I declared, wrinkling my nose and stepping away from them.

"Let her go, it'll only make things worse." I heard Enrico's voice, and it seemed Santino wanted to come after me.

That confrontation only confirmed what I wanted: to escape from Santino Vacchiano.

CHAPTER THREE

Santino

"If that girl runs away, I swear I won't be responsible for my actions," I growled, looking at Pietra.

"She's scared, and you can't keep your dick in your pants. What's the need to fuck the first woman who comes your way?" My sister jabbed her finger into my chest.

She spoke in a loud whisper so the child wouldn't hear. I grabbed her wrist, pushing her back, only to get shoved by Enrico, which made me stagger.

"Don't touch your sister!" Enrico defended her. "You little shit!"

He cursed me as he always did. Even when I turned thirty, Enrico would still call me a kid, just like he did with Valentino.

"Then tell her not to touch me. Before she's your wife, she's my sister," I growled at Enrico, the man I considered an uncle.

"No, that was before she became my wife. Control your impulses," he roared, taking a step towards me.

"Both of you stop," Pietra said.

My impulsiveness was nothing new to them. After all, I grew up this way. Between Valentino and me, I always had a tendency to be impulsive. My brother knew how to be sensible between us, as we were Vacchianos, heirs to the family's short tempers.

"I need to go. I'm going to get a soldier to tail that crazy woman. No one outsmarts me; this marriage has become a matter of honor," I declared, turning my back on the two of them.

"San." I stopped when I heard my sister's voice, turning to look at her over my shoulder. "Cinzia is my friend. Maybe it would be better to rethink this marriage. I'm sure Dad would understand; after all, he always understands everything you two ask for."

She rolled her eyes at her own words. Pietra was always very private, unlike me and Valentino. I think that's why she used to do things in secret, just like my crazy fiancée.

"I took too long to accept that I would marry that girl. Now that it's finally sunk in that my marriage to Cinzia will happen, whether she likes it or not, it will happen. I am loyal to the Cosa Nostra; this union will occur," I said, trying to maintain a calm I didn't even recognize.

I didn't wait to hear their response, forgetting even the document I had gone to get. I knew Enrico would find a way to deliver it to my parents' house, which was the headquarters of our mafia. I pulled out a pack of cigarettes, took one out, and as I watched the girl walking in the distance, she was nearing her parents' house.

Cinzia lived at the beginning of the street, the damn girl I watched grow up. She was no longer the same girl who left here; in fact, she was still the same, Pietra's scared little friend.

I lit the cigarette in my mouth, watching her turn her face as if she knew she was being watched. Her hair was loose down her back, and even from a distance, her blue eyes stood out with their intense color. She was beautiful; in fact, I had a huge urge to strip her clothes off, lift her skirt, and shove my hand between her legs. *Fuck!*

I knew my average for women was tall models; they were easy. I didn't usually have much patience with women. I liked to fuck one, two, three, regardless of how many. I just wanted to shove my dick into pussies.

My fiancée was different from all the women I'd had, but that didn't make her any less beautiful. In fact, I put her on such a high pedestal that Cinzia became too grand even for me.

I wanted her; I desired her. What man would deny a woman like her? But maybe her sharp tongue would be a problem because I hated women who thought they had the right to weigh in on a man's life. It gave me the itch every time I saw my father bowing his head to something my mother said, as if she owned the air he breathed. Obviously, Tommaso could never live in a world where Verena wasn't; their dependence was something that scared me.

I didn't want that kind of vulnerability.

That's why I wanted to marry Cinzia Bianchi. I'd have a woman by my side to produce an heir, and I could go out fucking other pussies. Being faithful to my wife was never a viable choice for me.

The girl disappeared from my sight when she entered her house. Cinzia was short; even though she was wearing a shirt with a square neckline, it gave me a view of her ample breasts, immediately bringing to mind everything I could do with them. The image of putting my face between them, fucking them with my dick...

Ah, it was hard to find a woman with big breasts to do a *Spanish*. Maybe I was a damned pervert, but I wanted to fuck that woman so badly, all because she thought she could be superior to me.

I entered my parents' house, knowing that Cinzia didn't know, but the house next to my parents' would be ours because after our marriage, we'd move out of our parents' residence. My father's house, the largest on the street, which was considered the headquarters of the Cosa Nostra, would go to Valentino and his fiancée, the hot little Latina.

I entered the residence, hearing the voices of Valentino, Dad, and Aldo Bianchi, my future father-in-law. Maybe encountering a member of that arrogant girl's family at that moment wasn't such a good idea.

"Where are you going?" My father asked as I walked past them.

"After my soldiers," I said, turning to the three men who looked at me confused.

Like me, Valentino was a *caporegime* of the Cosa Nostra. We had our soldiers; we were considered captains of the clan, as others were.

When my brother took the Don's chair, he'd change the entire hierarchy to his favor.

"Why soldiers, brother?" Valen asked, standing up from the sofa where he was sitting.

"To keep an eye on my crazy fiancée. Did you know your little girl is planning to run away and marry someone else?" I raised an eyebrow at my father-in-law, who widened his eyes in shock, making it clear he knew nothing about it.

"What?" Dad looked at Aldo.

"I'm as surprised as you are. I didn't know about this." The girl's father was astonished. "Let's expedite this marriage before Cinzia does something crazy. For God's sake, my only daughter is a disaster!"

"No one is expediting the marriage. I want that girl to run away because I'm going to drag her back by her hair! She'll understand she's dealing with a Vacchiano," I growled, seeing my brother's smile. He already knew what I wanted to do.

"Don't forget you're talking about my daughter," Aldo snarled.

"He should have thought about that when he gave her to me in marriage. I've always been clear about who I am. Now deal with the consequences. If I find out you told her I put soldiers on her tail, she'll be the one to suffer. Understood, father-in-law?" I was direct.

Aldo sighed and nodded. My father shook his head, suppressing a smile. The bastard knew I wanted to punish my fiancée, and I was going to do it one way or another.

If Cinzia thought she was clever, it was because she had never played against the best player in Sicily.

One should never make a deal with the devil...

CHAPTER FOUR

Cinzia

"Tommaso Ferrari! I've told you no!" Pietra scolded her son, who had jumped into the pool without his floaties. Both of us got up from the lounge chairs and rushed to the edge, seeing the boy emerging from the water with a loud laugh.

"Uncle Valentino taught me how to swim, mummia." The little boy splashed toward the edge, where Pietra quickly lifted him by the armpits.

"I want to punch those uncles of yours. I don't want you without floaties. Understand, my angel?" Pietra was quite the protective mother, and at first, it was strange to reconcile my friend being a mom, since Pipi had always been a bit wild.

But little Tommie changed her.

"But I know how to swim without floaties, Mom. Look..."

"No!" She grabbed him by the arm, stopping him from jumping again. "Mummia doesn't want to see..."

Pietra looked at me with a panicked expression. Tommie sighed longingly as she put the floaties back on his arms and jumped back into the pool, splashing water everywhere, including on us. I was wearing a loose dress, and the water clung to the fabric against my body.

I turned my face to see Enrico appearing, pulling a cigarette from his pocket. He had his sunglasses tucked between the fabric of his dress shirt, among the first open buttons. Next to him was a Vacchiano I didn't recognize.

"Are you leaving, dear?" Pietra asked.

"Yes, I'm going with Valentino to the center of Sicily. There's a suspicious shipment that arrived at the warehouse, and it shouldn't be there." Her husband confided in her.

"Why does the kid have floaties on?" the twin asked, moving to the edge of the pool.

"Because he's a five-year-old child!" Pietra scolded her brother.

"Yes, but he doesn't need them." Valentino's resemblance to Santino was striking. Even when Valentino had an accident, there was no scar to differentiate them physically.

"I'm his mother, and I decide what's best for him." Pietra crossed her arms.

"You're too protective, which makes a big difference." Valentino knelt by the edge of the pool, calling to his nephew.

"If you take them off, I'll punch what you call a member." My friend avoided saying the word in front of her son.

"Annoying as hell!" Valentino stood up and turned his attention to me. "Hello, sis-in-law."

"Hello, Valentino." I rolled my eyes as he took out his pack of cigarettes. As he moved, he revealed a smooth chest, lacking the tattoo Santino had. "No tattoo on your chest?" I asked, pointing out.

"Looking for differences, aren't you? Yes, I don't have a tattoo on my chest. San has a dragon on his back that wraps around his shoulder and finishes on his chest," he confirmed.

"There should be more differences," I murmured disapprovingly.

"If you want to give me some kisses pretending you mixed up the brothers, I'd love it. That would really piss off Santino," Valentino teased.

"I don't want any, let alone two." I curled my lip.

"Speaking of Santino, where is he?" Pietra asked.

"Around," Valentino answered.

He wasn't going to say where his brother was. The two could provoke each other, but they were loyal to one another. Maybe the teasing was due to their brotherhood.

"Let's go, Valentino," Enrico called, prompting the twin to follow him.

Enrico kissed his wife goodbye, and I was left alone with my friend. We returned to the lounge chairs, where I sat down, running my hand through my hair and making a bun on top of my head.

"The fact that Valentino didn't say where his brother is means he's up to something," I said to Pietra.

"I don't know. During the day, they handle Cosa Nostra affairs, but there's something I want to tell you." Pietra lowered her voice, looking around. "Last night, Enrico told me. My husband always tells me everything, although sometimes I have to extract some things from him. But Santino put soldiers on your tail, my friend..."

"What?" I interrupted her, looking around and seeing no one.

"You won't see them. We all know how well-hidden Cosa Nostra's soldiers can be," Pietra whispered. "Friend, you said you were going to marry someone else. Do you really think Santino would accept that quietly? He's waiting for your first misstep. Don't run, Cinzia, that's exactly what he wants."

I fell silent. Pietra was watching her son playing in the pool. Damn it! I shouldn't have mentioned running away. I had even thought that Santino wouldn't want that marriage, just like I didn't.

"I don't want to marry Santino," I finally murmured.

"Who is this other man?" my friend asked.

"Marco graduated with me. He's also in Sicily. He always knew I had a fiancé and gave me a ticket to Vegas where we would marry away from everyone's eyes. He's different; he's not like Santino. He's calm, attentive, loving, and fulfills all my wishes..."

"But you don't love him. You want him only because he's convenient. That's boring, emotionless," my friend twisted her lip.

"Maybe not everyone wants the hectic life you and your husband have," I retorted.

"Seriously, Cinzia? Everything you said about this Marco reminds me of one position in bed: missionary. Friend, Santino might be my brother, but he's a Vacchiano with Zornickel blood running through his veins. Do you really think that man is incapable of loving? He might be the devil eating mangoes, but deep down, he's a pit of jealousy. Be sure of this: he will love you. Just don't make the mistake of running away. If you do, Santino will hunt you down to the ends of the earth. If he can even do that, since he's already said that marrying you has become a matter of honor. Friend, there's no escape." Pietra sighed as she finished speaking.

"I'm not getting married, Pietra. He'll betray me. I don't want to be the wife who spends her nights alone while her husband is out there, coming home smelling like a whore," I whispered back.

"I'm your friend, Cinzia. I'll always do everything to protect you, but if you run away, you'll be doing something beyond my ability to protect you, giving him a reason. We grew up in the mafia. We knew from childhood that we wouldn't marry for love—although that wasn't my case. My friend, don't run away, please!" Pietra's fear was palpable in her voice.

"I'm already decided. I'm not marrying Santino," I declared firmly.

I would outsmart that Italian. If he thought he could put soldiers on my tail and assume I wouldn't find out, he was sorely mistaken.

The previous day, our brief encounter had made everything clear in my mind, especially after the article I saw that morning. There he was with a model, Santino and Valentino, both with that enigmatic look.

While his fiancée was back in town, he was chasing any woman who came his way, as if my presence were irrelevant.

I refused to marry and be the wife of a mafioso who cheated all over Sicily.

CHAPTER FIVE

Cinzia

It had been a week since I had returned to Sicily, a week of avoiding Santino. I didn't want to marry the man who spent every night with a different woman, as if he were a collector of trading cards. My wedding was scheduled for the following week—there was no escape, either I married him or I ran away.

Running away had never seemed so appealing.

I had always been a fearless girl, but the suspicion that I was being watched by soldiers made me anxious. What if it were true?

Pietra wouldn't lie to me; our friendship had always been stronger than her relationship with her brothers.

I couldn't involve anyone in my crazy plan. Everyone was loyal to Cosa Nostra, and being loyal to the clan meant supporting my marriage to Santino, which was why I was alone in this.

I heard a knock on my door and turned to see my mother entering the room.

"Daughter," her eyes sparkled as she looked me up and down, "you look beautiful."

I smiled, turning back to the mirror. I was wearing a blue dress that fell just above my ankles, with high heels on my feet. The dress had no cleavage, as it was closed around my neck, with the fabric rising up the sides of my armpits, leaving my shoulders exposed and the fabric closing at the nape of my neck. My straight blonde hair fell over my shoulders. I chose a light makeup look, simply enhancing my blue eyes.

The fabric hugged my body, accentuating my curves. I love wearing clothes that flatter me, that show you don't need to be thin and tall to be beautiful.

"Mom, could we say I'm coming down with a virus?" I asked, making a pout.

"No, how can we have an engagement dinner without the bride?" I rolled my eyes at Giulia's comment.

Of course, Giulia Bianchi was glowing about the wedding, just like my father. She also wanted it, after all, what better outcome for this marriage than to spread the word among all the mafia wives that her daughter was marrying a Vacchiano, the only daughter married to the future right hand of the Don.

My mother was a great mom, but she was ambitious. They didn't see that I'd be just another toy in Santino Vacchiano's hands. He didn't even want to marry me. The twins fought over who would marry me, until it was decided that Valentino would take the father's seat, which meant he would marry Yulia Aragón, and the leftover—me—would end up with Santino.

"Let's go then, Mom," I whispered, disappointed, as all I wanted was to escape that reality.

There was a time in my life, many years ago, when I was thirteen, that I thought Santino Vacchiano was my first love—such childish delusion, until I had that first kiss. Santino was the first man to kiss me, and by ironic fate, he wanted to be my first in bed as well. He might have been experienced and done all kinds of crazy things, but I always insisted that I would marry as a virgin, and I was a virgin, which was a huge waste. I had waited 23 years of my life to give myself completely to a man who could be in another woman's arms the very next day.

I followed my mother through the house. Dad was waiting for us, and we left together. Several cars were parked on the side of the street, indicating many guests.

It was supposed to be just a dinner, but I'd be forced to put on a million smiles.

I followed a step behind my parents, passing through the entrance of the Vacchiano house. The garden lights were on. Being a private condo belonging only to Cosa Nostra, there was no security at the entrance, as anyone there had clearly been through the entrance with an invitation.

As I passed through the entrance, I quickly spotted one of the twins. I knew it was Valentino. He hastily buttoned up his shirt, trying to hide this fact, which made me suspicious.

The enormous house was packed with people, most of whom I didn't remember. I had been away for five years—how could I remember all those people?

Mom immediately started handing out her smiles to everyone around me. Dad's hand touched my back. I saw Valentino approaching, having buttoned up all the buttons on his shirt. *Too late, dear, I already knew you'd try to pass for your brother.*

"Father-in-law!" With the most shameless attitude, he lied.

Even the way he spoke was the same.

What a damn bastard!

Valentino greeted my mother and father, placing his hand on my back, pulling me away from my parents, greeting most of the people present, to whom I only managed a forced smile.

"Where is your brother?" I asked with a smile.

"Who, Valentino?" He tilted his head, playing along with the charade.

"Employee." I stopped in front of him. Valentino lowered his eyes. I raised my hand, and he tried to block me, but I slapped his hand, which had a tattoo on his fingers, just like his damned brother. I unbuttoned his shirt to confirm what I already knew. "No tattoo. Why are you pretending to be Santino?"

Valentino shrugged, greeting a couple who passed by us.

"He's with some woman, isn't he? Protecting his little brother as always." I rolled my eyes.

Another detail about the twins: Valentino had a woody fragrance, while Santino's was musky.

"I don't know where he is. I just got a message to cover for him. Now let's do our part," he said with a chilling nonchalance. *What the hell, how could that be normal?*

How could I be at my engagement dinner while my fiancé was who knows where, having sex with some woman?

I turned my face and saw a familiar face coming from the back of the house. It was the damned Santino. He had sent Valentino to impersonate him, showing up with disheveled hair while smiling at a girl in a formal dress, clearly a guest at the party, whom he was fucking somewhere. His eyes met mine as he buttoned his shirt, revealing his chest tattoo.

I looked back at Valentino, who was lost in his thoughts. I didn't hesitate. If Santino could screw some random woman at our engagement dinner, I could put on a little show.

"Fiancé," Valentino looked at me, puzzled by the tone of my voice, "you said you'd accept a kiss to provoke your bastard of a brother. For all I know, it's Valentino..."

"Are you crazy?" Valentino didn't have time to push me away when I grabbed his shoulders.

He didn't make a scene, of course he wouldn't. If he did, it would make it clear that he was impersonating Santino.

The twin who wasn't my fiancé held my neck, pressing his tongue against mine in a slow kiss. He didn't refuse me, didn't make a fuss, returned the kiss, his mentholated breath adding freshness to mine.

"I'm going to smash your face, Valentino," the roar came from beside us.

I pulled away from Valentino, who had a smug smile on his lips, and wiped the corner of my mouth, pretending to clean the smeared lipstick.

"What?" I played dumb, turning to my actual fiancé, who had his mouth drawn into a straight line.

"You bitch, I knew he wasn't me," he roared.

"Sorry, I didn't know." I feigned innocence, watching my father approach with Don Tommaso.

"What's going on?" Tommaso asked.

"I'm asking the same thing, Valentino," Santino growled at his brother, who raised his hands in surrender.

"In my defense, I was attacked and I don't refuse a kiss, especially when it comes from my sister-in-law. And what a kiss..."

"I'm going to blow your brains out, Valentino," Enrico appeared from who knows where, holding Santino back.

"Cinzia, what have you done this time?" Dad huffed at me, making the men present look at me.

"Nothing. I kissed my fiancé. I can't help it if it was the wrong fiancé. The fault is his for being all over some woman. — I shrugged, looking at Santino, who still had his eyes narrowed in my direction.

"In that case, the guilty party is you, Santino. I've always said that switching places with your brother would cause problems." Mr. Tommaso came to my defense.

"You're coming with me, Cinzia," Santino made a move to escape from Enrico's hold.

"I'm not going anywhere with you smelling of some woman. I don't know where your mouth was minutes ago," I yelled, irritated.

"Trust me, you won't want to know..."

"And I really don't want to!" I cut him off sharply.

"See? She'd never kiss me willingly. She did it on purpose, knowing it wasn't me," Santino complained to his father.

"Maybe I did know, but next time keep your damn dick in your pants, and it won't happen again!" I stamped my foot, turning my body. "And I don't want you near me unless you've showered..."

I didn't even finish speaking, walking away from those men, hearing the laughter of Don Tommaso and the other twin, while all I could decipher from Santino was his growl.

CHAPTER SIX

Santino

I was buttoning my shirt in front of the mirror, my anger still gnawing at every muscle in my body. I heard a knock on the door and saw my mother's blonde hair; she had a small smile on her lips.

"Your father said you were up here," Verena said calmly.

"Yes, he did. What a drama over a fuck," I said, leaving the first three buttons of my shirt undone.

I walked to the bed, sitting down while putting on my shoes.

"It's not drama, Santino. It's your fiancée. Maybe you should show her a little respect. It's your engagement dinner, and this is how you repay her?" I heard the clinking of her heels echoing on the floor as she stopped in front of me, crossing her arms and staring at me with those evaluating blue eyes.

"What do you want me to do, humiliate myself? Apologize? Hell no, I don't know if you know, but she kissed Valentino knowing it was him!" I roared, getting up from the bed, running my hand through my damp hair, leaving it messy.

It was a short cut; you couldn't even tell it wasn't combed.

"Well, I knew, and your brother isn't sorry," I turned my body towards Verena.

"And does he regret anything? We're talking about Valentino, the guy who couldn't care less about the lives of those around him." I extended my hand to Verena. "Come on, Mom, unfortunately, I have an engagement dinner. Why are we doing this farce?"

"Any reason, but not sticking your member in any hole, my son." I shook my head, smiling at my mother's sweet way of talking about such a perverted subject.

I had my hand on Mom's shoulder; she was short and had a soft, sweet scent. We went down the stairs toward the living room, and as I looked around, I found my crazy fiancée next to my sister.

With them were Enrico and my father.

"Let's go over there. It's time to make amends..."

"Dream on, Mom. I'm not apologizing for fucking... Ow!" I ducked, taking an elbow jab from Verena.

We approached, and I was rubbing the side of my belly, giving a sour look at the short blonde.

"I'd forgotten that for someone half a meter tall, you've got quite a strong jab," I grumbled, knowing the people present would hear.

"Forgot that I'm the one who brought you into this world, and I still know how to catch you off guard."

"What happened?" Verena held her husband's outstretched hand.

"Nothing, Santino being a jerk as always. I keep wondering how I only produced ungrateful children, except for my little girl. She gave me my best gift." I curled my lip at my mother, smiling at Pietra.

"You're saying that now, but six years ago you were trying to kill Enrico," I mocked, putting my hand in my pocket, looking around for Valentino. "Where's Valen?"

"He must have found a hole," Enrico answered.

"I'll see if he needs help. Maybe he's hard to find." I made a move to turn around, grunting in pain at the nail that dug into my arm.

"Your place is here, little brother. You've already exceeded your quota for the night," Pietra said between gritted teeth.

"Don't forget you're still my sister, and I can give you a few slaps," I growled, pulling my arm back.

"Touch her and I'll make sure you meet the devil before your time." Enrico came to his wife's defense.

I rolled my eyes, stopping there, looking to the side and seeing the whirlwind named Cinzia Bianchi, my crazy fiancée.

Crazy and hot, damn, I could have fucked my fiancée that night instead of that woman. I didn't even remember her name, in fact, I didn't remember any of their names.

I spotted one of my father's associates approaching, with two girls by his side, too young to be his escorts; they must have been his daughters.

"Julian Velas." My father extended his hand to him.

Of course, my father and Enrico knew who he was. If Valentino had been there, I'm sure he would have known too; he knew everything. My brother was an encyclopedia, memorizing everything easily, unlike me.

Pietra passed in front of me, pushing me aside. I was surprised to notice that she did this because there were two young girls looking at me. In fact, I hadn't even paid attention to them; they were cuties, maybe my type, not picky, but at that moment, I wasn't in the mood for fucking anything.

"Don Vacchiano," they shook hands, "I brought my daughters. I know one of your sons is engaged..."

"The other one too," my father cut him off.

"Oh, I didn't know." The man deflated.

"He's engaged, but not dead," I declared in Valentino's defense.

The man didn't understand, but my family did and looked at me with narrowed eyes.

"You're impossible, Vacchiano!" The girl next to me sighed, irritated.

Cinzia moved, turning her body, making the scent of her perfume permeate my senses as she moved, her blonde hair swaying.

"Damn it! What did I do this time?" I declared, not understanding why she was leaving like that.

"Maybe he still needs to mature a lot," Enrico mocked.

"He's a Vacchiano; he'll learn only when he realizes he's losing," my father said, making that talk sound even stranger.

"You're crazy. Now that the crazy woman is gone, I'm going after Valentino," I grumbled, turning around and feeling Enrico's hand on my shoulder.

"I hope you don't need another bath. Control your dick and honor your family," Enrico grunted at me.

"This coming from the biggest fucker in Sicily..."

"Ex-..."

I rolled my eyes, moving away from them. Before Enrico declared himself my sister's little puppy, he was a tremendous asshole, just like my brother and me. The difference was that he swore he would never marry, unlike Valentino and me, who were forced to marry.

I could go after my brother, but something led me to the back door of the house, where I saw my fiancée walking alone on the lawn. She had her phone to her ear, turned to the side, the moon reflecting on her face, making me realize she was smiling as she talked to someone.

Cinzia said she was going to run away to marry another man. What if all that was true? What if she really loved another man?

Hell no, I spent five years of my life accepting that I had to marry the little girl I watched grow up, and then she was going to run away to marry someone else.

Fuck it, Cinzia Bianchi was mine, and no one was going to change that.

CHAPTER SEVEN

Cinzia

"The tickets are for tomorrow, my love," Marco declared from the other end of the line.

"You know I'm going, don't you?" I stated the obvious.

"Are you sure there won't be any problems for you?" Marco was worried.

"Everything would be easier if that lunatic rejected this union. Just me refusing won't help, because he's the one who needs to do it—mafioso rules." I sighed, watching the moon reflect on the distant sea.

"And how are you, my love?"

Marco was a good man, calm and understanding—everything Santino Vacchiano was not.

"I'd be much better if I weren't living this madness. There's nothing worse than arriving at your engagement dinner and finding your future fiancé fucking another woman," I complained, dissatisfied. Maybe I didn't need to mention that I had kissed Valentino.

"I miss our conversations..." I smiled, turning my body.

"I miss everything, except this place." I sighed through my smile.

Everything at college was light; my first years were chaotic, I enjoyed it, went to parties, knew I couldn't fall in love or get involved with anyone. But in the final year, I met Marco. He was my partner in many projects. There was never that passionate fire, but there was camaraderie. I knew he didn't love me, just as I never declared my feelings to him. It was strange; our relationship was always one of partnership.

"I need to go, Marco, they'll notice my absence soon," I said, saying goodbye to him.

I was still scared. No one knew I was planning to run away the next day. I gave Santino a chance to be different. I actually thought I could marry him, tell Marco I changed my mind, and he would understand. But arriving at that dinner and seeing him come out from one corner of the party with a woman made me realize that nothing would change Santino Vacchiano. It would always be like this: going to parties with him, my husband sneaking off to fuck other women, and then coming back to my side as if nothing had happened.

Definitely, this was not for me.

I went back to the party; the place was still crowded. Scanning around, I found the two twins together. They were facing away, one of them had his hand on a woman's back, both had the same tattoos on their hands, as if done on purpose to avoid obvious differences.

I wouldn't doubt that the one with his hand on the woman's back could be my future husband.

The other turned his face, as if looking toward the exit, waiting for someone, until his eyes met mine. That possessive look belonged to my fiancé. Valentino had a gentler look when it came to our relationship.

When he turned, I saw it was my fiancé because the open top buttons revealed the tattoo marks that Valentino didn't have.

"At least it wasn't the asshole with his hand on that woman."

I stood still as a waiter passed by offering a glass of champagne. I accepted, bringing the crystal to my lips, taking a small sip, feeling the tiny bubbles of the champagne burst, a delicious essence flowing down my throat.

"Ragazza," I removed the glass from my mouth, raising my eyes to the man in front of me.

"Which of the two twins am I talking to now?" I arched an eyebrow.

"Don't play games with me. I know you already know about the tattoos." He rolled his eyes, taking the glass from my hand and finishing the rest of the liquid that was mine!

"Hey, you know that was mine, and I didn't want to share with anyone," I emphasized, seeing another waiter stop by our side. I took another glass; Santino handed over his empty one and picked up a glass with an amber-colored liquid, probably whiskey.

"We need to talk," he declared.

"I don't want to talk to you." I wrinkled my nose, moving past him, feeling his fingers grip my wrist. We stood side by side.

I felt his lips close to my ear, his whisper bringing little jolts to my body, something I had never felt before.

"You're coming with me now. I'm not asking; I'm ordering," he growled. My treacherous body gradually surrendered to that hoarse and smooth timbre.

I turned my body, lifting my face. Our eyes were close to each other, his gaze turned one way, mine the other. Only our faces, facing each other, his hand gripping my wrist, his touch warm.

"I've never been good with orders. You won't be the first I obey." I smiled, not breaking eye contact with him.

Santino narrowed his eyes at me, growling at my audacity.

"You're mine, Cinzia Bianchi." His face moved even closer to mine, his lips pressing into a straight line, his grip on my wrist tightening.

"I'm not a piece of property to claim as yours! I don't want you, I don't desire you. All I see when I look at you is a scumbag. You'll never have me, Santino Vacchiano." I tried to pull my arm away, but his other hand moved to my neck.

I widened my eyes. He wasn't even sparing the fact that we had guests watching his little show.

Santino didn't release my wrist, gripping my neck tightly, knowing how to do it, as if he wanted to intimidate me. But all he was achieving was making me hate him even more.

"I don't give a damn if you love or hate me. You've been sentenced to be mine, and no one makes a fool of me, especially a *ragazza* as cheeky as you," he roared close to my ear.

From the corner of my eye, I saw the blonde woman approaching with her husband. It was Santino's mother.

"Darling, let her go now. Everyone is watching," Verena whispered.

Santino realized the spectacle he was making and released me, his eyes meeting mine, narrowed, with hatred clearly visible.

"The dinner is over, as the bride is indisposed," he declared in a tone loud enough for everyone to hear.

Mr. Tommaso went after his son. I touched my neck, feeling the tears of rage burning on my face. The asshole left, leaving the entire focus of his performance on me.

I didn't let the tears fall, as doing so would show everyone that I was fragile, and I am not like a crystal that breaks easily.

"Cinzia, come with me," Mrs. Verena said kindly, putting her hand on my waist and guiding me along with her.

In less than ten days since I returned, Santino had only made me more certain of how much I hated him and how much I loathed the fact that I needed to marry that imbecile.

What good was being as handsome as he was if he had the mind of an amoeba?

CHAPTER EIGHT

Cinzia

I checked my watch for the thirteenth time. I woke up early, put on jeans and a hoodie, trying to blend in. I left the condo through the back of my house, went behind the neighbor's house, and took another street. My fear was passing by the guardhouse; they asked for my name. I said I was going for a walk, but who walks around in jeans?

What a huge mistake on my part. I was only carrying a small backpack, hidden in a corner of the airport, scanning my surroundings for any sign of Santino.

I couldn't tell if there were Cosa Nostra soldiers on my tail. I knew nothing, only that my friend had warned me that Santino had men tracking me.

But I had never seen them. In all the days I'd been in Sicily, I hadn't seen a shadow of anyone. If he was really doing it, he was being very cautious.

I arrived at the airport early, which was why Marco hadn't arrived yet. But he knew I was already there. I asked him to wait because I was afraid my asshole fiancé might show up at any moment.

I knew how risky it was to escape like this, putting everything at risk—my family, Marco's life, even my own. But I warned Marco, and still, he was willing to help me, which was crazy considering how I knew a Vacchiano. They couldn't stand being outsmarted. Their gigantic egos prevented them from thinking clearly.

I bit the tip of my nail, anxious about being discovered, the tension in the air, my eyes constantly scanning everything around me.

Why did it have to be like this? Why did I have to be in this dead-end?

Everything would be so much easier if Santino simply abandoned this union, but he wouldn't. It was all about his ego, proving to everyone that he would fulfill his role in the Cosa Nostra. But I was never good at following rules.

That Italian didn't even like me, an egocentric, spoiled, bad boy, jerk... He had so many negative "qualities" that I couldn't think of a single good one.

I refused to accept that he would be my husband. How could fate be so treacherous, making me marry the first man I ever kissed?

The most humiliating kiss a girl could have. Maybe nowadays I might think he called me "sweetie" as a genuinely affectionate nickname, but that was in the past, the past of a girl who felt insecure about her body, which wasn't relevant at that moment.

I had grown up, discovering that I was beautiful just as I was, that many desired me this way. I looked at myself in the mirror, and all I saw was the reflection of a stunning woman. Santino could date as many models as he wanted, but none would ever compare to me. I could be the worst nightmare he'd ever had.

I saw Marco appear among the people from a distance. It was unavoidable not to smile; he hadn't seen me yet. Marco was a man of average height, with long hair, not fitting the muscle-bound stereotype. He was what we'd call an ordinary man, nothing special. But he was a good friend, willing to run away with me to help me. What man would do that?

Actually, what human being would do that for someone else?

I pushed away from the wall, my subtle movement catching his attention. Our eyes met. I took small steps toward him, he smiled at me, but the smile faded quickly as I tensed when I felt a pressure behind me, a hood being pulled off my head, a breath on my neck, long fingers moving my hair aside. I didn't need to turn my face to know who it was—my worst nightmare.

"Didn't anyone ever tell you that when you make a pact with the devil, he always comes back to collect the debt?" Santino's whisper made me even more tense.

I shook my head, signaling Marco to leave, even from a distance he could see Santino's presence. I knew my fiancé wasn't alone; he was the caporegime of the Cosa Nostra, always surrounded by soldiers.

"It was never me who wanted this union," I murmured, closing my eyes in my anger.

"Directly it wasn't you, but indirectly, just being born close to the mafia makes you property of the Cosa Nostra. Perhaps your birth had only one purpose—to be mine." His whisper made me turn my body, seeing the grim face of the jerk who would be my husband.

"I will never be yours," I declared through gritted teeth.

Santino growled, gripping my wrist tightly, his firm hold making me groan in pain.

"Your refusal only makes me more eager for the moment I will have you." A forced smile appeared on his thin lips.

"I hate you so much," I declared, seeing him pull me by the wrist.

I turned my face, realizing Marco was no longer there; he was gone. I tried to pull my wrist away, wanting the jerk to let me go, but my persistence only made him pull my arm harder.

"I want to see what our family will think about the escape of my future wife," Santino growled.

"Jerk! Leave me alone! What part don't you understand that I don't want you?" I yelled, irritated, as he dragged me through the airport. Everyone was staring at us as we passed. "If you don't let me go, I'm going to scream..."

"Do that and you'll regret being born." My fiancé, who was a step ahead of me, continued to drag me as he spoke.

"HELP! A MANIAC!" I screamed, seeing Santino's murderous look directed at me.

"You bitch," he snarled.

I was caught off guard when he effortlessly picked me up, placing me over his shoulder, my face hitting his back, the smell of musky perfume mixed with the nicotine scent from his cigarette.

"Damn it!" I punched his back. "Let me go!"

Santino didn't even huff, not even breathless from carrying me on his shoulder. His hand on my leg kept me pinned against his body.

"Know this, Cinzia Bianchi: when I have you, you'll beg me to stop, and I will never stop, because you're playing with the devil." His voice penetrated my ear, making me realize I was screwed, but I would never bow my head to that jerk.

We left the airport, of course, no one did anything. Only the posts that accompanied Santino prevented anyone from daring to approach. Not in Sicily, where people knew there were men in black suits who did evil. Despite many theories, everyone was afraid.

CHAPTER NINE

Santino

I was enraged, gripping the door handle tightly. Luckily, the girl fell silent and stayed quiet.

Seriously, did she think she could just run away and not be noticed? She really didn't know who she was marrying. The car was in motion, and we were sitting in the back seat, with a car in front and another behind us.

"How did you know?" she asked, but I chose to remain silent. "I'm talking to you..."

"Just shut your damn mouth!" I growled, trying to suppress the adrenaline coursing through my veins.

Damn it! No one makes a fool of a Vacchiano! I've never been, and never will be, patient.

The woman huffed. Out of the corner of my eye, I saw her cross her arms, pouting her lips. She didn't know who she was trying to run from, but I would find out who the bastard was that wanted to steal my fiancée. After all, he was messing with the future wife of a mobster.

"Know this: I'm not going to shut up." I turned my face abruptly, closing off the car's partition to give us privacy.

I released the door handle and gripped her neck. Her blue eyes widened as my sudden move caught her off guard. I placed one knee on the seat, with the other foot on the floor, bringing my face close to hers.

"I told you to shut the fuck up. Don't provoke me right now, because I can't be held responsible..."

"Fuck you, what are you going to do? Kill me? Maybe death is better than walking down the aisle with an asshole like you." Cinzia spat the words, causing me to raise my eyebrows.

"So your life is so insignificant, even to you?" I tilted my head to the side, releasing her neck and grabbing her hands as she reached for me.

My eyes focused on the redness I left on her neck. Cinzia had golden, sun-kissed skin. Even though she had lived in the US, she still maintained her tanned skin. I find tanned women beautiful.

"Think what you want." Cinzia moved her leg, brushing against my knee, which made me stumble forward, my chest pressing against hers, our lips almost touching.

Cinzia tried to turn her face away, but it was too late. She ignited in me the urge to kiss her lips.

"No!" she growled as I let go of her hands and held her face.

"So you kiss my brother without hesitation, but now that I'm your fiancé..."

"A fiancé I hate, abhor!" I roared at her words.

Cinzia acted like a wild mare, impossible to touch without getting kicked.

I sat back down on the seat, my impatience still evident. After a few long seconds, the car stopped in front of my house. Cinzia quickly opened her door, eager to leave. I followed, running after her and stopping her steps by pulling her by the wrist.

"Where do you think you're going?" I snarled, still angry, watching my parents approach from inside the house. Even her parents came quickly from their home.

"I'm going to my house since you've brought me back." The woman tried to pull her arm away.

"What's happening?" her mother asked.

"Why don't you ask your daughter? After all, she was the one with a trip to Las Vegas to marry someone else!" My fiancée looked at me with narrowed eyes, like a puma about to attack.

"Daughter..." Giulia, my mother-in-law, whispered in a shout.

"Let me go, Vacchiano!" Cinzia growled, trying to pull her arm away.

"You're not going anywhere. From now on, you'll be under my watch until this damn wedding happens." No one said anything; there was nothing more to be said. "Your actions will have consequences."

"Go to hell!" Cinzia managed to pull her arm away, but I quickly grabbed her by the hair, making her scream from the force of my pull.

"If anyone interferes, she will be the only one who suffers. This wedding was an agreement, and it will happen." For the second time, she looked at me with tears in her eyes, but she didn't let them fall.

I put my hand around her waist, placing her over my shoulder once again. I felt Cinzia's fists pounding on my back. She had a heavy hand, but it didn't stop me from turning my body and hearing my mother's voice coming from behind me.

"Santino Vacchiano, you're not going to be an asshole like your father was with me when we got married," Verena declared, irritated.

"Too late, Mom. Maybe being an asshole is in the blood," I declared, heading toward my future home.

"Santino, fix this now!"

Of course, my mother wouldn't give up easily.

I didn't respond to Verena, simply stopping when I reached the porch of my new house, setting my future wife down on the ground.

"What do you think you're going to do?" Cinzia tossed her hair back, about to flee when I grabbed her by the wrist.

"I'm the one who will set the rules from now on," I growled, not releasing her wrist, typing the code on the door and unlocking it.

"What are you doing? Who owns this house?" I pulled her inside.

"Mom, I want the wedding moved up to tomorrow!" I called out, looking toward the door where my mother was.

"That's impossible..."

"Move it up before I end up a widower before the wedding even happens," I growled, feeling Cinzia trying to pull her arm away.

Verena simply nodded, but before leaving, she said:

"Don't do anything you'll regret. Learn from your father's mistakes." She didn't give me a chance to respond before leaving.

The door closed. I dragged Cinzia through the house, which was already furnished, in light tones, just as Pietra had instructed.

"I'm not marrying you tomorrow." Cinzia yanked her hand away, glaring at me. "And what the hell is this house?"

"Our house!" I replied, releasing her. After all, she couldn't go anywhere.

"Weren't we supposed to live with your parents?"

"Living with them was never an option," I declared, heading toward the bar.

"How did I never know about this house?" I didn't look at her, hearing her footsteps follow mine.

"As far as I understood, it was meant to be a surprise for you. Well, surprise!" I was a bit snarky. The girl muttered something, calling me a name, but I didn't pay attention. All I wanted at that moment was a good dose of whiskey.

CHAPTER TEN

Cinzia

A house? Our house?
I looked around. The word "our" felt strange when paired with Santino Vacchiano.

I tried to run away and in return got an advance on my wedding.

"Where am I supposed to stay?" I asked, exhausted.

It would have been comical if the jerk had answered me, but he didn't, keeping his eyes on the whisky he was drinking.

I sighed deeply, heading toward the stairs. I grabbed the railing, climbed the steps, and saw a hallway with about four closed doors. I wasn't feeling up to exploring the house, so I went to the last door in the hallway, pushing it open. This should have been the master bedroom; it was huge, with a bed in the center, and on either side, there were French doors, both closed.

I was hot, really sweating in that sweatshirt. I took it off and left it on the bed, then headed to the bathroom, finding a double sink, and on one side, a bathtub with a glass wall overlooking the beach. Living on this side of the street had its perks, as my parents' house didn't offer a view of the beach.

I stopped in front of the bathtub, staring out at the distant sea for a long time, letting out a deep sigh.

I felt exhausted, never had I felt so drained, and I hadn't even gotten married yet. I could still feel his big hands pulling at my scalp.

My father did nothing, no one did anything, and they weren't going to because I was the one to blame.

If this happened, it was my fault. I ran away, I would face the consequences.

I turned my body, opening the cabinets under the sink to find hygiene products, bathrobes, and towels, all neatly organized. Maybe taking a shower wasn't such a bad idea; being under the water might help clear my mind.

I closed the door, locked it, undressed, grabbed the liquid soap and shampoo, and went to the shower, which was located opposite the bathtub. I turned on the water, letting the huge cascade cover my entire body. I closed my eyes, letting the tears fall in the silence of the shower. I needed to strengthen myself; I couldn't show my weaknesses to my fiancé. He was the type of man who used them to his advantage.

I took the soap, and since there was no washcloth, I scrubbed with my hands, washed my hair with the shampoo. I must have spent over half an hour, scrubbing every part of myself, hoping Santino had left the house, gone anywhere, even to the ends of the earth, and I wouldn't care.

I sighed deeply, turning off the water, stepping onto the rug, and grabbing the towel from the counter. I dried myself slowly, covering each part of my body. Finally, I dried my hair, leaving it a bit messy. I put on the bathrobe; it was too big, closing around my body. There was no size difference; they all seemed to be the same size, making me think that whoever organized the bathrobes either didn't know my weight or thought I wore the same size as my fiancé.

I didn't care about that because there was something else to worry about: not having any clothes.

I leaned over to grab my jeans, planning to get my phone and call my mother to bring me some clothes, but I couldn't find the phone. I was sure it was in the pocket of my jeans. *Did I lose it?*

I opened the bathroom door, exiting, and found my fiancé sitting on the bed, holding two cell phones, one of which was mine.

"You have two choices," he said without looking up from the screen of my phone. "Tell me the password to your phone, or tell me who the hell Marco is?"

Santino lifted his eyes in my direction, his gaze lingering too long on the oversized bathrobe.

"What an awful robe!" he declared about the bathrobe.

"Yeah, it seems either this house was supposed to be just yours, or someone thinks we have the same body. — I rolled my eyes, as it was normal for me to be given large clothes or have my curves undervalued because I'm not the standard size. I never cared because I know how beautiful I am.

"If someone did this, they will be fired," he said seriously, getting up from the bed. "Who is Marco? Why does this bastard want to know how you are?"

"It's none of your business." I moved toward him, trying to grab my phone.

"You won't be using your phone anymore; it will be confiscated!" Santino growled, putting the phone in his pocket.

"You have no right to do that!"

"I do, I have rights over everything concerning you." His body pressed against mine. "Know that if this Marco shows up in front of me, I'll kill him. You're lucky you didn't save his last name because right now I want to snap the neck of the bastard who wanted to steal my wife."

"You can't steal something that was given willingly. I don't want you, Santino!" I pressed my body against his with the sole intention of trying to grab my phone from his pocket, which was in vain as Santino felt my fingers.

He grabbed both my wrists, turning me around, and pushed me until I fell onto the bed. I landed awkwardly, his eyes traveling down my body. Terrified, I looked down, feeling the draft touch my breast, which I quickly covered.

Damn, the bathrobe shifted, showing him part of my breast. Before he could analyze my legs, I pressed them together, making the fabric stay closed.

Santino moved, holding both my arms above my head, his eyes locked on mine, with that intense green gaze.

"You can cover up, but know that when I decide you're mine completely, a bathrobe won't stop me," he growled.

"Why? Why all this interest in someone who doesn't even experience pleasure?" This time I wasn't being stupid; I just didn't understand him.

"Who said I don't? Who was the idiot who said that? I want you, *ragazza mia*, I desire every part of your body. You have no idea how much I want to do with you. Just thinking about it gets me hard." Santino got off me.

My eyes traveled down his body, and yes, Santino Vacchiano was visibly erect, marking the fabric of his pants. *Damn, damn, damn!*

"Your mother left clothes for you in that suitcase," he pointed to the suitcase. "Know that I'm keeping an eye on you; any slip-up will be added to when I fuck you hard," he declared, leaving the room, leaving me alone and still without my phone, which the bastard took with him.

CHAPTER ELEVEN

Santino

"Brother, are you sure about this?" Valentino asked, unbuttoning the top buttons of his shirt and crossing his legs as he looked at me with that accusatory gaze.

"Sure? Have I ever been sure about anything?" I huffed, getting up from the couch and pulling out a pack of cigarettes from my pocket. "What a pleasure to have my own house and be able to smoke inside it..."

"Your dream isn't going to come true, not now!" I lifted my eyes as my future wife came down the stairs.

She was wearing a loose dress, her legs exposed, the floral fabric in shades of red contrasting with her beauty.

"Who's going to stop me?"

"Please, San, don't smoke that damn cigarette!" Valentino grumbled, annoyed.

The doorbell rang, and before Cinzia had a chance to respond, she went to answer it. It must have been my sister. Cinzia had spent the afternoon checking the details of the dress, and tonight Pietra would come back so we could choose the wedding rings. My sister had the best contacts in Sicily, and she was in charge of bringing a selection of rings.

I saw my nephew run into the room, looking at my chest to identify his uncles.

"Uncle Samy." He ran and threw himself into my arms, and I put the pack of cigarettes back into my pocket, hugging him.

"Oh, heavens! What did you eat today, you're such a chunk." I pretended to drop him, seeing my brother get up from the couch and motioning for me to toss Tommie to him. "Let's see if Uncle Valen has the strength to catch you..."

Tommie let out a squeal when I threw him into the air, and my brother caught him. We both laughed as the boy enjoyed it; he always did.

"Oh God! You two better not start tossing Tommaso around!" My sister immediately warned.

"Catch, San!" Valentino ignored our sister and threw the little one back.

"More, more, more!" Tommie requested when I held him in my arms.

The kid was a featherweight; there was no way I'd let him fall to the ground.

"No, Santino! Don't throw him!" I smiled at Pietra, who stamped her foot as I tossed the boy, laughing at her reaction. "You idiot! Do that with your own child when you have one..."

I dodged the pillow that was thrown at me. Valentino put the little one down, and Tommie wanted more, but his mother prevented it.

"Here are the rings..."

"Pietra, did you talk to one of the family's housekeepers to furnish this house and provide everything it needed?" I asked my sister, who looked at me, confused.

"Yes, why? Is something wrong? Did they forget something? I can speak with Carlota; she'll be the housekeeper for you as well. I'm sure you'll like her, Cinzia." My sister smiled at her friend.

My parents' estate had a single housekeeper, unlike my sister's house, which would be shared with ours. We were even going to hire one for my residence, but Mrs. Carlota said she could handle both houses.

"There's nothing wrong, Pipi." Cinzia used the ridiculous nickname she always called my sister.

"There is something wrong because I went to check the bathrobes." Cinzia looked at me, frowning.

"What's wrong?" my sister asked, confused.

"There's nothing wrong with it, Santino." Cinzia emphasized again.

"Yes, there is. They got Cinzia's size wrong." Her face turned red, and Pietra understood what I was referring to. "I'm not accepting this because it could happen again, and if I find out who made this mistake, I'll have them fired."

I growled, knowing it was one of the family's maids, some of whom I had slept with out of boredom, someone who couldn't stand that Cinzia would be my wife. The truth was, no woman could match her beauty.

"Friend, Santino is quite a perfectionist, and he's right. I'll ask Carlota to look into it."

"I really don't care..." Cinzia said again, her face returning to its normal color.

"But I do care. She'll be my damn wife and deserves to be respected. If some joker thinks this is funny, I'll punch the face of that idiot." I walked over to them, standing next to Cinzia, tucking a strand of her blonde hair behind her ear and looking deep into her eyes. "She's beautiful, a woman worthy of being the wife of a mafioso."

I winked at Cinzia, hoping she would let me have her, damn it, I just wanted to fuck her daring little pussy.

"Your little seductive man game doesn't convince me. I don't need you emphasizing how beautiful I am; I know it already. People have been telling me that for ages." The bitch shrugged, narrowing my eyes as my sister tried to stifle a laugh.

"What are you talking about?" My whisper came out somewhat sharp.

"Your trick doesn't work on me, Vacchiano..."

"Are you still a virgin?" I asked, the question gnawing at me inside. After all, I initially thought she was, but I was starting to have real doubts.

"I wish I could say no, but unfortunately, I am." Cinzia wrinkled the tip of her upturned nose at me.

Her lips had that glossy shine, the *gloss* I wanted to wipe off with my mouth.

"Well, it doesn't seem that way. Don't try to fool me; there's a very effective method to find out." I tilted my head to the side, suspicious.

"I'm a virgin. Being a virgin isn't always synonymous with inexperience. Like you, I enjoyed my single life; I just saved myself in one place for my husband." The shrew continued, leaving me irritated, and I took a step toward her.

"So, you mean that..."

"No, Santino, you're going too far with your perverted mind." Pietra stepped between us.

"How do you know? It's not her!" I grunted, wanting my sister out of our way.

"Because we always share everything." Pietra looked into my eyes, wanting me to control myself.

"Hell! I'm starting to think it would be better to be the Don and marry the Colombian..."

"There's still time; Valentino hasn't been officially named yet." Cinzia emerged from behind her friend, mocking me.

"There's no time. That hot Colombian is already mine." My brother hadn't even met his wife yet and was already saying she was his.

"They say Latinas are the hottest, in terms of destruction too. Be careful, Valentino," Cinzia even mocked my brother.

"I'm not afraid." Valen shrugged.

"I pray she's so beautiful and destructive that she ends up ruining you." My fiancée made me roll my eyes.

"You know, right? Never leave your fiancée next to my hurricane," I declared, looking for my nephew. "Choose the rings; I'm going for a walk on the beach with Tommie..."

"No, Santino, he's already had a bath," my sister warned.

"It's fine, Mom, I'll bathe again later." Tommie ran toward the back door of the house, and Valentino followed me.

The beach was a bit far from there; we walked over a path of stones until we reached the sand.

CHAPTER TWELVE

Cinzia

In front of the mirror, I saw my reflection. The dress lightly touched the floor, a strapless style that accentuated my breasts. The corset shaped my waist, adorned with white gemstones. From the waist down, the dress flared out in fine silk. The hairdresser had just left my room; my hair was styled with all my strands gathered at the back of my head, with some curls created by the *curling iron*. My long bangs were tucked behind my ear, allowing them to fall over my forehead. The makeup was light, highlighting my blue eyes.

I walked to the French doors of my new room. Was there a chance I could shove Santino Vacchiano into the guest room? I refused to leave this room, and besides, he was the jerk.

He hadn't even slept at home that night, leaving me locked in, not even giving me the door code, which was no surprise. After all, if I had tried to escape once, who's to say I wouldn't try again.

Santino hadn't asked about Marco again, but I knew that hadn't stopped him. He wanted to know about the man I was planning to run away with, but I couldn't tell him; revealing that would endanger Marco's life.

I pulled the curtain aside, looking at the two gardens of the interconnected houses, the two pools with safety barriers around them, where the wedding was prepared. There wouldn't be many guests. It was late afternoon, the sunlight turning the sky an orange hue.

I spotted the twins, both in suits but without jackets, all buttons done up, which made me unsure. Which one was my fiancé? One moved his hand impatiently, while the other was calm, smiling at something he had said. The impatient one was Santino; Valentino was usually more reserved in his movements, showing no nervousness. The calmness of my future husband's brother was eerie; he was the only one of the brothers who inherited more of their mother's temperament. After all, Verena was a Zornickel. And despite how crazy that family was, I always heard my father say they were frightening, they thought before acting, silently, the kind who kills in silence, without much fuss. I believe that's why Don Tommaso preferred Valentino in charge of the Cosa Nostra, and Santino never wanted that position himself. He knew he had the explosive temperament of the Vacchianos, a short fuse. Valentino was the perfect dose to dominate the Cosa Nostra, and Santino the perfect right-hand man for the next Don.

It was as if the twins completed each other.

I heard a knock at the door and turned to find my father, dressed in a full suit. To think this all started because of him, an official member of the Cosa Nostra, handing over his daughter in a contract marriage, all because he thought staying in the mafia was best for me. But it wasn't; I never wanted to stay in it. I wanted out, out of this world that restricts women in every way. We have no voice; we must yield to men, if the man loves the woman, as in the cases of Tommaso and Verena, Pietra and Enrico, the husbands indulged their every wish. It was as if they had a say in the mafia.

A fact that didn't happen with my mother. I saw how Dad repressed her; she never had a voice, it was a natural occurrence in contract marriages within the mafia.

And I knew it was nearly impossible for Santino to love me, as I hated him, and would do anything to irritate him, which meant we'd have zero chance of anyone ending up in love.

"You look beautiful, my daughter," Dad said.

I simply smiled. I was angry with him, angry for never loving me as a father should love his child, for always seeing me as merchandise to be delivered to Vacchiano. I was sure I was never a calm teenager, but it was his duty to love and care for me, not to hand me over to Vacchiano, thinking that would make me stop.

It was always for the Cosa Nostra; the mafia always came first.

"I know that at some point you'll thank me for doing this; it's the best for you, my daughter..." He dared to say.

"How can you judge that this is best for me? Did you ever ask what I wanted? Did you ask if I wanted to stay in the mafia? No, so don't come talking about gratitude. Let's just get this damn wedding over with," I muttered, holding onto my dress as I passed by him. I had difficulty descending the stairs but didn't ask for help.

We passed through the back door, and I looked from a distance. Everything was arranged, everyone seated in their places. My father linked his arm with mine; I didn't remove mine because, at that moment, it was best not to make a fuss.

I knew Aldo wouldn't say anything; he was a wise man who had already noticed how irritated I was. There was no way to argue when he would come up with reasons for everything.

A wedding march began to play slowly as we approached. A path of small tiles led to the altar, the yellowish lights were on as night began to take over the sky.

There was no escape now. In front of the altar stood my fiancé, the man who had once been my first love, the same man I had seen grow up into a tremendous jerk for not being able to control his member.

Santino was handsome, extremely sexy, but he was not the type of man to marry, as he didn't know how to control himself and be faithful to just one woman. And I was about to marry my worst nightmare, the epitome of the man I had always sworn to hate. I wanted a marriage based on love, a husband faithful to me.

We stopped, facing him. Santino extended his hand to me, Dad placing my hand on his, as always his touch was warm, the watch on his wrist gleaming in gold.

"Wait a second," I said, holding one of the buttons of his shirt.

"What are you going to do, you crazy?" he growled softly, with everyone watching us.

"I'm not going to risk marrying the wrong brother, though it might be better. Anyone is better than you," I declared, seeing through the open button the tattoo on his chest.

"Crazy is an understatement for you!" He fastened the button, intertwining his arms with mine, in a forced gesture.

And at that moment, my worst torment was about to begin: a marriage with one of the biggest jerks in Sicily.

CHAPTER THIRTEEN

Santino

I slid the ring onto the little woman's fourth finger, the white nail polish contrasting with the delicate jewelry. Cinzia did the same, placing the ring on my finger; she was clearly nervous.

I believe that was the longest we had spent together without arguing, and that was because we had a priest in front of us performing the ceremony. Father José was the family priest; he was the one who blessed all the weddings, poor man was so old he could barely speak properly.

Finally, the words were spoken:

"I declare you, husband and wife. The husband may kiss the bride." The priest's slow voice released what I had wanted to do since the day Cinzia returned to Sicily.

I pulled her by the waist, but it wasn't possible to press my body against hers because of the volume of the dress.

"You're not going to kiss my lips," she whispered through clenched teeth.

"I'm not kissing your forehead; you're going to kiss me now, Cinzia!" I growled in my whisper.

"I hate you..."

"We're even on that score." I pulled her a little more forcefully, pressing my lips against hers.

Cinzia wasn't surprised, as she had already expected me to do that. My lips met hers, and I slightly parted my mouth, lightly touching her tongue; her touch was gentle. Her lips felt like two soft cushions; I didn't want to let go, I wanted to deepen the kiss, tear off that dress, fuck her with such force she'd never forget who she belonged to.

But not everything that glitters is gold, and the damn woman pulled away, holding my chest and pushing me slightly backward.

"I hope you enjoyed that because there won't be any more." She blinked several times, making it clear how unsettled she was.

"Admit it, Mrs. Vacchiano, your panties are all wet right now..." My voice died as I spoke close to her ear; she turned her face with wide eyes.

"It's drier than the Sahara Desert, maybe it's not as good as you think." Her tone was haughty.

"Then prove it..."

"Keep dreaming, your fingers will stay far away from my panties." I smirked at her words because I was going to have my fingers messing around inside her cunt.

"I always get what I want, and I want you, Cinzia. I'm going to spank your ass so hard you'll spend a week sitting and remembering what it's like to be in your husband's arms," I grunted.

"You're dreaming too big, Vacchiano." She turned to smile at the guests as if we hadn't just had a confrontation.

We linked our arms, I held hers firmly, looking at our family and some family friends seated in the white chairs. Because it was a hastily arranged wedding, there weren't many guests; I couldn't risk that crazy woman running away again.

Cinzia was going to run away; I had seen with my own eyes the craziness she was about to commit, and nothing would stop her. That woman was determined. But I could be ten times worse.

From the moment she mentioned another someone, I had my men keeping tabs on her. I even considered that she wouldn't be crazy enough to run away, thought she wouldn't be mad, because her acting was perfect. But she did run away, my men saw it, and I hadn't even slept yet; it was just another of many sleepless nights or light sleep nights. At the first touch from them, I grabbed my jacket and headed to where she was going. I should have waited longer to find out who this Marco was, damn it! It was driving me crazy just thinking she might love someone else.

Not that I wanted to be loved, but fucking a woman who thinks of another man is enough to make anyone go soft.

A wedding dinner was prepared at my parents' house. Pietra made it clear that no woman I had previously been with should be invited. Little did she know I always omitted half of those I had slept with; I couldn't help being impulsive. When I saw someone, I was already fucking them. I was tired of fucking in corners at mafia events and then finding out the woman was married. Well, that was never a problem for me, after all, I wasn't the committed man, which didn't justify being the betrayed one. Just thinking about the roles being reversed made me furious.

Cinzia would never be touched by another man, even if I had to monitor her 24/7.

We were the first to leave through the stone path, an elderly lady guiding us into the house. My wife was tense; I knew this because the hand she had on mine was still sweaty.

A dinner table was set, and we stopped by the door, receiving all the congratulations. One of the last was my brother, who had a smug smile on his lips. Extending his arm, I released my wife to give him a hug, with a pat on the back.

"I can give you a wedding gift if you want..." he said, flashing his mischievous smile.

"Do it, Valentino; you'll be doing me a favor," Cinzia said beside me, understanding what Valen suggested.

"I'm so envious of this wedding, my condolences, brother." I rolled my eyes as he touched my shoulder.

"Don't forget it'll be you in a while." I shrugged.

"Two years still, since the Colombian girl is in college. I'm thinking of paying a visit to my fiancée, after all, I've never seen her before." Valentino flashed his sleazy smile.

"You're going to get yourself into trouble with Aragón," I warned him.

"Isn't Aragón having problems with the Serbs? He said his sister would be at risk too. Well, I'll go check it out before it's time to take over the Cosa Nostra."

"In other words, you want to make sure the girl is a virgin, don't you? I hope she's smart and doesn't save herself for you," Cinzia retorted.

"Just like you were, sister-in-law?" Valentino shot back.

"I was pretty dumb, actually. I should've become a handrail like your brother, where everyone runs their hands over. Why is it that when a woman does that she's a slut, but when a man does it he's a player? I'm disgusted by you, Santino. What if you pass some disease to me?" I growled at the girl, and Valentino burst into loud laughter.

"Man, you're so screwed." Valen shook his head as he left.

We stayed alone for a while. I pulled her by the arms, speaking close to her ear:

"I'm being very patient with you, but know that if you don't stop, I'm going to punish you, and that's not a bluff!"

"Then punish me, Vacchiano, because I'm not going to bed with you." Cinzia pulled her arm away and resumed smiling at the guests as if nothing had happened.

CHAPTER FOURTEEN

Cinzia

Luckily, dinner was over. All I wanted at that moment was my bed—a solitary bed, far from Santino Vacchiano, far from his insinuations and the threats he constantly made.

We said our goodbyes to everyone, and Santino's parents' house was empty, with only them remaining. Even my parents had left; I didn't talk to my dad—I didn't want to talk to him at that moment.

"Can we go?" I asked impatiently, knowing there was no escape; either I went to my new home or slept on the street.

"Yes, let's go," Santino agreed.

"Can I trust you, son?" Mrs. Verena asked.

"Don't trust me, mom." He shrugged like the spoiled kid he was.

I rolled my eyes, holding onto that heavy dress which was already irritating me. We moved towards the door; I didn't wait for him or even hear what his mother said to him. Nothing his parents said made Santino change his mind; he was a fool, a jerk, and it was in his blood. It was as if he heard in one ear and it went out the other, without filtering anything.

The front door was open. I walked through it onto the sidewalk, hearing Santino's footsteps behind me. I entered the path to our house, walking quickly, not even noticing when my heel got stuck between two stones.

"Ouch!" I twisted my foot, falling, my hands crashing to the ground, tears of pain welling up in my eyes. "Damn it!"

Panicking with all that fabric in the skirt, I pushed it aside until I saw the man stop beside me, helping with the fabric. His hand touched mine, finding my heel, and easily removing it from my foot, leaving it there, picking me up into his arms.

"I can walk," I grumbled, making a pained face.

"Yes, I imagine."

I held onto his shirt. My fiancé stopped in front of the door and typed in a sequence of numbers, which was so quick I didn't even manage to catch it.

"Are you going to make me your prisoner by not telling me the house code?" I asked as he entered the house, heading straight for the stairs, where he climbed the steps.

"Until you prove to me that you're trustworthy, you'll stay here, locked up, with no visitors, nothing." Santino walked down the hallway and entered our bedroom—the same one I had slept in alone the night before. I didn't know where my fiancé had been or if he had slept with another woman, but he hadn't been home.

Santino laid me down on the bed, his eyes meeting mine.

"You can leave, I'll manage on my own. I don't want to see your face today, and know that you'll need more than a door code to keep me your prisoner." His eyes narrowed when he half-closed them.

"This room is as much mine as it is yours..."

"I slept here alone last night, so I claimed it first." I cut him off, trying to sit up, but my foot hurt from the movement. "Damn it..."

I sighed, trying to contain the pain.

"Let me see it..."

"No!" I swatted his hand away when he tried to touch my foot.

"I'm just going to take a look. Is all this fear about having me close to you?"

"It's disgust, actually..." My voice trailed off as he huffed, ignoring my protests, pulling up the mound of dress fabric. "I'm wearing tights..."

Saying that, he easily tore the delicate fabric of the tights, removing them from my foot. He ran his hand over the other foot, taking off the heel. I almost thanked him for doing it, as my toes were all squashed.

His fingers held onto my foot, a jolt of electricity running through every part of my body, making me part my lips, a sigh escaping.

"I'm going downstairs to get an ice pack; your ankle is a bit swollen," Santino said, getting up and leaving the room.

That was my chance to get up and lock the door. I managed to lift one foot at a time, trying to stand, but I didn't expect my foot to hurt so much when it touched the ground, causing me to lose my balance and fall again.

"Damn it..." I whined, searching for my ankle, but the infernal dress was in the way.

Tears began to well up in my eyes, tears of anger, tears from that damned huge dress that was suffocating me.

I wanted to reach around to unfasten the buttons on my back, but there were so many—various ones. Who the hell invented this stupid dress?

"What are you doing on the floor?" Santino appeared, kneeling beside me, ready to help me up.

"Undo... undo these damn buttons on my back," I stammered through my choked voice.

He didn't say anything, positioning himself behind me. He didn't unfasten the buttons; he simply grabbed the sides, pulling hard until the buttons popped off. With his help, I managed to stand.

"Pull down the fabric and don't look at me!" I demanded, hearing him huff behind me as I leaned on my good leg.

I felt his fingers slide over my skin, causing small shivers—a gesture he noticed. As he felt the fabric move over my breasts, I covered them with my hand since the dress was designed without a bra. I turned my face away as he pulled the fabric down, letting the heavy skirt fall to the floor.

I gasped as he lifted me out of the dress, my butt pressing against his pelvis.

"I told you to close your eyes." I looked for something to cover myself with.

"You were being quite naive if you really thought I would turn my face away and not check out the size of your ass..."

"You bastard! Ouch..." I tried to place both feet on the ground, collapsing onto the bed.

My husband smiled maliciously. I grabbed a pillow, covering my breasts with my hand and forearm, then quickly replacing it with the pillow.

"Get out, Santino!" I roared, feeling humiliated and in pain.

"I'm not going anywhere." He shrugged, holding my leg and placing it on the bed, picking up the ice pack from the floor and placing it on my ankle. "Do you need anything else?"

"Yes, I do." He looked at me, his beautiful green eyes contrasting with his tanned skin. At that moment, I wanted to throw myself into his lap and beg him to touch me, but it all passed in seconds when I remembered what a jerk he was. "Get out of my sight!"

"Then deal with your swollen ankle on your own..."

"I don't need your help with anything! NOTHING!" I screamed as Santino got up and left the room.

"I'll leave. Maybe I'll find a hot model around..."

"Go ahead, Santino Vacchiano, do what you do best—be a jerk," I said, a bit worked up with my eyes full of tears, but I didn't let them fall.

CHAPTER FIFTEEN

Santino

I stopped in front of the bar under the stairs, which had been converted into a minibar with the whiskies I drank the most. I grabbed a glass from the rack, took the first bottle that came to hand, and filled the glass.

I downed it in one gulp, the only way to swallow Cinzia and her big ass. *Damn it*, I felt it rubbing against my cock. I wanted to grope her, but I was sure that if I did, the crazy woman would scream. I only like loud women in bed.

The glass shook when I set it on the counter. I could go back upstairs and insist on sleeping in that room, but I didn't; I didn't even feel like going on a hunt. I didn't want another woman, I wanted my wife, damn it, my wife and all her delicious curves. *Hell*!

My phone vibrated in my pocket. I took it out and saw a message from my brother:

"**Sorry to interrupt your hot night, but we need to go to the distribution center.**"

I let out a long sigh, putting the phone back in my pocket. I didn't even bother to tell Cinzia. If Valentino sent the message, it was urgent; my brother wouldn't text about something trivial.

I headed for the door, about to open it, when I heard footsteps coming from upstairs. I looked up and saw my wife in a robe that fit her perfectly. She hadn't showered yet; she hadn't had time to do so in such a short period.

"Where are you going?" Cinzia asked, stopping at the top of the stairs. I glanced down at her ankle, still swollen as before.

"I have matters to attend to..."

"Going out to fuck another woman during our honeymoon has become a matter to attend to?" Cinzia arched an eyebrow.

"Funny, because I didn't even know we were on a honeymoon, and if I remember correctly, you insisted I go after someone else, or am I mistaken?" I gripped the door handle. Cinzia pulled her hand out of the robe's pocket.

My eyes didn't stray from her intense blue ones, her hair slightly tousled from a once-perfect hairstyle.

"I'm going to give you a chance because I need to honor at least my first night married. This will be your only chance, Santino. If you walk out that door, there won't be another." The blonde bit the corner of her plump lip, lips I wanted to devour, to feel on mine.

My phone vibrated again. I took it out, seeing a new message from Valentino:

"Damn it, let's go, Santino!"

Hell, my eyes lifted to my sweet wife, her curves coming to mind, that *big ass* I wanted to spank, squeeze, hit, and fuck slowly, hard... I closed my eyes, frustrated.

Frustration overwhelmed me completely, the anger at being interrupted in my one moment of having my wife all to myself.

"I'm sorry to disappoint you, but my duty will always be to the Cosa Nostra," I declared, not going into details.

"Jerk..." That was all I heard from her lips as I left our house.

In front of my father's house, there were already four cars parked. Valentino had recruited all his men and brought some of mine; that's why my presence was necessary. I ran towards the open door, quickly sitting down and seeing my brother holding a gun, which he extended to me.

"You'll need this; you left it at headquarters." I took it, placing it between my legs.

"What's the problem?" I asked, giving one last look at my house where I left my *little hurricane*.

"Do you remember that shipment that arrived unannounced?" Valen asked, and I nodded. "It wasn't a coincidence; it was planned. They wanted to use our port. We don't know who they are yet, but we're about to find out. That port belongs to the Cosa Nostra; it's the only place goods can come and go. The first time, they didn't succeed because our men were on guard. I spoke with Dad and asked him to clear the port and put men on watch. I just got the call that they were there. Whoever it is, we'll find out which mafia they're working for, even though we already have an idea of who it might be…

"The Serbians," I whispered, knowing that Darko Cosic, the Serbian mafia godfather, might be seeking revenge for his father's death.

He was silent; no one had ever seen his face, but he was trying to rebuild the mafia that had been destroyed by the Cosa Nostra, led by my father. The Swiss mafia, In Ergänzung, led by my cousin Yan Zornickel, and the Los Sombríos Cartel, led by Ferney Aragón, my cousin's husband and also Valentino's future brother-in-law, as he had married his sister off to the future Don of the Cosa Nostra. My brother was going to marry Yulia Aragón, sealing the alliance between the Cartel and our mafia.

"Something tells me that if it is indeed Darko behind this, he won't be here, as the bastard wouldn't show his face like this," I whispered.

"That's why we can't kill everyone; we need some of them alive to find out Darko's plans," Valentino said, and I nodded.

We both fell silent, watching outside as the car sped away.

"I hope I didn't interrupt you," Valentino finally said.

"Actually, you did, quite a lot. I could be between my wife's legs fucking her right now, but here I am, pissed off, with blood in my eyes wanting to kill the Serbian bastard who possibly interrupted my one chance to have sex without a storm-level Cinzia hurricane," I grumbled, still thinking about her disappointed blue eyes.

"So she was going to give in?" I turned my face, looking at my reflection as another person.

"She was, she said it would be my only chance..."

"Let me guess, you left without even explaining that you were going on a mission?" I shrugged, making it clear. "Damn it, Santino, why didn't you explain? Sometimes you're really stupid; it was just a matter of explaining..."

"Go fuck yourself. When it's your wife, you can do whatever you want." I shrugged.

"Idiot!" He shook his head.

We both went on high alert as the car slowed down, the headlights turned off. We exited the cars quietly. Like me, Valentino signaled to the men; they couldn't tell us apart in the darkness of the place. Voices were present inside the warehouse. My brother went in the opposite direction from me, surrounding the intruders inside. From the corner of my eye, I saw them using flashlights, unloading a boat, trying to bring some illegal goods into Sicily.

"The house is falling apart," my brother said as the car headlights lit up, revealing the men who quickly started shooting at us, not knowing where to aim as the car lights blinded them.

For us, it was easy, shooting nonstop and watching them fall to the ground.

"We need at least one alive, circle around and take one hostage," I whispered to my soldiers asking them to check, as Valentino instructed them to do the same.

I approached my brother, still aiming my gun in case any of them were alive.

"I think we've killed them all, damn it!" I grunted, irritated.

"There was no avoiding killing them; they were shooting at close range. Let's see if we can find the Serbian symbol," Valentino said.

I approached them, a lifeless body covered in blood, the red liquid draining from the countless holes we had made. With my shoe, I pushed the dead man's head to the side, seeing what we wanted—the Serbian symbol.

"We've got what we suspected," I murmured.

"But we don't have anything on Darko; they're all dead. The bastard is still a mystery." Valentino was irritated, kicking the already dead man on the ground.

"*Capos?*" We both looked up at the soldier who approached. "We found this..."

He threw a man in front of us.

"Take him to the hideout; we'll meet there," Valentino declared.

We were still not convinced about that idiot; there was a risk he would die without talking, and we didn't know how loyal he was to his clan.

CHAPTER SIXTEEN

Santino

"He's not going to say anything..." Valentino's irritated voice invaded my hearing as I let out a long sigh, watching the blood of the idiot drain from my hands.

"As long as he's breathing, I'll keep trying," I growled, feeling the knuckles in my other hand.

I was with one of our soldiers torturing the man who hadn't even given his name. We knew he spoke English, but everything he said was in Serbian, still laughing in our faces. The soldiers said he spoke English at the distribution center. But the bastard was loyal to Darko Cosic; he hadn't uttered a single word to give us any clue.

"Finish him off, Santino," my father said, making me look at him.

Valentino was next to our father, as were Enrico and Aldo. Enrico was my father's second-in-command, while Aldo was the advisor. As usual, Valentino was by Dad's side, as if he were indirectly always training to be the Don, a burden I never wanted. I liked getting my hands dirty, feeling the blood of others on my hands.

Both of us were trained to kill, but beyond that, Valentino was trained to lead, and I was to be his right-hand man. I didn't even want that, but I knew my brother needed me.

I turned my gaze back to the man's mangled face on the floor; he didn't even have teeth anymore but continued to smile, a damned masochist who seemed to take pleasure in his own pain. I grabbed my gun from my back, aimed at his head, and fired a shot right through the middle. The man fell to the side, his hands still chained.

"And with that, we have nothing, absolutely nothing on that Cosic bastard!" I declared, putting the gun back on my back, removing the knuckles from my other hand, and handing them to one of the soldiers. I looked at the men standing there, arms crossed, staring at the dead man on the floor.

Like me, they were outraged. How could someone slowly take over territory and never show their face?

"We still have nothing, but the little devil is trying to invade territories that aren't his. At some point, he's going to make a mistake, and at the first one he makes, we'll be there. What matters now is that all our territories are safe. Send messages to our men in Vegas, inform Yan Zornickel and Ferney Aragón about the near invasion, they need to know that Darko Cosic is continuing his damned father's legacy."

We all nodded at my father's words. After all, the three clans had united to kill Bojan Cosic when he kidnapped my cousin Amélia, wanting to take the triplets from her womb, making one of them marry his son Darko, a son no one had ever seen. Bojan was going to kill Amélia, remove the babies from her womb, leaving only one alive while the other two would die. It was a union of the Cosa Nostra, In Ergänzung, and Los Sombríos that killed Bojan and all the men with him, about thirty Serbian mafia men, leaving the mafia without a godfather.

What we didn't expect was that a year later, his son would make it clear he was taking over the Serbian mafia, slowly making moves, and we knew either he was going to seek revenge or stay quiet. But to try to infiltrate Sicily, staying quiet was not what he wanted, because everyone knew Sicily was our territory; we dominated all of it.

"So while we do nothing?" I asked suddenly.

"There's nothing to be done, brother. We're not going after someone whose whereabouts we don't know. He's not even in the same place in Germany where his father was; he's in another place, another country, no one knows, there's no way to know. Darko Cosic will gain territory before showing his face..."

"Or he may never show it." I sighed, cutting off my brother's speech. "Well, I'm going home, I'm filthy."

I headed toward the exit door of the hideout.

"Dispose of this body and keep the distribution center clean; we don't want any trace of those bastards," Valentino ordered the soldiers.

I heard footsteps behind me when I opened the door. The hideout was at the back of the estate, near the rocks leading to the sea sand. We called it a hideout because it was on a rock, a place that anyone passing by would barely notice as a torture center for the men we captured, like our enemies.

Everything was dark; my feet touched the grass. It was so quiet, it hardly seemed like there had been a wedding there hours earlier; there was nothing left, the organizing team had already cleaned everything.

"Mom, are you awake?" I was surprised to see the house light on; usually, Mom wouldn't stay awake while we were torturing someone because she didn't like us doing it but preferred us to do it at home rather than on the streets.

In fact, Verena might try to instill some sense into us, but she couldn't do it with someone born to kill.

"Your mother is awake; she's with your wife..."

"My what?" I turned my face to my father, who had now joined me.

"After you left, your mother went to your house; she wanted to see how Cinzia was, even though she said it was nothing. Verena brought her to our house, concerned about her swollen ankle. We called our doctor to assess the severity; Dr. Ferrer left here shortly before you returned, gave her some medication, but it was nothing serious; she's fine..."

"Yes, I knew she was fine," I rolled my eyes at their exaggerated concern.

"Understand, Santino, now you're Cinzia's husband. You should have called the doctor for that injury. It wasn't anything serious, but it could have been more severe; it's your duty to take care of your wife!" Dad was straightforward with his words.

"And I know that," I declared as we approached my parents' house, which was also the headquarters of the Cosa Nostra.

"I hope you do." Tommaso sighed, knowing it was pointless to argue since we had the same strong-willed nature.

I entered the house, finding my mother who wasn't even startled to see me in such a deplorable state. Verena was so tired of complaining that her 24 years as the mother of mobsters had made her more resilient.

"Where's my wife?" I asked.

"She just went to your house..."

"I hope you didn't tell her the house's code," I growled.

"No, dear, I don't want to cause more problems for my daughter-in-law by letting her know the son I have." I rolled my eyes, stepping away from her.

CHAPTER SEVENTEEN

Cinzia

I typed the code into the door, leaving it unlocked, as Mrs. Verena had helped me lie to Santino. My own mother-in-law, my husband's mother, was the one who helped me with this. Who was I to go against her decision? Verena was the strongest woman I had ever known; she went through everything with her husband, saw him betray her, was rejected by him, and still overcame the difficulties with style. She made the mobster fall madly in love with her and became the most envied woman among all the women of Cosa Nostra, simply by being at the Don's side and having great influence over him.

Everyone knew that Don Tommaso did everything for his wife; he might as well have licked the ground she walked on. The man who was the biggest womanizer in Sicily became the most faithful of all.

But I knew I couldn't handle it. I knew I would go crazy when Santino betrayed me; it was as if I was already expecting it, as if my mind was preparing for his possible betrayal—a fact that would make me so angry. I can't handle betrayal or lies; for me, honesty is what matters.

I headed towards the stairs, knowing I had left the door unlocked, so he wouldn't even suspect I used it to get in.

The medicine Dr. Ferrer gave helped ease the pain in my ankle. He said it might be sore for a few days, but that I'd be better soon.

I went to my room; the bed was still impeccably made. I knew Santino hadn't gone out with anyone because his mother told me he was on a mission with Valentino. What confused me was why he left the house without telling me where he was going, making it seem like he didn't want to be by my side?

What was really true for Santino was that it was all just carnal pleasure; he wanted sex, and nothing more.

I was going to give myself to him. I knew my duty as a wife was to give myself to my husband on our first night, but he left, left without explaining where he was going, all because of his ego, as if he wanted me to understand that he would be with another woman.

I believed that my marital role had become a distant hypothesis because at that moment, I wanted to slap the beautiful face of that damned mobster. What was the use of a lofty demeanor, a beautiful face, an extremely hot body if it came with a horrible personality?

I was heading to the closet in search of pajamas since I had already taken a bath before going to Mrs. Verena's house. I needed to release that hairstyle that was driving me crazy, which is why I bathed before going to my mother-in-law's house, who had come to my home to check on me.

I turned my face when I heard movement entering the room. My eyes widened at the sight of my husband in such a deplorable state. He was still wearing the same clothes from the wedding, the shirt that had been white hours earlier was now stained red with blood, his hair disheveled, and there was blood all over his hand.

"Oh, heavens..." I whispered, concerned. "Did you get hurt?"

A smile formed at the corner of his lips, that beautiful smile capable of melting any underwear. Damn, why did I always feel wet when it came to him? Why did those delicious shivers only happen with him? I wanted to know what it would be like to have more of that, but having more of those shivers, those delicious twinges meant giving myself to my husband. But how could I do that with someone who saw me only as an object?

I should be used to it, as that's exactly what it means to be the daughter of a mobster: to be treated as an object.

Santino walked slowly towards me, not saying a word, raising his hand with bloodied fingers wanting to touch my cheek, which made me take a step back.

"Are you worried about me, wife?" he whispered with his usual hint of mockery in his tone.

"I just wanted to know," I said nonchalantly.

"Just 'wanted to know'? I don't want to talk." He shrugged and headed towards the suite.

"Asshole," I muttered.

"If you admitted that you were worried..." Santino opened the suite door, ignoring me.

"Why would I worry about someone who doesn't worry about me?"

"Who said I don't worry?" Santino stopped just inside the suite, his eyes half-closed, looking at me.

"You. I don't need anyone to tell me things when I see with my own eyes. If you really cared about me, you wouldn't have had sex with another woman at our engagement dinner, you wouldn't have stayed out all night, and you wouldn't have left without giving me an explanation. No, Santino, you don't care. In your twisted view, you might think you do, but when it comes to women, the first one who spreads her legs, you think of nothing but your own pleasure. I was going to give myself to you, I was going to do what I was obliged to do since they gave me to a bastard like you, but the fact that you left like that only made me realize that I was right all along; you're a bastard who only cares about himself," I said all at once.

He didn't say anything, just listened, his eyes analyzing my reaction, until he finally exhaled and said:

"Is that what you think? Did you come to that conclusion based on what?"

"Don't come at me with that bullshit; you're no saint..."

"You were gone for five years and still think you know everything about me?"

"I grew up in the same environment as you, I saw you go out with various women, I saw you become a man, I'm best friends with your sister. What else is there to know about you?" I crossed my arms, raising an eyebrow.

"Everything you know about me is basic. We haven't talked in years; to be honest, we never had a civilized conversation, it was always just jabs because for some reason, you never liked me. On our first kiss, you acted crazy and threw me into the pool. What do you really know about me? Nothing! Admit it, Cinzia Vacchiano, you know nothing!"

He threw it in my face; Santino still remembered our disastrous first kiss.

"Then prove it, because all I have about you are samples of how much of an asshole you are..."

I was panting, he looked at me thoughtfully, as if he was really considering what I said, until he fiddled with the door, signaling to close it, but before doing so, he said:

"Alright..."

And he closed the door, leaving me alone, staring at the closed door. What did he mean by that?

CHAPTER EIGHTEEN

Santino

I wrapped the towel around my waist, leaving my hair damp as I came out of the bathroom. I made sure to throw those clothes away—no one deserved to wear something soaked in someone else's blood.

I noticed the French door to the bedroom was open as I left the suite, the white curtain fluttering in the breeze.

Cinzia wasn't in the room, which led me to believe she was elsewhere. I walked toward the door, my bare feet touching the floor, and saw the sun rising over the vast sea in the distance, night giving way to day.

What a hectic honeymoon, and not for the reasons I wanted, because all I desired was to hear Cinzia moaning with her daring lips.

She heard my footsteps and turned around, my eyes trailing down her baby-doll dress. *Damn! What an amazing woman!* The short, lacy panties, the shirt highlighting her ample cleavage, the sunrise reflecting off her hair, making it more golden, her gaze meeting mine. She could be considered a woman with a sweet demeanor, that is, when she wasn't opening her mouth to provoke me.

"The sunrise is beautiful from here," she said with shining eyes.

"It becomes even more beautiful with your presence," I said, playing the charming man I could be.

Cinzia rolled her eyes. *Damn, why do my lines never work with her?*

My wife returned to appreciating the sunrise, as if even a mere landscape was better than my presence, ignoring me. I moved closer, her body flinching when I placed my hand on her waist, pressing her against my chest.

"I thought you wanted to get to know me better," I whispered, pushing her hair aside and blowing into her ear.

"The word 'know' doesn't always mean pressing your body against mine and rubbing your ass on me."

It was impossible not to smile at her honesty.

"We can use it both ways, intimately knowing each other." I held the soft silk of her baby-doll, touching her stomach. Feeling her smooth skin under my fingers, sliding down to the waistband of her shorts, my action was interrupted when she grabbed my hand, tightening her grip on my wrist.

"Right now, I don't want to get to know you intimately." Cinzia turned to face me. I instinctively lowered my eyes to her cleavage, right there, close to my hand; all I had to do was move a little higher, and I'd touch them.

"I want to fuck you, Cinzia Vacchiano," I said without diverting my eyes from her breasts, hearing her soft laugh.

"What did you say, Vacchiano?" She seemed not to have heard me.

"I want to eat you out." I was straightforward, meeting her eyes. "And I know you want it too..."

"No, I don't want to..." She tried to appear indifferent, but the way she was breathing, her eyes constantly shifting, the slight sweat at the corner of her forehead, even the way she swallowed hard at that moment, proved otherwise.

"Then prove it, or I'll find out for myself." My hand tightened around her waist.

"Find out for yourself? How exactly would you do that... Hey..." I smiled as she tried to step back, trapped by the balcony's railing.

My smile grew wider as, without her permission, I slipped my hand inside her shorts, feeling the damp fabric of her panties. She was so wet that my cock started to throb under the towel that was constricting it.

"My proof is right here, *ragazza mia*, your mind might not want me, but your pussy is crying out for my cock." Cinzia breathed heavily. "Tell me, my *little hurricane*, has anyone ever made you come just by whispering words in your ear?"

"That's technically impossible." Cinzia didn't remove my hand, but I knew she would soon.

I circled my finger over the fabric of her panties, feeling her button, the wet slit. I closed my eyes, imagining what it would be like to sit her on that balcony and fuck her hard.

"Well, the word 'impossible' doesn't exist for me." I pressed my member against her thigh.

I bit her ear, listening to her soft gasps.

"You know we're neighbors, right?" I growled, hearing my idiot brother's voice. Damn, this was the second time Valentino had interrupted my fucking.

Cinzia quickly blushed, not even looking down where my idiot brother was, running toward our room. I stood there alone, looking down, seeing Valentino's grin.

"You piece of shit," I complained.

"Good thing we're the same," he mocked.

"Don't you have anything better to do?" I leaned over the railing, talking to him.

"I'm heading to my fiancée's college. I found out she's at Columbia, so I'm going to visit my future wife..."

"You know that's in the United States, right?" I cut him off, frowning.

"Yes, I know. I'll soon become the Don. I'll have big responsibilities; this might be the only time I can go after my Colombian nymph..."

I knew what Valentino wanted to do. He'd never seen Yulia Aragón in person, only in photos, and the girl was beautiful. He knew better than anyone that Valentino wanted to go scare her because Valentino would never accept a wife who wasn't a virgin. And from what Amelia, our cousin and Yulia's sister-in-law, said, the girl was more advanced than me and Valentino combined. If I was having a headache with my *little hurricane*, I was sure Valen would suffer twice as much.

"If her brother finds out..."

"I couldn't care less about Aragón. If his sister isn't a virgin at our wedding, I won't marry her." Valentino was emphatic.

"Do you know when you're going?" I asked.

"Now. Our private jet is ready. I also want to stop by Owen and Yanni's club." I nodded.

Owen and Yanni were our cousins from the Swiss mafia. We were all family, an alliance between the two mafias when my father married Verena Zornickel, the woman who was the sister of the former Don of In Ergänzung.

"Just don't do anything crazy; that's my job," I mocked.

"Maybe I'll hit some parties and bang some American college girls." He gave me his roguish smile.

"I'm going inside because you've ruined my night two times in a row."

"Maybe it just wasn't your turn." The bastard laughed.

"Go fuck yourself!" I flipped him the bird, turning and going into my room. I closed the door, finding my wife lying on the bed. In the middle, she had made a pillow wall so each of us had our side.

Damn! I couldn't believe it. Me, Santino Vacchiano, sleeping with a fucking hot woman with a pillow wall between us? If she thought I was going to accept that, she was very wrong!

CHAPTER NINETEEN

Cinzia

"If you take down the wall I made, you'll sleep on the floor!"
"In your wildest dreams will I accept this Berlin Wall between us..."

"As if you knew anything about history," I interrupted, my voice dripping with mockery.

I turned my face away as Santino started throwing the pillows on the floor. I sat on the bed, my eyes wide open.

"You're not sleeping in just your underwear!" I declared, irritated.

"Do you prefer me without it?" He made a show of pulling down his boxer briefs slightly, revealing the V of his hairless, smooth abdomen. His ripped abs were every woman's fantasy. The good thing was, I hadn't been sane for a long time.

"If you take that off, I'll scream." I turned my eyes back to his face; I was breathless, my voice betraying me, and he noticed.

Damn it! Santino was a machine—a machine that could do everything. Well, I only needed to find out if he knew how to use all of his functions, a fact I didn't want to discover. *What a big liar I was; I did want to find out.*

But it was different. We were husband and wife. If he were a man who showed even a hint of fidelity, I'd have given in. But how could I live with the man I lost my virginity to, only to discover two days later that he might have gone to bed with another woman?

I wasn't born to be a mafia wife, but I became one.

"Shall we find out how your scream will sound?" he said, sliding his underwear down his member.

Damn, damn, damn!

Santino's penis was huge, the biggest I'd ever seen, not that I'd seen many—maybe three—but that was a good amount to compare. The fabric sliding off his member made his cock spring up, touching the tip of his abdomen. My husband, who was kneeling on the bed, sat down, removing his underwear.

Without hesitation, he knew exactly what he was doing, showing himself completely, and damn, he was even hotter without clothes. The tattoo on his chest was a flame starting from his back, rising over his shoulder, ending on his chest. One of his arms was entirely covered in tattoos.

I swallowed hard; maybe the only dry thing about me was my throat, because my pussy was not only wet but soaking, so wet that I could feel my juices dripping down my folds.

"You're not going to sleep like that," I whispered, trying to find my voice.

"I'll sleep how I want; my house, my rules..."

"Our house, and you're putting on shorts, even the underwear!" I exclaimed, horrified, looking at that hard, throbbing monstrosity. I was a virgin girl; I should act like one.

But no, all I wanted at that moment was that cock. I might be a virgin, but I was sure I had given oral pleasure to other men and let them pleasure me by touching my pussy, but that was it. Nothing more, because I could never marry someone who wasn't a virgin, which was a big mistake because that was my chance to leave the mafia.

It seemed that even indirectly, something inside me knew I wanted to be in the mafia, even though I always emphasized that I didn't.

"Are you sure, *ragazza mia?*" The bastard slid his tattooed hand over his vein-marked cock, squeezing the tip.

The bastard knew exactly what he was doing, how to tease me, that I was breathless, that I wanted him. Oh, how I wanted to feel my husband's cock; being with him was my greatest test of endurance.

I always wanted to know what it was like to have complete sex, what it would be like to have a man penetrating me. I was 23 years old; all I knew about sex was the foreplay, just that.

"I wanted your hand here, my *little hurricane*" he whispered in a rough voice. I moistened my lips, biting the corner of them. "I wanted to feel your mouth around my cock, your plump lips sliding over my dick..."

His voice faded as his eyes closed, continuing his movements, going up and down, as if imagining my mouth there.

I gripped the blanket, wanting to touch him like a child wanting that toy.

I was weak, I wasn't going to resist. I was going to touch him; I wanted to touch him, wanted to feel that tingling and his touch on me. But suddenly Santino stopped masturbating, his smile becoming gigantic for me.

"See? You want my cock; you're having an internal battle, but you know, I don't want you right now. I gave you your time, but you took too long. Now deal with your anguish because I'm leaving." Santino got up from the bed.

"Oh, no, you're not!" I leaned over the bed, grabbing his wrist, my nails digging in. "If I find out you went to bed with any woman, you risk waking up without that precious thing of yours."

I glanced down at his still-erect penis, making it clear what I was talking about.

"As far as I remember, you're a woman too..."

"You know what I meant, Santino Vacchiano!"

"Fine..." Just like the first time, he said simply, "fine," grabbing his underwear from the bed and heading toward the closet.

I watched his small, round butt, the dragon tattoo covering his back, and the brown hair on his legs. Santino disappeared into the closet, emerging minutes later in a pair of gym shorts and a tank top.

I strained my eyes to see that.

"Where are you going?" I asked, confused.

"Running..."

"But you haven't slept yet," I interrupted.

"I have insomnia and a hard-on. I need to release this endorphin somehow," he said, looking at me as if expecting me to invite him to bed and have sex.

"Well, have a great run, husband, because I'm going to lie down and maybe touch myself and sleep very peacefully." I smiled at him with a hint of malice.

"But you're not! If you don't want to have sex with me, you're not going to masturbate!" Santino crossed his arms.

"Go run then; there's no way you'll know." I smiled again, lying down on the bed.

Santino took off his shirt, throwing it on the floor.

"Suddenly I'm tired. I'm going to sleep, and if you touch yourself, my cock will slide into your pussy without meaning to!"

He quickly lay down beside me, and I huffed. How foolish I was, missing the chance to touch myself while thinking about my mischievous husband's delicious body.

CHAPTER TWENTY

Cinzia

"Wow, is Santino still sleeping?" Pietra asked, sitting on the stool with her hands resting on the white granite island in the middle of the kitchen.

"Yes, is that a problem? When he's sleeping, he's an angel, doesn't bother anyone." I shrugged.

"I've never seen my brother sleep so much. San suffers from insomnia; he's always wandering around." Hearing Pietra say that reminded me of how he wanted to run instead of sleep.

Maybe it was his anxiety that kept him from sleeping, or maybe he didn't even try, since he didn't try to sleep before leaving—he just left. He only stayed because I had become an obstacle for him.

"Well..."

"Did you two do anything?" She was dying to know.

It was past noon. Pietra was the one who brought us food. She entered the house without ringing the doorbell, and just as I was coming down the stairs, she came in with the plates. I had already eaten and put the dishes to wash; apparently, everyone knew the code to my house, except for me.

"We didn't do anything." I pulled up a stool, facing her.

"What do you mean? He didn't even try anything?" We were both whispering.

"He knows that if he tries, I'll scream and make a scene. I'll only give in to him when I feel confident, or..." I smiled, remembering my husband's delicious cock, "when I can't take it anymore."

"Did you two do something?" Pietra deduced from my smile.

"No, we didn't. Just your perverted brother got naked in front of me." I rolled my eyes.

"And knowing my naughty friend, you liked it."

"With all due respect, I know he's your brother, but he's well endowed." Pietra laughed, making me cover her mouth. "Pietra!"

"I know, I know, I've seen those two naked many times, never seen them like that, but they're my brothers. I lived 20 years in the same house with them. There's no way not to bump into them with their cocks barely staying in their pants." Pietra shook her head, both of us seeing the man walk into the kitchen, quickly silencing us.

"I can't believe you were talking about cocks, including mine. Your whispering actually sounded quite loud. I didn't need any effort to hear it." Santino was shirtless, running his hand over his sculpted abs, standing in front of the fridge, looking at me. "Is this how it's going to be, always talking about everything with my sister? I'd prefer you omitted the part about my cock."

He made a funny face, causing Pietra and me to laugh.

"Little brother, you arrived late. We always talk about everything. Your member isn't the first we've discussed. After all, Cinzia has seen several to compare yours to a bean..."

"How many has she seen?" he growled at me.

"Well, I thought you knew..."

"What did I know, Cinzia Vacchiano?" Santino growled again, clearly irritated.

"I think I said too much. I'm going to head out." Pietra stood up, slipping away.

"Thanks, Pipi," I muttered, noticing my husband walking toward me.

"Cinzia?"

"There's nothing to hide. I've always known I wasn't purely innocent to you. Did you forget that day in this room? You wanted a virgin wife; you'll have that, but innocent, never." I touched his chest, standing in front of me, wanting to push him back, unsuccessfully.

"Be more specific..." His voice trailed off with the growl he gave.

"Oral, masturbation, fingering..."

"Did someone finger you?" His hand gripped my thigh, spreading it and lifting the fabric of my skirt.

"Not that kind of fingering, just massage, you know?" My breathing became ragged as Santino's hand began to move up my leg.

"Still not sure." He was playing, and I was falling, his fingers touching my pussy over my panties. "Like this?"

I closed my eyes as Santino moved the fabric aside, sliding through my folds. Just his rough whisper made me excited.

"Yes, like that..." I whispered, opening my eyes to meet his.

"And like this?" Abruptly, he shoved two fingers inside me.

"Ah!" I held onto his chest, pushing him away. "Asshole!"

He gave me that cocky smile.

"I thought you were lying and needed proof." He even had the nerve to say.

"Of course, the liar here is you!"

"Have I ever lied to you? As far as I remember, no. Now you're playing hard to get with your pussy, as if you're afraid of being discovered. Sometimes I think you're no longer a virgin; I saw the way you looked at my cock." I stood up from the stool, walking towards him, trying not to punch his beautiful face.

"I don't want you, because I don't want to wake up the next day and find out that my husband slept with me and then with someone else," I declared, pointing my finger at him.

"Didn't I say *okay* when you asked for that?"

"Okay? What does that mean?"

"It means okay, I'll do what you asked..."

"I doubt it. I doubt it. You'll just have me and then go back to those women you flaunt on all those tabloid sites. I'm not blind, and it doesn't take much to see that you probably just want me to have a child because I'm not your type of woman..."

"Don't start with that. Don't come at me with the crap that I don't like you because if I didn't, *ragazza mia*, I'd simply ignore you, fuck you hard, and that would be it! But I'm not insisting; I'm being patient. Don't tell me I don't find you beautiful because I've talked about that with you. I want you, Cinzia. I won't promise that I can be faithful because I've never done that before, but I need to fuck you. I need to know what it's like to slide my cock into your pussy..."

"I'm not falling for the gong strike. You just made it clear that you don't know if you can be faithful. I'd rather have a marriage without sex than a shared marriage. Until you're certain, you won't have me because I prefer to be scared and avoid the risk."

"So what do you want from me? This is who I am. How can you change something in someone..."

"I don't want you to change; I want you to prove that you can be faithful to one woman!" I interrupted, somewhat irritated.

"I'm not going to be faithful to someone who doesn't even make an effort to be in the same bed as me. It's all clear to me now; you love that other man and want him, but now I'm yours, and I won't give up what's mine. I'm leaving. Meanwhile, stay locked in here reflecting on your thoughts. Not even my sister will be allowed in. And just in case, I'm going to have the house code changed. My mother tends to help the oppressed, and you wanted my worst side. Now you'll get it. You didn't want me of your own free will, so know that I'm going to find someone who does!" he growled, leaving me speechless as he left the house and left me alone.

CHAPTER TWENTY-ONE

Santino

I entered my parents' house, my knock on the front door made them both notice my presence.

"Where are you going, son?" Mom asked as I passed through the living room.

"Anywhere away from my wife," I declared, frustrated, knowing I had messed up my words and if I had any chance of having Cinzia, I blew it by mentioning I would look for another woman.

"What's the problem this time?" my father asked, getting up from the couch where he had been sitting.

"Cinzia is the problem. No matter how much I try, she won't let her guard down. I'm tired, simple as that, tired." I shrugged.

"Tired after one day of marriage? Is that what I'm hearing?" My father, who was the only male role model I had, spoke up.

"Nothing I do makes that woman lower her guard. She's infuriating. Cinzia wants something from me that I've never given to anyone." I ran my hand through my hair, furious.

"That's called marriage. You have the choice to go there now, be aggressive, and get everything you want from her, but if you haven't done that yet, it's because you don't want to go down the path of aggression, am I right?" I continued walking towards them, sitting on a couch facing the one my mother was on, while my father stood behind her, holding her shoulders.

The perfect couple. Tommaso always protecting his wife from everything, and she always by his side for everything, as if Verena was the balance to my father, the madness and the calm.

"I don't want to resort to aggression. I might be a damned arrogant, but I know if I force myself on Cinzia, she'll never look me in the eye again. I grew up with that woman; I saw how she reacted when I stole a kiss from her when we were teenagers. I know the hurricane I have by my side..."

"Wait, I didn't know about that kiss!" It was my mother who spoke, somewhat amazed.

"I don't think anyone knew because it was kind of a bet between Valentino and me." I shrugged.

"So she has a greater reason to hate you?" Mom asked.

"Maybe. The truth is, I don't even know what she wants from me. All I can think is that she loves another man, and maybe I made a big mistake agreeing to this marriage. I should have talked to you, but I thought it was a matter of honor. My wounded ego made me go ahead with this union. That's why I asked for this marriage not to be postponed, but if Cinzia was ready to run off with someone else, it's because something was very clear: she loves this other guy, a certain Marco." I sighed, knowing the name of the man.

I didn't recall having any enemies named Marco, and even though I could grab that phone and force her to give me the password, I didn't want to. That could be violating everything I consider privacy, even though keeping her phone with me would be quite obsessive.

"Well," Dad stroked his beard, scratching it, "you didn't do anything wrong. You fulfilled your duty to the Cosa Nostra. You're an honorable member, one of the most loyal men to our clan, and this girl, Cinzia, is the woman for you. A more delicate girl would be broken by you. I know the son I have. You, Santino, have all the traits of the Vacchiano, and if you're trying to control yourself, it's because you see something in her. The fact that she loves another man is something beyond anything I can help you with right now."

I remained silent, running my hand through my hair irritably, Cinzia's words echoing in my mind. How could I give something I didn't know how to give? I've always had all the women I wanted, and if a woman appeared in front of me, I had doubts about whether I could resist. I could lie to her and say I would be faithful just to get what I wanted, but that's not for me. I don't like being lied to, and that's why I don't lie.

"Valentino went after the Colombian, didn't he?" I asked, changing the subject.

"Yes, he asked, and I authorized it. When he comes back, we'll start preparing for your initiation as the new Don, and we'll need you here." I nodded, knowing I would have an influential role alongside my brother.

"I want a mission," I said, seeing my father narrow his eyes, confused.

"What do you mean?"

"Send me away, anywhere. I need time away from Cinzia." My mother let out an audible sigh.

"And do you think running away from your problems will make things better?" Verena inquired.

"At this moment, yes. There's no way to be around her without fighting. There's no possibility of having a relationship without arguments. I'd rather take myself out of the game..."

"You want to go far away? I'll send you on a mission then, but know that if I find out you're posing for photos with women or sleeping with women, I'll put an end to this marriage myself. I would send Valentino on this mission, but I see that won't be possible with him going after the bride. This separation is for you to reflect, at least once in your life. Stay on course, focus only on your mission, and honor your wife. Don't betray her, as it may make you regret it in the future," my father declared, and I already knew where he was going to send me, as he had been talking about it all week, saying someone would need to go to Las Vegas to monitor our casino.

"You're sending me to Las Vegas? That won't help much with his relationship with Cinzia..." My mother let the sentence fade, looking up at her husband who was behind her.

"Yes, I'm sending you there. Santino wants distance from Cinzia, and he'll have it. It will be fifteen days there. He will make all the decisions and will know that everything he does could reflect on his relationship with his wife. Do you want to go, son? Go, but know that every action has its reaction." I nodded, getting up from the couch, knowing that this was exactly what I wanted to do.

"Okay, I still have clothes here. Have a suitcase packed for me. I want to leave today, preferably now," I said, determined, knowing that all I wanted at that moment was to be away from Cinzia Vacchiano.

CHAPTER TWENTY-TWO

Cinzia

"Dear?" It was night when I heard Mrs. Verena's voice entering my house. I got up from the couch, seeing my mother-in-law enter the room.

"Hello!" I replied somewhat awkwardly upon noticing Mrs. Verena's expression.

"Well, I came because Santino went on a mission." She looked around, letting out a long sigh.

"Mission?" I was puzzled by that.

"Yes, it was necessary to have someone trustworthy in Las Vegas, and since Valentino isn't in the country..."

"Ah, I believe there's no need to make excuses for him. Santino asked to go on this mission, didn't he? He wants to stay away from me." I sighed as I finished speaking.

"Yes, my dear, it was him who asked. I tried to make him stay, but he said the two of you have only been fighting." Mrs. Verena walked around the room, stopping in front of me. "Tell me, Cinzia, my dear, do you love someone else? Because Santino believes you do."

I remained silent. I could lie and say yes, but Mrs. Verena had always been so honest with me, and even though her children were troublemakers, she always took the right side of things, even if it meant going against her own children.

"No, I don't love anyone. Santino thinks I love Marco because he's the man I was going to marry, but it wouldn't have been a marriage out of love, just something to get out of this situation. Marco, unlike Santino, always listened to me and showed he wanted the best for me," I declared the truth.

"So you were only going to run away to get rid of Santino?" my mother-in-law asked, and I nodded with a tilt of my head. "Santino will never be a patient man, even if he wants to be, he won't succeed. He's intense like a Vacchiano. I really wanted your union to work out, but maybe, after what Santino said today, it should never have happened. He said he shouldn't have agreed to this union, that he did it out of honor. San went to Las Vegas and promised his father that he's going far away to think about this marriage, making it clear that he won't get involved with anyone out of respect for you."

I shook my head, biting the corner of my lip. He was indecisive; maybe he didn't want our union.

"So he's not coming back home?" I asked in a whisper.

"It's fifteen days away." Mrs. Verena blinked her blue eyes at me.

"Okay."

I was embarrassed because, even though I wanted Santino away from me, he left without saying a "goodbye," simply disappearing. A feeling of abandonment filled me.

"Cinzia, may I ask you a question?"

"Yes." I nodded, noticing that the woman wasn't thinking about the matter, just speaking.

"Do you want this marriage? Because if you don't want it just like Santino doesn't, we will ask for an annulment. When my son returns from his trip, Tommaso will talk to him. It's clear that neither of you like each other. I don't want to see my son unhappy in a relationship, and I don't want to see you unhappy either. I watched you grow up, and we made a grave mistake thinking this could work out."

Mrs. Verena waited for my answer. *Were they going to annul the marriage?* After so much begging, no one did anything, but with Santino taking a simple step back, they were considering annulling that damn marriage. When I said I didn't want him, that it wouldn't work, no one listened to me.

Did they make me go through all that humiliation for this?

"Yes, anything is better than being with Santino," I declared, blinking rapidly to hold back angry tears.

"The password for your house hasn't been changed; it remains the same. You have the right to come and go as you please." I just nodded.

Mrs. Verena was at a loss for words, as it fell to her to give the news that her son was thinking of rejecting me. Perhaps it was what I always wanted—his rejection—but feeling it wasn't as good as I had hoped.

I was left alone in that huge house, tears streaming down my face. Whenever I was alone, I allowed myself to cry.

Santino was gone; he didn't want me anymore. And I was still a virgin, a virgin because I didn't want him, because apparently, I demanded too much from a man who couldn't give anything.

I headed to my room...

THE ROAR OF THE MOTORCYCLE caught my attention. I ran to the window, futilely hoping it might be my husband, but it was obvious it wasn't; it was just Valentino on his black bike. Santino's bike was white, and both of them had those big motorcycles.

Even though they crashed and got hurt with those monstrosities, neither of them ever gave up those things.

It had been twenty days since Santino left, with no news from him, no communication—he had simply vanished. That is, as far as I was concerned, because Pietra said he was in contact with everyone in the family, just not with me. Valentino had already returned from his trip to New York to visit his fiancée, but there was still no sign of Santino.

Mrs. Verena had said it would only be fifteen days, but those fifteen days had turned into twenty, and no one knew when he would come back.

Santino hadn't appeared in the newspapers anymore; he was keeping his promise to his father.

The house phone rang, and I rushed to answer it:

"Hello?" I said breathlessly.

"Friend?" Pietra's voice made my shoulders slump.

"I don't know why I still expect that idiot of your brother to call," I grumbled, my daily frustration taking over.

"He said there's still no set date for his return," Pietra said.

"Tell that cowardly idiot to at least say where my cell phone is." I rolled my eyes.

Santino hadn't even left the cell phone with me. I searched the entire house, looking through all his clothes, hoping he might have left it there.

"Friend, Santino's mood is worse than when he left. I don't know why he hasn't come back..." Pietra said.

"Because he's an asshole! Jerk!!!" I declared, irritated.

"I'm calling you to come take a dip in the pool with me. Maybe Tommie will lift your spirits," Pietra said kindly.

Everyone looked at me with pity, as if I were the rejected wife, always trying to include me in everything. Fortunately, I had Pietra. She was my true friend, always speaking plainly, even telling me things I didn't want to hear.

"Nothing better than the beautiful smile of my godson. I'm on my way," I confirmed, bidding her farewell as I headed towards the stairs to put on a swimsuit.

CHAPTER TWENTY-THREE

Santino

A Few Days Later...

The soldier parked in front of my parents' house. It had been thirty days in Las Vegas; what was supposed to be only fifteen had doubled. I didn't want to come back, but I returned to resolve what I had pending.

Being away from Cinzia helped clear my mind, and make the decision I needed to make. I didn't want it; all those thirty days, there wasn't a single day I didn't think about my *little Sicilian hurricane*, but it wasn't working anymore. We were wearing each other down, and when we were together, it was like fire and gasoline—the more you throw, the more it burns.

I wanted Cinzia, I desired her, but there was no way for us to stay close. She loved someone else, and I hate everything that goes against my will. If we continued in that madness, either I'd end up killing her or she'd kill me, which would be nearly impossible.

I walked past the sidewalk of my parents' house, soon hearing Tommaso's reprimanding tone with my brother:

"You're going to honor what's between your legs and stay here, got it?"

I entered the living room to find the two of them in that standoff.

"Did I miss something?" I asked, meeting their gazes.

"Damn, brother, finally!" Valentino came toward me, giving me a tight hug.

"Now that you're back, Santino, make your brother understand that he shouldn't be going after his fiancée. The time for their union hasn't come yet. I wanted to meet the Colombian girl; you did, now he's not allowed to set foot outside this place, because the Cosa Nostra chair is waiting for him." Dad was firm.

"What's going on?" I asked, crossing my arms and looking at Valentino, who gave me one of his half-smiles, that typical smile of ours that's worth nothing.

"He went after the Aragón girl, but wasn't content with that; he participated in an orgy right at the fraternity where the girl lives, and even spread it around that Yulia Aragón is his fiancée and that anyone who gets involved with her will have their dick cut off. The girl got a bad reputation, and on top of that, a fiancé who betrayed her," Dad said, trying not to laugh.

It wasn't the same for me, as I burst into laughter. This was so typical of Valentino—marking his territory and then moving on to appreciate others.

"Damn, Valentino, seriously? An orgy?" I shook my head.

"Well, in my defense, when I arrived, everything was already happening, and you know how I am—I can't deny female bodies. I didn't even remember that there was a fiancée, but at least now I know she's still a virgin, and if she doesn't marry as a virgin, I'll punish her on our wedding night..."

"The punishment will be the poor girl having to marry you," I mocked, shaking my head. "But how was she? Did you meet her?"

"Yes, a beautiful girl, but with a sharp tongue." Valentino rolled his eyes. "I'm going to keep some handcuffs, ropes, whatever it takes to tame that Colombian beast."

My brother shook his head, his eyes shining as if remembering the girl.

"And how did you end up in an orgy?" I asked, curious.

"I arrived at the fraternity, looked for Yulia, she snubbed me, as expected, said I shouldn't be there, that I'd have to put up with her for a lifetime already. After that, I found out there was a party at the fraternity where she lives. I went around telling everyone that she was my fiancée and that if anyone wanted to keep their dick, they'd stay far away from her. I pressured one of her friends who told me Yulia was still a virgin and was thinking of losing her virginity with some guy named Louis. I went to him and threatened him, and that's how the news spread. Yulia wanted to kill me. Well, I was about to leave when I walked into a room with several people, and before I knew it, they were pulling me into the middle of it. The next day, I disappeared from the fraternity, but the rumor that the poor girl had a fiancé who threatened everyone and participated in an orgy spread," my brother said with a sense of casualness.

"Man, you're crazy..."

"I'm going to marry a virgin and pure girl for me. If Yulia Aragón isn't a virgin on our wedding night, I'll make her bleed with a beating!" Valentino was direct.

Just like me, he valued a woman's innocence highly, although my Sicilian hurricane was far from innocent.

"*Okay*, but why was Dad fighting with you?" I asked, confused.

"Because I just wanted to stop by again, make sure my plan worked..."

"No, Valentino! Ferney Aragón already called, instructing us to stay away from his sister. For that reason, you'll stay here and prepare for your future role as Don." Dad was direct.

Valentino shrugged his shoulders. He was clearly crazy about that girl, but they could only marry after she graduated, as stipulated in the contract. Valentino demanded in the contract that the girl remained a virgin for him, but considering what my brother said, and judging by the fact that she was a college student, anything could happen, just like with my crazy wife.

"*Okay*, tell my future brother-in-law that I'll stay far away from his little sister." At that moment, both of them looked at me.

"Now tell me about yourself, son. Have you decided?" Dad asked.

"Yes," I whispered, running my hand through my hair. "Did you do what I asked?"

"Yes. The papers are in my office. You both just need to sign, and the marriage will be annulled." I nodded.

"I'll get her and take her to my house. As soon as we talk about it, Cinzia can go back to her place, return to her routine," I declared resolutely.

"Are you sure, San?" Valentino asked.

We've always had a strong connection, and he must have noticed in my reaction that I wasn't completely sure about what I was saying.

"I'm not sure, because I want that woman, but it's not working. She's like a rose with thorns. Every time I try to get close, she pricks me, as if we can't be close..."

"That's not the solution, as there's always the option to change. If you want her, don't let her go, or you might lose her forever. I know my two sons see my marriage to your mother and feel disgust, fear of falling in love and becoming vulnerable. But love isn't bad; it's a good thing that takes hold of us. It's like the sun that rises after a storm. I hope you're sure of what you're doing, Santino. It goes against all the rules of the Cosa Nostra. Aldo might want to marry his daughter off to someone else. Don't think that by annulling the marriage, you'll be freeing her, because Cinzia is part of the mafia, and women mostly have the role of bearing our children," Dad said, making me reflect.

But nothing anyone said would make me change my mind.

CHAPTER TWENTY-FOUR

Cinzia

Thirty days. It had been thirty days since Santino left home and didn't give me any more updates. Those thirty days were accumulated with a tremendous rage, wanting to punch that perfect face of that jerk.

I fastened the button of my denim skirt when I heard the sound of the door. Something made me think it could be him, after all, no one visited me in the morning. I lowered the fabric of my shirt and left the closet without even putting on anything. I headed towards the stairs and spotted my husband, or at least I thought it was him; from behind, it could even be Valentino. I descended one step at a time, seeing him head towards the bar. I knew he must have heard my footsteps, but he didn't bother to turn his face.

Santino placed a stack of papers on the bar counter, his eyes finally turning in my direction. Facing his cold gaze, I knew it was my husband; Valentino had a more relaxed expression when talking to me, after all, we didn't have any clashes to nurture hatred towards each other.

"I thought you wouldn't come back." I crossed my arms, watching him turn around with a glass of whiskey in his hand.

"Hello, Cinzia." He didn't even notice that I hadn't greeted him, and maybe I wouldn't. "I have a proposal for you..."

"A proposal?" I inquired, raising an eyebrow, noticing his loud sigh when I cut him off.

Santino's eyes traveled slowly down my body, not a quick movement, but a deliberate one, as if he was analyzing every part. Noticing the hand holding the whiskey glass, I saw several bruises on his fingers.

"If you let me speak and don't interrupt." He took a few steps towards me, and I stood still, watching him. "First, either you lie down with me, without reservations, and let's fulfill our roles as husband and wife."

"And what's the second option?" I asked about the other alternative.

"If you refuse once more—" Santino turned back towards the bar, picking up the papers he had before and extending them to me—"we annul the marriage. I still have the chance to annul it and pretend we were never married. After all, I haven't even touched you properly."

"How many?" I asked suddenly.

"What?" He didn't understand, raising an eyebrow.

"How many women did you sleep with? After all, we both know someone like you doesn't go without sex..."

"Three." He answered bluntly without even counting.

That infuriated me. How did he think he could come back after being away for a month, sleeping with more than one woman, and still think I would accept that madness?

"Where do I need to sign?" I asked, heading to the bar, knowing there was a pen holder.

"So, you're opting for the annulment of the marriage?" he asked, making me turn towards him.

"You stay away for thirty days, THIRTY!" I exclaimed, approaching him and slamming the papers against his chest. "You come back saying you've been with three women and think I'm going to welcome you with open arms? Every time our marriage is in crisis, you'll go around, sleep with other women, and come back as if nothing happened? Go to hell, Santino!"

He grabbed my wrist, stopping my arms, his grip was strong.

"I lied, okay, I didn't sleep with anyone..."

"And I believe in Santa Claus!" I forced a laugh in my nervousness. "Why would you lie? What's the reason? There isn't one, don't be contradictory, Santino!"

"Maybe I wanted you to think that, sign this, and let's end this marriage once and for all," he growled, releasing my arm and pushing me back.

"I never thought I'd agree with anything you say." I took a step back, losing my balance.

I turned back to the bar, searching for a pen.

"I hope you know, you'll be free of me, but nothing will stop your father from giving you to another man." He threatened me again.

"Anyone is better than a jerk of a husband like you!" I threw it in his face.

"I'll do you a favor and help you find an old man." Santino spoke again.

"I don't care." I shrugged. "Maybe an old man will be more faithful than a new one like you," I declared, looking for any pen. I finally found one, took off the cap, hearing my husband's footsteps next to me. *Or should I say ex-husband?*

"I'm giving you the chance to sign this, but you know it's final. Don't come back later begging me to take you back, because it won't happen! When your father gives you to a man who will certainly not spare you, who will rape you, because we both know I could have done that and forced a child into you," Santino declared next to me, as if trying to scare me.

"Your psychological pressure doesn't work on me." I turned the papers over, finding my name on the line.

I stared at it for long seconds, about to become Cinzia Bianchi again, a single woman. I bit the tip of my lip. I had thought that I could be Santino's wife, that we could be a couple, but I didn't believe what he said. Santino went away just two days after our marriage, couldn't handle it, and went to betray me, even if he said otherwise, there were enough reasons not to believe him after the long list of women he had been with.

"I hope you regret what you're doing..."

"I thought the idea of annulling the marriage was yours," I declared, placing the pen on the line, signing my name, finally becoming a single woman again.

"I thought I could be smart and refuse."

"Maybe I'm the dumb one then, but a dumb one free of you, asshole!" I left the papers on the counter.

"Don't forget you're still talking to a mafia member!" He pulled me by the hand with a snarl.

"A useless member," I grumbled, trying to affect him. Santino growled, raising his hand around my neck, squeezing hard, making me lose my breath.

"You insolent girl! I should have raped you!"

"We both know you'd never be able to do that," I mocked, playing with danger. "Now let me go and go fuck as many women as you want, we have nothing left."

I don't know why, but seeing him there in front of me, so handsome, with veins in his neck standing out with his anger, the man who had once been my husband and was now nothing more.

"Get out of this house and never show up in front of me again." He pushed me, almost making me lose my balance, but I stayed on my feet, heading towards the front door.

CHAPTER TWENTY-FIVE

Cinzia

"Friend, it's been a week," Pietra said, sitting on the edge of the pool while playing with little Tommie in the water.

"A week of freedom," I declared, tossing the plastic ball to the little boy who jumped to catch it.

"A week of you complaining about seeing my brother going out every night. You spy on him from your bedroom window, Cinzia Bianchi!" my friend said in a reprimanding tone.

"He's a jerk..."

"But he's not going out with anyone."

"A conscious jerk." I shrugged.

It had been a week since Santino and I had annulled our marriage. Since then, we hadn't looked at each other, and I only monitored him every night from my bedroom window because my parents' house was close to the condo's exit, and practically every night Santino left on his motorcycle with his brother.

I didn't know where they were going, but he never appeared in the magazines with any famous models. The Vacchianos were famous in Sicily, even though they were mobsters; people seemed to idolize what they did, despite living outside the law. It was as if they created their own laws and had all the powerful government men on their side.

Of course, my father was furious about the marriage being annulled. Of course, he wanted to hand me over to someone else immediately, embarrassed by the rumors spreading. But the truth was I didn't care. Why should he?

For the first time, I saw Mom stand up for herself, asking him to leave me alone for at least a few days since I had gone through a horrible experience. At that moment, I realized my father respected her, but Giulia was so submissive to him that she accepted everything my father said.

"Shall we leave, Tommie?" my friend called to her son since we had been there for a while.

Little Tommaso went to his mother, complaining. I walked to the edge, moving along the side, grabbing the robe that was there. My friend's pool was deeper at the end, where I usually didn't go because I didn't know how to swim. I put the robe on my arms.

"*Boo*" the whisper near my ear startled me, causing me to lose my balance and fall into the water.

I went straight down, the weight of the robe dragging me to the bottom, flailing my arms, trying to get back up.

"I don't know..." was all I managed to say as I put my head out of the water, the robe falling off as I moved my arms.

That's when someone jumped into the pool. My futile attempt to get to where I could stand was interrupted when I felt strong hands holding my waist, pulling me to the shallow end with a firm chest against me. I didn't swallow any water, as the rescue was swift.

I opened my eyes and saw my ex-husband, my suspicions confirmed when I noticed his tattoo.

"Asshole! Why did you do that?" I pushed his chest, which made him release me, but I still couldn't touch the ground, so I clung to his shoulder. "Get me out of here, now!"

"You don't know how to swim?" the bastard had a tone of amusement in his voice.

"Go to hell! Get me out of here," I pleaded, feeling humiliated by clinging to him.

His wet hair, his green eyes playful towards me.

"Who would have thought, Cinzia Bianchi can't swim." His mocking smile was evident.

"Take me to the edge, what do you want, huh? I thought we were ignoring each other!" I gripped his shoulder tightly, feeling his firm skin.

"I was curious to hear the side effects of Hurricane Cinzia." He mocked again. Santino was shirtless, probably having taken it off before jumping into the pool.

The jerk made as if to let me go again, which is when I clung to his waist with my feet circling around him.

"If you let me go, I'll punch you. Get me out of here, Vacchiano!" I demanded, my eyes wide when his hand slid down to my butt. "Hey! Get your hands off me!"

His strong grip made me gasp.

"I think I've been wanting to do this since we got married..."

"We're not married anymore!" I cut him off.

"Cinzia, *ragazza mia*, we might not be married, but your body still shivers at my touch..."

"Go to hell! Do what you said you'd do, stay away from me! Jerk! Do you think I don't see you going out every night?" I said without thinking.

"You're watching me?" The mobster still hadn't removed his hands from my ass, and I was at his mercy at that moment, his hands moving down my butt, squeezing it from underneath, rubbing against his member that was starting to harden.

"My room faces the street," I declared, tilting my head.

"I might be going out every night, but the only pussy I want to fuck is yours, my *little Sicilian hurricane*." His voice had turned husky.

"But I don't want you," I stated, sighing as his cock pressed against my pussy.

"I haven't even seen your pussy clearly and I already want it so much. Will you give me your virginity, Cinzia Bianchi?" he asked, bringing his lips close to my ear, sending shivers down my spine.

With that tone of voice, he could have asked for the world and I would have given it to him.

"You had your chance and squandered it," I murmured with a faltering voice.

"So what are you going to do?"

"Remain a virgin for my future husband? Or maybe go to some club and pick up the first guy who comes my way, lose my virginity to anyone, never see him again, and move on. Maybe doing that will make my father stop bugging me about marriage," I declared, determined.

"So you're saying it's better to lose your virginity to anyone but me?" His voice had grown tense.

Finally, Santino did what I was asking, taking me to the edge where we both got out. I was a step ahead of him, feeling his eyes on me.

"Great, thanks to your little prank I'm without a robe, jerk!" I complained.

"You could walk around like this. My eyes appreciate it; it's quite a sight. I wonder what it would be like to fuck that delicious ass." I closed my eyes at his words.

"Go to hell, Santino! Maybe I should do that after all..."

"There's no fucking way you're going out like this. What's mine is not for anyone else to look at." I turned my face away from his words.

"Yours? I believe there's a misunderstanding..."

"You'll always be mine, *ragazza*." His obsessive tone made me wet.

"No, I'm not yours, and you'll find that out when I lose my virginity to another man and not to you!"

"If you do that, I'll punish you." We walked towards each other.

"Forgot that we're no longer husband and wife?"

"Maybe I made a grave mistake because your pussy still belongs to me..."

We were interrupted by Pietra, who appeared with a furrowed brow, witnessing the two lunatics in a standoff.

"Is there a problem?" my friend asked.

"Your brother, he's the problem!" I huffed, heading towards the house door.

"You're not fucking leaving here like that," he growled, grabbing my wrist, which I pulled away.

"Go to hell, Santino! We annulled the marriage, we have nothing left, go be with the models you're used to and leave me alone!" I shouted in frustration and confusion.

"Come on, friend, let's get a towel." Pietra grabbed my hand as Santino released the other one.

I felt all those tremors, the way he looked at me, how I still desired him, but all we ever did when we were together was fight.

CHAPTER TWENTY-SIX

Cinzia

The ride-sharing car stopped in front of the nightclub. It shouldn't be so hard to fit in here again; there was a time in my life when I knew everyone around, made friends, was considered the popular girl, all because I lived among older people, using fake identities.

One of the reasons my father promised me to Santino Vacchiano and sent me away for college. Marco wasn't in town; he said he was traveling to Greece but would return in a few days. My friend was happy about the annulment of the marriage. I called him a friend because it was almost impossible to consider him a boyfriend after everything I had been through.

It still felt like Santino's hand was forcefully groping my ass, his big, strong fingers.

I looked around as I headed toward the nightclub's entrance. I had no friends in Sicily; the ones I had lost contact with. Pietra couldn't come along because her husband was too jealous to let her out, and rightly so.

The atmosphere was dark, fluorescent lights spinning through the light show, a DJ playing electronic music. I wove through people dancing energetically, approaching the bar where I ordered a shot of tequila.

"Hello!" I heard a male voice in my ear. I turned to see a familiar face—"Cinzia Bianchi?"

"Elton?" I smiled, recognizing one of my classmates.

"Long time no see. We're over there in the corner; I believe you'll recognize some people." He smiled enthusiastically.

I took the tequila handed to me, feeling Elton's hand on my back, guiding me to the corner where his friends were. I greeted everyone, some of whom I recognized from having studied with me.

I was soon included in the group, chatting with the girls, drinks being handed to me constantly. The truth was that none of those men caught my attention; none of them had that malicious glint that damned Vacchiano had, not to mention the green eyes of that bastard, the tattoos spread across his body, the beard that marked his face, even that chiseled abdomen, his cock touching his belly... Hell! Even if I got completely drunk, I wouldn't forget that asshole's sculpted body.

I grabbed another drink, not knowing what it was, and downed it in one gulp.

"Look at those two twins coming over," one of them said, making my blood run cold.

"Don't you know who they are? They're just the hottest guys in Sicily. They say they're amazing in bed but that their family is like a bunch of mobsters. Some say it's a rumor, others say it's true, like they're camouflaged behind a company. Mobsters or not, I'd love to bed any of them," the other said with a mischievous smile, looking at the men.

I was facing away, so I didn't need to turn around to know who they were talking about.

"Cinzia is blocking the view."

Oh, sure, of course.

I rolled my eyes, turning to leave, only to hear one of them say:

"One of them is coming over..."

Her sentence trailed off when that one locked eyes on me. From the squint of his eyes, I knew it was my ex-husband. What a coincidence; did he think I was bluffing? Or did he follow me?

Given the chat we had earlier, I wouldn't be surprised if Santino followed me.

I raised an eyebrow at him; he continued walking, passing by the guys in our group. I didn't see where Valentino went; my focus was elsewhere.

"Following me, Vacchiano?" I asked over the music.

"I needed to see with my own eyes if you were going to do something crazy," he said close to my ear.

"Wow, Cinzia is so lucky," one of the girls said behind me, making me roll my eyes.

I passed by Santino, grabbing a drink from someone's hand, about to bring it to my lips when the bastard intercepted me and took it away.

"Hey, I came here to drink!" I complained, looking up at his V-neck black shirt, revealing the tattoo on his chest that only he had.

"Drink? Are you out of your mind? You're going to lose your virginity to just anyone, and drunk?" he scolded, throwing the cup on the floor.

"Cinzia, is everything okay?" Elton approached, noticing our brief argument.

"Yes, Elton, I'm fine. It's just a family acquaintance..."

"Husband!" Santino growled, making me look at him.

"Husband my ass!" I retorted. "It's fine, Elton."

I only said that to get him to back off because all I wanted that night was to dance a lot, get drunk, and kiss a few lips. Sex was not on my agenda. But what plans? Santino had just thrown all mine down the drain.

"Who do you think you are?" I shoved his chest, turning my back and moving away from him.

I managed to shake off my ex-husband, stopping near the stage and looking up at the dancers performing in the cage with a pole dance bar. Next to the stage was a ladder, and I stood there, listening to a remix of "Sweet but Psycho" by Ava Max, closing my eyes and dancing to the rhythm of the music.

I smiled at the girl who shared her drink with me. This time, the liquid was sweeter, and I soon felt the effects of the alcohol in my blood, the boldness taking over me.

I never claimed to be a saint, especially with alcohol in my veins.

The girl on stage signaled for me to come up, extending her hand. I took it and climbed the steps, adjusting my dress slightly as it kept riding up, almost revealing my ass.

At that moment, I forgot I had an ex-husband. I was guided into the cage, dancing there alone, seeing the lights focusing on me at various times, aware of the many eyes on me, which made me dance even more, gyrating to the electronic music until my eyes opened with the new person who joined me in the cage.

"Damn it, Cinzia! You're going to kill me," Santino growled over the music, and I smiled in my drunken state.

I grabbed his chest, bringing my face closer to his.

"See how everyone desires me, only my husband prefers to stay away for a month instead of being in my presence," I declared, turning around, raising my arms, and rubbing my ass against his legs.

"Let's get out of here. You're too drunk to have a civilized conversation..."

"No, you leave. I want everyone watching me, see what Santino Vacchiano lost." I made a move to step away, but the mobster pulled me by the wrist.

"There's no fucking way I'm letting these vultures stare at my wife..."

"I'm not your wife anymore." I tried to push his chest, but he stopped me, pulling me out of the cage and lifting me over his shoulder, forcibly removing me from there.

"You'll always be my *ragazza!* Get the fuck out of my way!"

He cursed those around him, my face pressed against his shirt, smelling the mix of perfume and nicotine.

CHAPTER TWENTY-SEVEN

Santino

I pushed through the crowd, feeling my wife's—or should I say ex-wife's?—slaps on my back. What the fuck!

Just thinking about those men looking at her, hearing one of them say "*that hot little blonde*" made me furious. No one should be looking at her, not in those clothes, not with her ass almost on display for everyone.

Damn, the way Cinzia danced, how her body moved with the music, a sex nymph, the hottest woman I'd ever seen, with her ass almost completely exposed to everyone around her.

I reached the outside of the club, setting my little hurricane down on the ground. Stumbling, she grabbed my shirt to keep from falling.

"You"—her small blue eyes meeting mine—"are a hot bastard, but I'm going back in there."

"You're not going anywhere. You're coming home with me." I grabbed her by the wrist and headed toward my motorcycle, which I'd parked next to Valentino's.

My brother came along, knowing what I was going to do. As soon as we arrived, we split up. I asked my sister where her friend was going, just the thought of another man taking her virginity put me on high alert.

It seemed that when she was mine, there was no fear, but after I annulled the marriage, it appeared, always beside me, with Cinzia's unpredictable behavior.

Damn it, dancing on stage? With everyone watching?

"Are you crazy if you think I'm getting on that thing?" she pointed at my motorcycle, stumbling over her own feet.

"Yes, you are." I took the spare helmet from the bike's rack, which I'd brought along under false pretenses.

"No, I'm going to fall off." I released her wrist when I realized she wasn't going to run away.

I turned my face to see the pout forming on her lips.

"I'll never let you fall, *ragazza mia*," I said, tucking her hair behind her ear.

"I don't like you, but I don't like that you make me want to attack you every time I see you, and I feel like a caged animal for wanting to attack someone..." Her sentence trailed off as she lost her balance on those high heels.

"What would attacking someone be like?" They say intoxication always brings out the truth.

"You know, pulling hair, tearing clothes, biting, scratching, and... having sex..." The girl bit the tip of her lip, which I kept staring at, wanting to touch.

The word "sex" matched the sweet freshness of her breath. I texted Valentino to let him know I was taking my crazy wife home.

Maybe I should never have signed that annulment.

I took off my leather jacket, knowing she hadn't brought a coat. Cinzia stayed quiet, her body swaying like one of those inflatable dolls that move with the wind, but with one exception—there was no wind. I zipped up the jacket, grabbed the helmet I had placed on the seat, and put it on her head.

"Do you want me to take your virginity, Cinzia, or would you prefer another man?" I asked, taking advantage of her drunken state.

"I always wanted it to be you, but as we know, you're an asshole..." She rolled her little eyes.

I put my helmet on, took the key from my pocket, and sat on the bike. I extended my hand for Cinzia to climb on. She did, hugging me tightly around the waist, at least she did that without arguing.

I started the bike, leaving the club's parking lot. Our house wasn't far from there; I didn't drive fast, feeling her head resting on my back, her leg wrapped around my waist. Luckily, my jacket was large enough to prevent others from seeing my *ragazza's* ass.

I still couldn't come to terms with Cinzia's actions, with her showing herself off like that to everyone. Damn, she was even crazier when drunk, and I was starting to become fascinated by all her madness.

That day, when I startled her, seeing her fall into the pool and struggling to get back up caught me off guard. I never imagined she didn't know how to swim. I jumped in right after her, taking advantage of the situation as I grabbed her ass. She had a body that drove me crazy, making me want to lick her all over, taste her, the damn woman who was supposed to be mine, but whom I had pushed away.

My bike was recognized, and soon the condo gates opened for me. I nodded to the security guard who shone his flashlight in my face to make sure it was me. I drove through the streets towards my house, the house that should have been ours, a house I didn't stop living in after Cinzia left it.

I pressed the button on the remote control attached to the bike key, opening the garage gate, which I drove into, parking the bike next to one of my sports cars. I turned off the bike, the garage falling into darkness as I closed the door.

"*Ragazza?*" — I called her when I noticed that her arms didn't even move on my back.

"Leave me here," she mumbled, her voice still slurred from the alcohol.

"Come on, let's get out of here." Carefully, without letting go of her arm, we dismounted the bike.

I pulled her by the hand, heading toward the door, opening the one that led into the living room. The lighting made Cinzia blink several times.

"This house isn't mine, it's yours!" she declared, pulling her arm away and heading toward the exit of the house, walking through the living room.

"Hey!" I ran after her. "Are you sure you want to come home like this? What do you think your dad will say about his drunk daughter?"

"I'll sleep on the sidewalk, but far away from you..." Maybe her intoxication was wearing off "because all I want to do now..."

Her blue eyes traveled down my chest. Apparently, Cinzia was still pretty drunk, and dealing with out-of-control women isn't my style.

"Well, I'll let you attack me, but first, you'll have to go up the stairs with me." Before she could say anything, I picked her up and put her in my lap.

"You have this annoying habit of picking me up, I feel like I'm too light in your arms..."

"And who says you aren't?" I winked at her.

Cinzia sabotaged herself by not having a *standard* body, but that's what made her beautiful, so beautiful that I couldn't keep my eyes off her. She was perfect, that is, when she wasn't arguing with me.

I entered my room, our room, setting her down on the floor. The girl stumbled over to the bed, throwing herself down and lying face down.

"I miss this pillow," she whispered, making me go to her. I removed her high heels, made her turn on the bed, and opened her jacket. "Vacchiano, I should attack you... *meow*..."

She mimicked a cat's meow, moving her fingers, which made me laugh out loud.

"Believe me, I'd love to be attacked by you, but not like this, all messed up."

"I'm pretty sober." Cinzia smiled.

"I'm going to get one of my shirts so you can take off that dress," I said as I took off my jacket from her.

I went into the closet, grabbed a long shirt, and returned to the room, where I found the crazy girl taking off her mini dress. *Damn!*

Cinzia wasn't wearing a bra, her full breasts right there, ready to be groped, pinched... Damn alcoholism.

"You can dress me now, Sammy." Her sweet, drunken eyes met mine.

"Damn it!" I grumbled as I walked toward her. "You drunk are my greatest downfall..."

I let out a long sigh as I struggled to put the shirt over her head without looking at or touching her breasts. It took all my self-control.

"Don't you want me, Sammy?" A pout formed on her lip.

"Believe me, I want you very much, but I'm fully aware that once you regain your sanity, you'll go back to hating me," I grumbled as I helped her lie down.

"Sammy?"

What the hell was this "Sammy" she was calling me?

The only person who called me that was her, and we were just kids.

"What is it, Cinzia?" I asked, trying to keep my dick calm in my pants.

"Will you sleep here with me?"

Even knowing she was drunk, I couldn't say no to a request like that. I nodded, took off my shirt, then my shoes and pants, leaving only in my underwear.

I might have to face the Sicilian hurricane when I woke up, but it didn't matter because I'd get to smell her for an entire night.

CHAPTER TWENTY-EIGHT

Cinzia

I squeezed my eyelids shut, opening my eyes and looking around the room. Through the curtains, I saw the daylight illuminating the room, a room I immediately recognized. Feeling that strong hand on my waist, I turned abruptly, waking the man beside me, startled. Santino's green eyes opened wide at me.

His hand moved away from me, as if trying to avoid a potential conflict.

"H-h-how?" I stammered, closing my eyes against the irritating headache.

From the dry throat and the hellish headache, I must have drunk way too much.

"How did you end up here?" His voice was low and raspy.

"Yeah." I opened my eyes again.

"A long story that involves you dancing in a packed nightclub, showing your ass to almost everyone..."

"Oh, heavens! Did I really do that?" I murmured, sitting up in bed and running my hand through my hair. "Maybe the fact that I'm wearing your shirt is the least of the problems it seems..."

"Aside from you taking off your dress in front of me and practically begging me to dress you, no," he declared, sitting up on the bed.

"Oh, no way! Did I do that too?" At that moment, I felt humiliated by myself.

"Wait, your exact words were: '*Dress me now, Sammy.*'" I turned my face away as he sat on the bed, causing the blanket to slide over his defined chest.

"I got naked in front of you?" I lowered my face, feeling a little relieved to be only in his shirt and panties.

"That really worried me. Do you always do this, Cinzia? Drink and lose control? You drunk are quite *cute*, but all I can think about is, what if I hadn't been there and it was another man? What if someone had raped you? Damn it, Cinzia!"

He was right, so I stayed silent, lowering my head and biting my lip. I had crossed all boundaries, not even remembering how I ended up in that house.

Maybe the fact that he was there made me angry enough to take everything that came my way, and I wasn't proud of it. Santino moved beside me; I didn't look at him, just staying quiet.

"Damn it! Of course Valentino would record that, imagine how many other people recorded it?" I turned my face, horrified, taking the phone from his hand.

There I was, dancing in the nightclub cage, I didn't even recognize myself. As I moved, the dress lifted, showing the curve of my ass, it was very sensual, I didn't even know I could do that. Soon in the footage, Santino appeared with everyone complaining as he carried me out of the nightclub.

"I... I..." I handed the phone back to Santino without looking him in the eyes.

"You really don't remember, and that makes me furious, damn it!" Santino got up from the bed. I raised my eyes to see him walking in front of the bed, wearing only black boxers.

I didn't know how my purse ended up next to the bed, I grabbed it, taking out the phone with fear.

First, I saw a message from my friend:

"Cinzia Bianchi, I don't know what you did to get that drunk, but Enrico said your dad is furious about the news of his daughter dancing on stage and being carried out by Santino. Call me when you can, I'll tell you the details, but I'll give you a heads-up, crazy Aldo said he's going to look for a husband who can handle your craziness... his words. Love you, call me!

I didn't open anything else, throwing the phone on the bed. *Damn it!*

I wiped away some tears that had fallen down my cheeks. *Another husband?* My dad must be crazy if he thinks that will happen; I didn't want another husband, didn't want any husband at all. All I wanted was to finally be free.

The bed sank in front of me, and I rubbed my eyes, drying my tears.

"Go on, Santino, say whatever you want to say, I admit I messed up this time." My voice came out choked, and I raised my eyes to meet his.

"I'm not going to judge you, I'm just terrified. Do you understand the gravity of the situation?" His hand lifted to touch my cheek, wiping away a tear.

"Yes, I understand, and it looks like I'm in for a big lecture from my dad about potential marriage candidates," I grumbled, averting my gaze from his.

"Your dad is looking for new husbands?"

"I just wish he'd understand that I'm 23 and can take care of my life without needing a man by my side." I ran my hand through my hair, irritated, feeling that hellish headache. "In the end, you were right; I might be able to get rid of you, but I can't escape the fate of ending up married to a mafia man."

I swung my legs out of bed, one at a time, getting out from under the covers.

"Where are you going?" Santino asked as I stood up, brushing the shirt that had fallen down my legs.

"Home?" I looked in his direction. He got up too, shirtless and wearing short gym shorts, as if he had put them on in a hurry.

"If you want to stay here, you can. I bet Aldo must be spitting fire every time he opens his mouth. I've already informed Valentino that you're at my place, so they don't need to worry about you." He shrugged.

There was a husband I didn't know, a caring man who wasn't introduced to me while I was married.

"Thanks, I think I'd like that, but I need a painkiller for my headache, I'm about to explode," I asked, and he motioned for me to follow him to the kitchen.

I went down the stairs, admiring his broad back and tattoos. Santino was the epitome of a handsome man. We entered the kitchen, and he went to the first aid kit, handing me a pill and a glass of water.

I first placed the pill in my mouth and then swallowed it with the help of the water.

"Can I take a shower?" I asked awkwardly. This wasn't my home anymore, maybe it never had been.

Santino nodded, so I turned and headed towards the stairs.

"Cinzia?" I looked back over my shoulder. "When you're ready, you can attack me, and preferably imitate a cat like you did yesterday."

"Oh, heavens! Did I really do that?" I shrank further in my embarrassment.

"Yes..."

"I think I'm never going to drink again in my life, I've exhausted all my shame reserves."

"They say when alcohol enters, the truth comes out, and you said you want to lose your virginity with me, Cinzia Vacchiano," he called me by his last name.

"Keep dreaming, Vacchiano, keep dreaming!" I climbed the stairs, resolving in my mind that I would never drink alcohol again after all that embarrassment.

CHAPTER TWENTY-NINE

Cinzia

I stood in front of the mirror, my damp hair hanging loosely. I opened the drawer and found my comb that I had left there. I held it in my hand, running it through my hair. My face looked a bit pale, the moral hangover still lingering. Even a long, hot shower hadn't made it go away.

I put on Santino's shirt again; it was long, covering my body down to just above mid-thigh.

I went without panties, something nobody needed to know, as I refused to wear the same pair. I left the suite and found the bed still messy, letting out a long sigh as I headed towards the stairs. I went down and noticed the mobster sitting on the couch, still in the same clothes, his feet propped up on the coffee table, fiddling with his phone.

"My sister stopped by and left a cake for you. It's on the island," he said without looking up at me.

Since he didn't look at me, I didn't respond. I went to the kitchen and found a piece of chocolate cake, my favorite. I grabbed a fork from the drawer, headed to the island, and sat on a stool.

I took out my phone and saw a message from my friend:

"A cake to lift your moral hangover."

Pietra knew me so well. I didn't understand how my father hadn't come over to drag me by the hair. Aldo had always been a good father, but like every mob father, he thought the best thing for his daughter was a good marriage.

I took a bite of the cake, which tasted delicious, my eyes closing as I chewed.

"It seems good." I opened my eyes to see the mobster entering the kitchen, resting his arms on the island next to me.

"Want some?" I took a bit on the fork and brought it to his mouth, which he opened, his lips brushing against the fork.

Santino chewed as I pulled the fork away, watching his lips move in a slow, sensual motion. Or was I just seeing something sensual? Damn it!

I lowered my eyes to the plate, feeling my face flush. He noticed my embarrassment, taking the fork from my hand and placing it on the granite countertop of the island.

His tattooed hand picked up a piece of cake.

"Look at me, *ragazza mia*," he said, and I lifted my gaze. Santino brought his hand to my mouth, his fingers brushing my lips. I took the cake from his fingers and then sucked on them. "Holy shit..." he murmured, making me smile at his focused gaze on my lips.

I chewed the cake without breaking eye contact, which remained fixed on my lips.

"Is there anything else I need to know that I did yesterday?" I asked.

"Well, I think you're aware of the worst parts. The dancing was what pissed me off the most. I'm still processing the fact that all those men were watching my wife! Do you realize I heard more than one man calling you hot? And then I come home and hear you asking me to attack you while you were imitating a cat. Cinzia, you pushed all limits, and I'm an expert in doing that! — Santino growled. — I wanted to punish you so badly last night, my hands itched to slap your ass hard."

"Sorry?" I murmured, biting the corner of my lip.

"If you keep biting that lip every time you mess up, I'll tear it off!"

"How did we end up here?" I asked, wanting to know one last thing.

"By motorcycle. And I thought it couldn't get worse..."
"I came by motorcycle? On that thing?" I interrupted, alarmed.
"Cinzia Vacchiano, you're testing all my limits of sanity, damn it! Don't you remember how you got here?" Santino snarled at the end of his sentence.

"*Okay, okay*, I won't drink any more alcohol. I think..."
"Think nothing, you're not drinking and that's final! Damn it!"
"And stop calling me Vacchiano, because we're nothing anymore." I pouted as I finished speaking.
"Funny, because last night you wanted to attack me..."
"Go to hell!" I grabbed the fork and took another bite of cake. "Eat, Santino!"

I shut him up with a smile as I fed him the cake. He continued to smile as he chewed.

I took a piece of cake to my lips, trying to remember having ridden on that monstrosity of a motorcycle. Even I was worried about that. Damn, there must have been something very strong in that drink because I didn't remember anything, not even how I got to his house.

"There's a piece of cake here," Santino said, making me lift my eyes to him as he lowered his face, getting closer to mine.

I stayed silent, hypnotized by his gaze as he came closer, his lips brushing against the side of my face, his tongue sliding over the cake that had gotten there. He literally licked it off.

I parted my lips, gasping at his proximity.

"There's another piece here..." he whispered, knowing there was nothing, his hand spread out in my hair, near my neck.

His tongue brushed over my lips, biting the lower one and pulling it back, squeezing it with his teeth, causing me to let out a whimper of pain.

"This is for biting your lip every time you're testing me," he whispered, pulling away from my lip.

"And what do I get for dancing like that in front of everyone?" I provoked, my eyes fixed on his.

"Do you really want to find out?"

"Yes..." My voice came out in a barely audible whisper.

We were startled when the doorbell beeped loudly. Santino grumbled and pulled away from me. I looked up to see my friend appearing.

"Don't you know what a doorbell is, Pietra?" Santino grumbled.

"I do, but why would I use it? It's not like I came in and found you two having sex." My friend looked at me, her eyes narrowing. "Cinzia Bianchi, were you going to give yourself to this pervert? Friend?"

"Well..." I bit the corner of my lip, knowing that if it weren't for her, I might have been about to face quite a punishment—a punishment I wanted.

"Do you want to come to my place? After all, we both know you're no longer married. You know the mess you're making, right? Well, no one here is a child, I'm not going to force anyone to come to my house. I brought clothes for you, friend; after all, wearing Santino's shirts isn't decent attire. And if you're going to leave, go through the backyards, because your father doesn't know you're here," Pietra said all at once.

"Now it makes sense why he didn't come here; he doesn't even know I'm here," I whispered.

"This is the last place he would think you are. After all, he thinks you two can't stand each other. In fact, that's what we all think. You're both crazy!" My friend handed a change of clothes to Santino. "I hope you know what you're doing..."

Pietra left the kitchen as quickly as she had come, like a whirlwind, but not before saying:

"If you're going to take her virginity, Santino, at least be considerate!"

And so, we were left there alone once more.

CHAPTER THIRTY

Cinzia

"That was a sign," I murmured.

"A sign of what exactly?" he asked, placing the clothes Pietra had brought on the island.

"No punishment, I'm going to put on this outfit and go to Pietra's place." I jumped off the stool, pulling down the shirt.

"Or..."

"Or?" I lifted my eyes to see him coming closer.

"Let me punish you without taking your virginity?"

Santino positioned himself in front of me, pulling me by the waist, pressing his body against mine. I knew this was a mistake; after all, with him, it would never be just a man, as I felt strange things every time we touched.

"You're making me curious..." My voice trailed off as he squeezed my butt.

Before I could say anything, he easily lifted me onto his shoulder, making me gasp as I let out a squeal.

"Asshole! I'm not wearing panties!" I pounded his back, hearing his laughter, feeling his hand slide over my exposed butt due to the shirt he had lifted.

"This way is better." A slap landed on my butt.

Santino climbed the stairs, keeping his hand on my butt, caressing it all the while. He entered his bedroom and laid me down in the middle of the bed.

"Stay there!" He turned and went toward the closet, where I heard the sound of chains.

He returned holding a metal chain and a pair of handcuffs.

"You're not seriously going to do this," I said, sitting up on the bed, terrified. When he mentioned punishment, I thought it would be just a few spanks.

He quickly moved toward me, preventing me from moving.

"What did you think it would be?" I widened my eyes as he positioned himself over my body, holding my wrists and raising them above my head.

I tried to pull my hands away but lacked the strength. Before I knew it, I was handcuffed to the headboard.

"Wouldn't a punishment just be a few spanks?" He smiled at my panic. "Get that chain off me!"

"I'm going to make you feel the frustration I felt when you danced for all those people. I never said it would just be spankings..." He moved my arms on the bed.

How stupid I was! Santino lifted the shirt I was wearing, pulling it over my arms and covering my eyes, tying it there, depriving me of any sight. My arms were pressed above my head, restricting my movements even more with the shirt tied.

"Santino!" I scolded him, the lack of sight making me extremely frustrated. The sound of the chain was making me anxious.

He pulled me by the waist, making me lie down on the bed. He passed the chain around my neck, lifting it and pressing it against my mouth.

"Open your mouth, or I'll do it myself..." When I didn't, he did it himself.

Forcing my jaw open aggressively, I didn't know what he was doing; I just felt the metal of the chain on my mouth. He pulled the chain, tightening it further.

I realized he had made a binding so that when he pulled, it would tighten even more around my mouth, running the chain down between my breasts, resting in the middle of my pussy.

"Oh, little whirlwind, you don't know how much I wanted you like this, vulnerable, completely at my mercy." The ambient air touching my skin made me fear what he would do.

"I'm going to punch you..."

"Are you? Tell me how," he mocked.

I felt the bed sink; he was moving, and I knew he was walking around the room. Suddenly, everything went silent. Santino left the room. Was he going to leave me alone? Was this my punishment? Naked, tied up, alone?

But soon the footsteps returned. He came back. I heard something clinking, the bed sank again, and I believed it was his legs around my waist, all that anxiety making me apprehensive.

"Oh!" Something cold touched my breasts. "Is that ice?"

He didn't say anything, but I could hear his smile as he slid the ice cube over my swollen nipples.

"So tasty, and surrendered to me..." he whispered, sliding the ice over my other nipple, circling it. "It would be so easy to fuck you like this."

"Asshole!" I murmured, enjoying all that tension.

Santino lowered the ice, and I heard it clink, indicating he was replacing it. He left the previous one on my belly button. The sound of the chain made its presence felt again. I didn't know what he was doing.

"Ah!" I let out a little scream as he shoved an ice cube into my pussy through the end of the chain.

The chain tightened further in my mouth, and I couldn't stay still. The ice at the end of the chain made me writhe, the cold inside me leaving me incredibly aroused and tense. The more I moved, the tighter the chain squeezed my mouth, preventing me from speaking.

"You're feeling anxious, aren't you? Seeking inevitable pleasure, it won't come, because the ice is just meant to keep you tense, just as it did to me yesterday..."

Santino picked up another piece of ice, running it over my lips compressed by the chain. He stepped back, the ice still inside my pussy was small. From the rustling of his pants, I knew he was removing them.

His body came back on top of mine. I felt his penis touch my stomach, soon feeling his hand gripping both my breasts, pressing something in between. That's when I realized he was sliding his penis between my breasts, performing a "Spanish" move.

It was incredibly sexy; of all the times I had gone further with a man, nothing compared to this.

I sought more friction from the almost-melted ice inside me, making the chain slip out. Santino loosened the chain in my mouth, allowing me to speak again.

"Do you want an orgasm, ragazza mia?" he asked, sliding his penis between my breasts.

"Yes..." I murmured, my jaw aching.

Santino grabbed ice, stopping his movements, placing it back inside my pussy, just like before, making me writhe with that friction as I moaned loudly, throwing my head back, the chain tightening around my mouth.

"Where's your dirty mouth now? You don't know how delicious you are, given up like this..."

He resumed sliding his penis between my breasts, this time faster, squeezing my breasts tightly.

I didn't stop writhing; the chain brushing against my pussy was just as he said, the ice gave me pleasure but made me delay.

"I'm going to come; tell me I can cum on your face."

At that moment, he could ask for my virginity, and I would give it. I nodded in agreement, unable to speak, just affirming vehemently with my head.

It didn't take long for him to grunt, and I felt the hot jets being splashed on my face as he came between my breasts.

"Fuck! What a hot woman!" He pulled out from between my breasts, spreading my legs, and removing the ice from my pussy amidst that torture.

I could feel his cum running down my face, but having Santino's tongue on my pussy made me forget everything. He slid it all over, leaving the chain aside so that as I moved, it didn't tighten my mouth.

I wanted to touch him, but I couldn't, so I writhed against his lip, seeking more of that friction, his tongue taking me completely without even inserting a finger. I was so wet, so surrendered.

"Go on, my little Sicilian whirlwind, give yourself to me, give me your honey," he requested, and I surrendered.

The spasms made me moan loudly, like waves of electricity coursing through my body. Santino sucked everything up until he got up, leaving the bed, and leaving me alone. Damn, was he going to leave me like this, or was he?

Asshole!

"I'll be right back, the doorbell is ringing," he said from somewhere, leaving me in that state and walking out.

CHAPTER THIRTY-ONE

Santino

The doorbell rang again. I grabbed a shirt hastily from the closet, smoothing the fabric over my abdomen. I only put on shorts without underwear due to the rush. I stopped in front of the door, opening it to find none other than Aldo Bianchi, my ex-father-in-law.

"Where is Cinzia?" he asked immediately, looking over my shoulder.

"I don't know if you remember, but we're no longer married, so I don't see how I can help you with that." I leaned against the door, making it clear he wasn't welcome to enter.

"Funny guy, weren't you the one who helped her leave the club?"

"It could have been Valentino too, after all, we're identical." I shrugged casually, little did he know the taste of his daughter's pussy was still quite pleasant in my mouth.

"You and your brother think you own the world..."

"We don't think, we are," I cut him off casually.

"I'll keep an eye out. If Valentino shows up at home without my daughter, I'll break down this place you call a house."

"Fine, but you'll be wasting your time. I don't know where your crazy daughter is."

Everything was planned. Valentino was staying at Pietra's house, probably spending the day sleeping after partying all night. No one knew where he was except us, so Aldo might think his daughter was somewhere with Valentino.

"I need to know where Cinzia is. If you see her, send her home. There's a suitor coming to my house tonight. My daughter has no sense of caution!"

"Oh? A suitor? Who would that be?" I asked, feigning disinterest.

"Marco Lombardo. He's not directly involved in the mafia; his uncle is one of the associates. Since he's outside the mafia, my daughter might calm down and accept this marriage. From what his uncle told me, Marco is a calm man and accepted without hesitation..."

"My father approved? A marriage with someone outside the Cosa Nostra is not allowed!" I was somewhat harsh in my words.

"No, your father doesn't know yet, but I will talk to him, and I know Tommaso will understand my desperation."

"I hope he doesn't, because marriages outside the mafia are not permitted," I growled, slamming the door in his face and hearing the lock click.

Hell!

When he mentioned Marco, only one thing came to mind—the Marco she was planning to run away with. I didn't know if it was the same person, as I didn't know his last name, but I wouldn't allow that marriage to happen in any way.

I went back up the stairs, moving not quickly but silently, entering slowly, seeing the chain in her mouth, trailing down her body, the shirt over her eyes, and the handcuffs binding her to the bed. From her rapid breathing, I knew she was still awake.

My cum was dripping down her flushed cheek. Damn, I had come on her face, my cock had slid between her ample breasts.

"Santino?" Her voice was breathy through the chain.

"Yes, amore mio," I murmured, moving towards the little whirlwind, running my hand over the chain, undoing the knot, and removing it from her mouth as she closed her lips, moistening them.

"What did my father want?" She knew it was Aldo. "I heard his tone of voice but didn't understand what was said."

I leaned over the bed, entering the code on the keypad, unlocking her cuffs and removing them from her wrists. She moved, and as she did, she pulled the shirt back down over her arms, putting it on again.

"Your father was looking for you," I said as her eyes blinked several times, adjusting to mine.

"He doesn't know I'm here?" she asked, looking around. She was searching for something to clean her face.

Cinzia got up from the bed, briefly losing her balance. I held her by the waist, smiling at her wobbly legs.

"Be careful, ragazza mia," I warned close to her ear as I stood up behind her.

"Stop calling me those sweet names. We both know you're not sweet." Quickly, the woman regained her composure and headed towards the suite.

I followed her movements, analyzing her thick thighs, her ass creating a delicious curve. Just thinking about my cock rubbing there made me hard.

I stopped at the doorway, watching her wash her face with soap.

"Remind me never to accept your punishments again. You're crazy." Her eyes met mine in the mirror's reflection as she rubbed her cheeks.

"But you really enjoyed being tortured, and that's not even a third of what I know how to do." I smiled at her, watching her open and close her mouth, curiosity sparkling in her eyes. "You want to know, don't you?"

"A little? Tell me more." Cinzia gave one of her typical half-seductive smiles.

"I have a chain of clamps that goes on your nipple, descending into an anal plug. As you move, the plug vibrates, making you writhe and pulling the clamps on your nipple..."

"*That... that...* doesn't hurt?" She turned around, intrigued.

"Pain and pleasure can go hand in hand. Haven't you ever tried it?" She shook her head. "My brother and I are part of a BDSM club here in Sicily. He participates more than I do because... how can I explain? I lose patience, and the last time I hurt a woman for real, her moans gave me a headache. Valentino likes these things more; in fact, he has a hidden apartment from our parents all equipped for that, but he doesn't only have sex in that style; he practices 'normal' sex as well."

"And no one knows about this?" she asked, curious, and I shook my head. "Not even Pietra?"

"No one, Cinzia, and if anyone finds out, I'll know it was you." I was direct.

Valentino and I always shared all our secrets, including the fact that we were part of that club. My brother was more sadistic than I was, but it was a fact we hid so well that no one ever found out.

"And why did you tell me?" Cinzia turned back on the faucet and bent down to rinse her face.

As she bent down, her shirt rode up, showing the curve of her ass. I turned my face to the side, my hands itching, moving up to her, rubbing my hard cock against her delicious ass.

"Santino Vacchiano, who gave you this freedom?" She couldn't turn around because she was rubbing her face, which allowed me to take advantage of the situation, lifting her shirt for a clearer view of her ass.

My cock was almost poking out of my shorts simply because I wasn't wearing underwear.

Cinzia finished washing up and turned to me quickly.

"This is madness. Stay away from me. We were married and didn't even think about having sex. What do you want now?" she asked breathlessly.

"Actually, I always wanted to fuck your pussy." I shrugged.

"Tell me what my father wanted?" She went back to the subject, making me sigh loudly as she moved away, returning to the bedroom.

"It seems that tonight your new suitor is coming to your house..."

"WHAT?" She let out a shriek, looking at me with wide eyes.

"That's right. Just as you heard." I shrugged.

"He didn't mention a name?"

"He did, but I forgot." Damn, I wasn't going to mention that asshole's name.

"No, I don't want to marry someone else," she whispered, sitting on the bed and running her hand through her hair.

"Well, we could run away to Las Vegas and get married." Cinzia raised her eyes, squinting at me.

"You're crazy, Vacchiano! Why would I do that with you when we were already married?" She rolled her eyes. "Or I could tell my father that we had sex, lost my virginity, and I might even be pregnant. What man would want to marry a woman who might be pregnant by someone else?"

"Your plan is great, but I won't accept that lie if it doesn't become reality." I walked towards her, Cinzia lifted her blue eyes to me.

"What do you mean?"

"I want to take your virginity, I want to cum inside you and put a baby of mine inside you," I grunted, pushing her onto the bed, covering her body with mine.

"That would be madness even for us..."

"Madness would be if we lied about something we both want." I gripped the hem of her shirt, lifting it.

"Santino," Cinzia sighed, "what if I really get pregnant?"

"Don't think, just let me fuck you for the first time," I pleaded with a breathy voice, knowing I was doing it out of selfishness, wanting to put a baby inside her because the man who was coming to her house might be that Marco she was planning to run away with, and damn it if Cinzia belonged to another man who wasn't me.

I'm a damn arrogant bastard. I made the mistake of losing her once, but I was determined to make up for it.

"Yes, Vacchiano, don't make me think. Just be my first man..." she consented through her breathy voice.

CHAPTER THIRTY-TWO

Cinzia

Santino slipped the shirt over my head and tossed it aside. His face descended upon mine, his hand caressing the side of my cheek.

"First time wild or gentle?" he asked, brushing his lips against mine, making me gasp.

"Gentle." I smiled, lifting my hand to touch his neck, pulling him towards my lips, initiating a slow kiss. Our lips matched, his tongue caressing mine.

"Maybe I could make an exception for the virgin pussy..." His voice trailed off as he pulled away.

I watched him remove his shirt and stand up to take off his shorts. I turned on the bed, lying back on the pillows, and Santino came over me.

"So?" I asked, feeling uncomfortable for the first time in this situation. "It's not like I don't know how sex works, but losing my virginity like this was never a life goal. After all, I saved myself for my husband..."

"*Schiii...*" His lips covered mine, silencing me with a kiss. "Don't think..."

He positioned himself between my legs, trailing kisses down my neck, leaving a path of kisses as he moved, stopping over my breasts, which he squeezed and brought to his lips.

I felt his tongue circle my nipple, my eyes slowly closing, feeling the small spasms, his hands causing that intoxicating frenzy.

His hand descended between my legs, touching my pussy, flicking my vaginal lips, sliding easily over my pleasure as it flowed.

"So wet," he murmured, inserting a finger inside me. "So tight..."

He panted, his eyes meeting mine, his lip coming into contact with mine again.

"Don't fall in love, Vacchiano," I teased as his teeth grazed my lip, pulling it with force.

"To fall in love, you'd have to agree to everything in sex..."

"Good thing I'm a puritan then," I teased, though I'm curious enough to agree to anything in bed.

Santino replaced one finger with two, moving them inside my pussy. Entering and exiting slowly, his lips constantly on mine, as if he couldn't keep them away.

He removed his fingers, looking at me tenderly.

"It's impossible to get wetter than this," he murmured.

He supported himself on his knees, his cock touching my pussy, pressing with a bit more force. I touched his shoulder, squeezing it, our eyes locked on each other, his hand touching the side of my cheek, caressing with his finger.

With a bit more vigor, he penetrated me. I closed my eyes tightly against the pain, as if I were being torn apart.

"*Amore mio,* open your eyes." His request came in a rough kiss.

I opened my eyes, feeling them misty with tears from the sudden pain. He withdrew from me and penetrated me again, this time going even deeper.

"Oh God! It hurts so much," I complained, seeing him smile as he lowered his lip and touched mine.

"Did someone say it wouldn't hurt?" he asked lovingly.

"It's your fault. You should have chosen someone with a smaller cock," I teased, meeting his eyes which had risen to mine.

"Don't be deluded, ragazza mia, you're mine, you've never stopped being..." His sentence trailed off as he withdrew from me, penetrating me again.

His movements, coming in and out, became increasingly urgent, as if I were adapting to his size. Santino kissed me again, a slow, wet kiss. The kiss made me forget the member tearing me apart, until the pain was replaced by pleasure, just like when he sucked me, taking me completely.

"Can I fuck you with a bit more force?" he asked, as if those movements were the limit of his anguish.

"I thought you didn't know how to do anything faster," I provoked, meeting his eyes.

"Do you want to be fucked hard, amore mio?"

"Don't call me that," I murmured. "Now shut up and do the full job..."

"That's the hurricane I know." He smiled.

The movements became faster, reaching the end of my pussy, with the certainty that he wasn't even putting it all the way inside me.

I dragged my nails down his back, pulling his body closer to mine, running my hand down the curve of his ass, feeling it. He smiled against my lip.

"I've always wanted to do this..."

"Always is a very strong word..."

"But it's the word that fits correctly." He arched his gaze, staring at me, not moving away.

His thumb caressed the side of my cheek, feeling the spasms touching my body, knowing I wouldn't last long under his intense gaze. It was as if, at that moment, something took over me, his cock entering and exiting, taking me urgently, making us one.

I surrendered, gripping his back, moaning loudly, writhing.

"Santino..." I whispered his name, rolling my eyes, seeing him do the same.

"Fuck!" His hot jets shot inside me.

I knew there was no turning back after that. Santino came inside me. We did it in the heat of the moment, but what were the chances of getting pregnant on the first try? My mother took almost a year to get pregnant with me.

His heavy body fell on top of mine, and we stayed like that for long seconds, his face in the curve of my neck.

"What's this story about always wanting to do this?" he asked, still with a tired voice.

"I'm not telling," I declared, smiling as he pulled out, feeling his liquid running down my legs. "Looks like I'm no longer a virgin..."

"Don't dodge the question," he interrupted me.

"It's nothing." I turned, lying on my side.

"No one stays 'forever' wanting to grope other people's asses," he declared playfully.

"*Yeah, yeah*... Even though you and your brother are the same, I've always liked your impulsive nature more. Pietra used to nag me for not asking about both of you, just about you, but you can lower your expectations because I stopped doing that once you started hopping from bed to bed..."

"So does that mean I've always been your target?" he asked casually.

"It's your fault. You were always the one circling around me, or did you forget that it was you who gave me the kiss?"

"I was your first kiss, your first man. Cinzia Bianchi, you're destined to be mine," he murmured, jumping over me, extending his hand to help me up.

I grimaced as I held his fingers, feeling discomfort between my legs.

"Does it hurt?"

"A bit sore..."

"Come on, let's take a shower, I'll take care of you." He gave me a flirtatious wink.

I looked at the sheet, finding the trace of my virginity, the red stain on the white sheet.

I was no longer a virgin; I lost my virginity to a man who wasn't even my husband…

CHAPTER THIRTY-THREE

Cinzia

We both came out of the bathroom together. I put on the dress Pietra had left for me, a floral dress of mine that I had left at her house one day when I went for a pool bath.

"What time is it?" I asked, hearing my stomach growl.

"It's one in the afternoon. Do you want to sneak out and have lunch somewhere?" he asked with that suggestive smile while buttoning up his black shirt.

Santino was wearing a black dress shirt along with his usual black dress pants. *He looked so sexy in those clothes.*

"I'm not getting on that thing you call a motorcycle," I declared, making a face.

"You liked it when you were *tipsy*," he teased, coming towards me, pulling me by the waist, his hand sliding up, brushing my hair aside.

"Remind me never to drink again." I rolled my eyes.

"Don't worry, the image of you gyrating like that in front of everyone won't leave my mind anytime soon."

"Was it really that bad?"

"Cinzia, I wanted to kill everyone who called you a hottie. Is there anything worse than that? You lose all your inhibitions when you're drunk." His eyes narrowed in my direction.

Maybe I really did go overboard. I still couldn't understand how I got so drunk that I ended up like that.

"Can we change the subject and go eat? How are we getting out of here?" I asked as he gestured for me to follow him.

"We're going in one of my cars," he declared, holding my hand, leading me through the house to the garage.

Why didn't I know this version of Santino when we were married? Why was he being so attentive? Why only at that moment?

I headed towards the driver's side door. His car was low, a sporty BMW model. The door opened automatically when he pressed the remote. I sat in the passenger seat, and he did the same next to me.

"Get down so there's no risk of your dad being on the street and seeing us..." I nodded as he ran his hand over my neck, pressing me against his legs.

"Hey!"

"You can give me a blowjob if you're interested." Santino opened the garage gate.

I held onto his thigh, my face pressed against the bulge of his growing cock as he reversed out of the garage.

"Damn, your dad is right on the sidewalk in front of my dad's house. They're talking," Santino whispered, but didn't give up on the plan, accelerating towards the exit.

It was clear he was tense.

"That forbidden feeling is making me so excited," I declared, sliding my hand over his erect cock that was pressing against the fabric.

"Cinzia, don't tease me..."

"Now that I'm no longer a virgin, could I fulfill my fantasy of having sex in the car?"

I knew he had passed the exit of the condo because he sped up. I slid my hand along the fabric, unbuttoning his pants.

"You're no longer a virgin, but you must be sore..."

"A little pain doesn't hurt. — I bit the corner of my lip. — Can I get up?"

"What's your hunger level?" he asked, growling.

"Can we make a stop first?" Santino glanced down.

He signaled, turning onto a dirt road abruptly. I lifted my head, knowing he was heading to a place almost no one went. By the time we reached the destination, I unzipped his pants, his eyes never straying from the road, his hand gripping the steering wheel tightly. Then he suddenly braked, stopping the car, reaching his hand beside the seat, pushing it back.

"What to do with you, *huh,* little tornado? I don't have sex in this car because it's my pride and joy, but I might make an exception for your little pussy..." Santino pulled me onto his lap.

The car's ceiling was low, but there was plenty of space on the sides. Santino lifted my dress, my legs on either side of his waist, and he lowered his pants enough to free his cock.

"No foreplay?" He raised an eyebrow, confused.

"Just fuck me, Santino. I'm hungry for food and for you," I declared, hearing him laugh, that delicious laugh echoing in the car.

"You're crazy, and in a good way, an incredibly delicious kind of crazy." His hand slapped my ass while he held his cock with the other hand.

Holding him up, I slid my sore pussy from our first time. I closed my eyes, feeling completely invaded, going as far as I could.

"Move that sexy ass of yours over my cock... that's it... like that," he panted.

I was still a bit sore, but nothing was going to stop me from having a second round with Santino Vacchiano.

I wrapped my arms around his neck, bouncing my ass on his pelvis, his hands spread across my butt.

"Ah..., Cinzia..., if you knew how much you drive me wild." Our eyes locked.

A desperate kiss started. I began to grind faster on his cock, letting out many moans into our kiss. He was big, and it felt even deeper that way.

"Santino," I whimpered his name amidst the kiss.

"Give me all your moans, a*more mio.*" Despite my pleading, he kept calling me *my love.*

It wasn't his love, and he probably said that to all of them, but one thing couldn't be denied: Santino knew what he was doing. One of his hands moved to my neck, pulling my hair back, his lips descending down my neck, leaving wet kisses.

"Ah..., Sammy," I whimpered with a choked voice, his fingers sliding over my stomach, moving from my ass to touch my pussy.

The moment he touched my pussy, it was like a spark that surrendered me to pleasure, moaning loudly, rolling my eyes, feeling the spasms. Santino pressed his cock deep, coming inside me again.

"Ah, *amore mio*..." he groaned, hugging me tightly.

We stayed like that for long seconds until I finally spoke.

"How am I going to clean up? I hadn't thought about that," I murmured, turning my face to meet his eyes.

"There's a shirt of mine in the back seat, grab it. — I looked over him, extending my hand, taking it and feeling his hand caressing my butt. — Hand it to me, when you get up I'll put it underneath, so it doesn't drip on my black pants and leave a mark..."

I nodded, getting up. Santino placed the fabric over my pussy, preventing the liquid from touching his clothes. I sat in the passenger seat as he reached into the glove compartment for a tissue to clean his cock, while I used the shirt to clean myself and put my panties back in place, having only moved them aside earlier.

I turned my face, and Santino looked back at me.

"Are you still hungry?"

"Now just for food," I declared with a lazy smile.

"Let's go have lunch then." He winked and started the car.

CHAPTER THIRTY-FOUR

Santino

I parked in my garage, stepping out of my car and lifting my eyes to see the most beautiful blonde who had ever been in my arms exiting from the passenger side. Cinzia let out a sigh.

"It seems like there's no avoiding it. It's time to go home."

I headed towards the garage door that led to my living room. Opening it, I looked at the curtain of the window, noticing that night was beginning to fall. I had spent the afternoon with Cinzia; she had asked to stay at the beach after we had lunch because she didn't want to return and face her father's decisions.

I agreed to her wish because I wanted that too—to be by her side, to hear her delicious laugh, her hair in the wind. Damn, Cinzia Bianchi was becoming my redemption, and she could have been mine, but I sent her away out of sheer selfishness.

Maybe it was the thrill of the forbidden that made me want more. I wanted more of her and couldn't keep my hands off that woman.

All I wanted was to deny that feeling, but I was falling for it like a fool.

Cinzia walked past me, and I watched her walk, my eyes analyzing her curves. I had always been a one-night guy, I'd sleep with girls and then send them away. Since my marriage to Cinzia, I hadn't slept with anyone else, which was beyond crazy because I used to sleep with a woman every night, and now it had been almost 45 days without sex. *What the hell was that witch doing to me?*

I had annulled the marriage precisely for that reason, and yet, I couldn't. It was as if I was searching for Cinzia Bianchi in every woman. What was impossible to find because there was only one Cinzia Bianchi, and the crazy girl was right in front of me.

I quickened my pace, pulling her by the waist and pressing her body against mine.

"Why did you need to lose to change?" She sighed, resting her head on my chest.

"Because I'm an idiot," I grumbled, squeezing the fabric of her dress and pulling it up.

"What do you plan to do, Vacchiano?" she asked, trying to turn, but I stopped her, pushing her onto the backrest of the sofa.

I leaned her over the high part of the sofa, letting the dress fall over her back, her ass sticking up towards me.

"I want to fuck you again, *ragazza mia*," I said, caressing her skin.

The panties covered part of her ass. I grabbed the sides, wanting to pull them down but needing her approval.

"Santino..., I shouldn't, but I want to..." she whispered, her face turned sideways, her hair falling onto the sofa seat.

We were at the back of the sofa, which made it easier for her to keep her ass up for me. I pulled down her panties, watching them fall to her feet, then opened my pants, lowering them just enough to free my cock, which was rock hard at that moment.

Not even my hand could span her entire ass; it was large and delicious. Damn, I was crazy about Cinzia Bianchi's ass.

I rubbed my cock across the length of her ass, sliding it to her wet entrance, so moist it seemed to shine. I closed my eyes at the sensation of slipping my cock slowly into her pussy, hearing her sigh.

I was getting her used to my size; Cinzia was tight and embraced my cock as if it were hers. I dug my fingers into her ass, reaching deep into her pussy, my eyes focused on her expression, biting my lip as I entered and withdrew.

I moved one of my hands down, stimulating her folds, feeling the texture of her pussy on my fingers as I slid in and out with my cock.

Cinzia was moaning louder than before, which made it clear that maybe we were pushing the limits for her first time. But I was selfish, and I wanted her, I desired her, I wanted to fuck that pussy all the time. And with this, it would be three times coming inside Cinzia, three times to make sure I got her pregnant. When she found out I knew who the man her father wanted to promise her to, she'd hate me.

I started fucking her harder, pounding my pelvis against her ass. Cinzia moaned, sighed, gripping a sofa pillow tightly.

"Santino..., I..." She squirmed, closing her eyes, surrendering.

I lowered my gaze, the image of her ass, my cock entering and exiting her pussy, grazing her ass—the most perfect image. Her walls squeezing my cock was enough to bring me to climax.

I plunged deep one last time, hitting the end of her pussy, groaning loudly as I came inside her.

Damn!

I squeezed my eyelids shut, releasing a sigh as I opened my eyes.

I pulled my cock out a few seconds later, seeing a strand of my cum sliding down her leg from inside her pussy. Damn, what a breathtaking sight.

I helped the girl up, her lazy eyes meeting mine.

"Wasn't it supposed to be just once?" she whispered with a lazy voice.

"Well, the first time was a mutual decision, the second time you asked for, I couldn't miss out, so I asked for a third." I smiled, pulling her by the waist, pressing my body against hers. "I want you, *amore mio*...

"Don't call me that when you clearly call all the others the same way." Her eyes met mine.

"Who said that?" I asked.

"It's totally your style, calling everyone affectionately to get what you want..."

"I don't need to be affectionate; I always get everything I want, and most of the time it's through aggression." I lowered my face, touching my lips to hers.

"So why this change only now?" Cinzia avoided my kiss.

"I don't know, the feeling of possibly losing you is taking over me, and besides, you've also let your guard down a bit. We both know that when Hurricane Cinzia is activated, no soul is left untouched," I said, seeing a small smile on her lips.

"I hate you, plain and simple..."

"I thought I was your favorite," I teased, recalling what she had said.

"My favorite to hate the most." She shrugged, trying to brush it off.

"My Sicilian hurricane, you can't deny it, we both know that you want me as much as I want you..."

"You want me, Sammy?" I looked at her features—her cheeks always flushed, slightly full lips, blue eyes contrasting with brown lashes, her face roughly at the height of my chin.

And the way only she called me that made me completely hard.

"You still ask? When the answer is obviously yes."

"Do we really need to go?" She changed the subject drastically, pouting.

"Can I come with you?" I asked.

"I think it would be nice to have someone by my side."

Little does she know that the man her father wanted to give her to was supposedly the same man she loved.

CHAPTER THIRTY-FIVE

Cinzia

For the first time, I liked having Santino by my side; it was strange, we went from zero to a hundred in a matter of seconds. I could still feel my intimacy pulsating, a slight burning sensation. The last time we had sex was a bit uncomfortable, but not bad; it was good. *Who was I trying to fool?* It was wonderful, but the problem came after; for a first time, having sex three times might have been pushing all the limits.

We walked toward my parents' house, where I noticed a car parked in front of the house. My supposed suitor was already there; my father didn't waste any time handing me over to another man. He always thought I was a problem, so it's easier to pass the *problem* onto someone else.

The perks of being part of the mafia, I thought with irony.

Santino was by my side, and suddenly his body tensed, his hand holding mine gripping a little harder. I climbed the steps to the porch of the house, and before entering, I released my hand from his. I was taken by surprise when his fingers touched my cheek.

"*Amore mio,* I'm sorry for taking your virginity today. I know how you were saving yourself for your husband, but I'm selfish enough to know that if a child of mine grows in your womb, no one will make me leave your side." His eyes didn't even divert from mine, as if he knew something I didn't.

"What are you talking about?" I asked, somewhat astonished.

"Let's go inside." His lips quickly met mine in a chaste kiss.

We pulled away as I entered the house first, fully convinced that Santino was walking behind me and had left the door open, as if he was doing it on purpose for someone to see him inside.

My father came toward me as soon as he heard my steps, his eyes fiery as if he wanted to kill me with just a look.

"What are you doing here, Vacchiano?" he asked, grinding his teeth as he always did when he was angry.

For him to call him Vacchiano meant he didn't know which of the twin brothers he was talking to.

"I came to accompany Cinzia," Santino spoke with that mocking tone.

"Dad, we need to talk..."

"Now is not the time to talk. Come on." He practically dragged me by the arm; I could hear Santino growling behind me.

I entered the living room, facing the two men there, but what caught my attention the most was recognizing a familiar face among them.

"Marco?" I smiled as I spoke my friend's name. He stood up from the sofa and came toward me.

We embraced, a strong hug, reminding me of college days, something that seemed distant, even out of my reality, as if it no longer was part of me. Marco had always been important since the moment he entered my life, but his touch didn't provoke the same crazy sensation that the damned Vacchiano caused.

Thinking of Vacchiano reminded me that he was still there.

"What are you doing here?" I asked, suddenly alarmed, pulling away from him.

"I found out that my uncle is an associate, so I was able to get to your father," he said with that sparkle in his brown eyes, his beard always with disheveled hairs messing up his face.

He wasn't Santino; I couldn't compare them. Santino was an extraordinary man, and in addition, vain, unlike Marco, who never cared about his appearance.

"Wait, so my suitor is you?" I asked, even more surprised.

"Yes, it's me..."

I turned my face abruptly to Santino. He knew, he knew that my suitor was Marco, which is why he asked me to run away, to take my virginity, and apologized because he was already anticipating my anger.

"Did you know?" I asked, looking into his eyes. He nodded, reaching into his pants pocket. "You lied to me about not knowing?"

"And I got what I wanted." He shrugged in that arrogant way.

"Why?" I was trying to control myself not to blow up at that bastard.

"Remember when I said you were mine? Well, I just made you see that, and Aldo Bianchi, my father will never approve of a marriage with a member outside the clan." He was even more arrogant with my father.

"Your father will not influence a decision about my daughter. Marco is the best for Cinzia and is willing to do anything for her." My father was direct.

At that moment, a new person joined us, the Don entering the house. His eyes met his son's, and beside the Don was his wife, always impeccable, Verena, the epitome of calm for the Don of the Cosa Nostra.

"I'm not going to influence what exactly, Aldo? Could it be that for the first time in over 50 years of partnership and loyalty, you went against one of my orders?" The Don spoke seriously.

"You say that because your daughter is already engaged, while mine is tarnishing the family with news of her dancing almost naked for everyone to see." I widened my eyes, looking at my father.

"Sorry, Daddy," I whispered, feeling guilty.

"It's no use apologizing for something that has already happened, Cinzia! You couldn't even maintain a marriage with the damn

Vacchiano. No one wants you, and that's why you will marry Marco Lombardo!" My eyes filled with tears at all his harsh words.

"She's not marrying him, damn it!" Santino raged.

"I assumed she wasn't with you. I'm seeing the tattoo on your chest; they might have hidden it for an entire day, but Cinzia will marry Marco!"

"I'm not, Dad! Sorry, Marco, but I can't," I murmured to him as he looked at me confused, after all, this was what I wanted in college.

"But I thought that..."

"She can't marry anyone if she's expecting a child of mine." Everyone fell silent at Santino's words, various gazes directed at me and Santino.

At that moment, no one understood anything, since we had always hated each other; how could I be expecting a child from him?

"What are you trying to say?" Dad asked, stunned.

"You know how babies are made, right? Your daughter is mine, and she could be carrying my child, and there's no fucking way I'm letting her marry someone else," Santino growled at my father.

I was still angry with Santino, feeling deceived, as if he had taken my virginity knowing that my new suitor was Marco.

"I can't believe it, you saved yourself for 23 years just to give it up like this?" Dad looked at me discontentedly.

"That's not a problem; if it happened today, there's the morning-after pill. I don't care about that," Marco suddenly spoke up.

Everything happened in a fraction of a second. Santino moved behind his father, pulling out the gun that was on the Don's back, aiming it at Marco and walking quickly, stopping right in front of him with the gun to my friend's forehead.

"What part of this don't you understand? Cinzia Bianchi is mine, and I don't bluff when I say I'll kill the damned bastard who stands in my way," he growled in a way I had never seen before.

I ran toward Santino, tears beginning to stream down my face. I had never been one to cry, but I felt deceived, ashamed, and as always, limited, with my fate being determined by men.

"Enough!" I begged with my hoarse voice, holding onto Santino's tense shoulder. "If you don't put down that gun now, I'll never look at you again!"

He lowered the gun, his eyes fixed on mine.

"Sorry, *Ragazza mia*," he whispered, pulling away but speaking loudly for everyone to hear. "If I find out that Cinzia took the morning-after pill, this entire family is dead, and I couldn't care less if he's my father's *consigliere*, because I am the future of the Cosa Nostra, and if it's not now, your death is certain, Aldo Bianchi."

He spoke directly to my father; I had never seen Santino so agitated.

"Santino!" Tommaso tried to stop his son.

"Fuck off, Dad, I want this pile of shit away from my wife..."

"She is no longer yours," the Don declared with regret.

"For now, because she never stopped being mine," Santino said, looking into my eyes.

"You lied to me, Santino," I murmured.

"I lied because I knew you wouldn't want me if you knew who the damned suitor was," he tilted his head slightly as he spoke.

"How do you know? Now I don't want you, you lied to get what you wanted, lied out of selfishness, always for your own sake." I wiped the tears that kept falling from under my eyes. "I'm not going to take the pill, but know that if I'm not pregnant, regardless of what's between us, I'll never want to look at you again, you bastard!"

I walked past all of them toward the stairs, not wanting to see anyone anymore. The culmination of all the recent events was overwhelming me—the news, losing my virginity, Santino's lies, Marco's return.

Would I have agreed to marry Marco if Santino hadn't taken my virginity? Probably yes, but not for love, because my damned treacherous heart belonged to that arrogant, bastard mafioso.

"I need to be alone, please leave me alone!" I pleaded as I climbed the stairs, locking myself in my room, letting the tears flow copiously as I sat on the floor, leaning against the door.

CHAPTER THIRTY-SIX

Santino

Cinzia climbed the stairs with tears in her eyes, and at that moment I realized I had made a mistake, but it was a mistake I didn't regret making, because I would do it a thousand times over. I wanted to go after her, climb those stairs, take her in my arms, and soothe the tears streaming down her face.

I had never seen her cry like that, and for that reason, I knew how hurt she was with me. Cinzia had always been a strong woman, and she came back even more resilient after leaving college. She had changed, transformed, from a little girl who left Sicily to a woman full of curves, beautiful and perfect.

Hell! I turned my body wanting to go after my wife, until I felt my father's hand on my shoulder.

"Don't go after her!" he growled in that way he always did when I screwed up.

"Did you see her state?" I looked alarmed in his direction.

"Yes, I saw, and that's exactly why you're not going after her." Tommaso narrowed his eyes at me. "I know the son I have; you're not going after her. I know you'll end up fighting if you do."

"Don, we need to talk because we're talking about my daughter. You need to understand that Cinzia is with a suitor who understands her temperament. I can no longer bear the consequences of a 23-year-old girl who doesn't know how to behave..." Aldo's words were interrupted when my father cut him off.

"My friend, I will not approve a marriage between a non-official member of the Cosa Nostra. Our rules are there to be followed, and Cinzia will only marry an official member of the clan, not a relative of an associate." My father's words were direct.

Tommaso always adhered strictly to all the customs of the Cosa Nostra.

"Rules can be followed, but that never included your son, who left my daughter at the first obstacle," Aldo growled.

"I will resume my marriage with Cinzia, whether she's pregnant or not!" I roared, making everyone look at me, but my eyes were fixed on Aldo. "And if I find out that you married her off to another man, you can consider yourself a dead man. I couldn't care less if he's my father's *consigliere*, because I am the future of the Cosa Nostra, and I'm only leaving this fucking house when I'm sure that pile of shit is far away from this condominium and far from *my wife*."

I emphasized "my wife," growling as I looked at that man.

"Santino, remember..."

"I'm not going to remember any fucking thing, Dad. This woman might not be married to me at the moment, but she's my fucking wife!" I roared, directing my gaze at Tommaso.

Everyone looked at me as if I were the crazy one, but the crazy ones were them, thinking I was bluffing.

Knowing Marco Lombardo's name, I was going to research everything about him because nobody has such an absolute desire to steal someone else's woman out of love. Who in the fucking universe would commit such madness for such a foolish feeling?

I didn't know what they had lived, didn't know the intensity of that love, but every time I looked at that bastard, I felt an absolute urge to blow his brains out. Damn! I was jealous of the fucking bastard for having her love and attention.

Attention that I had had all to myself that day—the sweet smiles, the small blue eyes in the face of her smile, the droplets of sweat that spread across her body. Damn, I wanted Cinzia Bianchi like I had never wanted another woman before, and the fucking way her mouth was so bold always left me wanting more.

"I'm sorry for the inconvenience, Marco," Aldo said to that bastard.

"It's fine, I love your daughter. We had wonderful times in college, and I know that with aggression, I won't get anything from her." His eyes met mine, making that indirect remark explicit.

"Well, know that with aggression, I got everything from her, including something that you, who claim to have been by her side for so many moments, couldn't get," I mocked in a terrifying way, making even him take a step back.

"I always respected her, and I don't care if she's no longer a virgin or even if she might be pregnant with someone else's child because who raises her is the father..." That was enough for me to move toward him.

I was pulled back by my father's arm lock.

"Damn it, son, control yourself!" my father roared.

"Stay away from my wife if you don't want to feel the heat of hell," I growled, my words faltering against my father's forearm that was suffocating me.

"Both of you get out of this condominium now," Dad declared authoritatively to Aldo's guests.

Tommaso didn't let me go, clearly knowing that I had blood in my eyes and wanted to take that bastard's life. I was going to find out everything about him; nobody faces me and gets away unscathed.

That Marco guy left accompanied by another man. When he passed by me, I felt my mother's delicate hand on my shoulder, trying to calm me. Verena had a calming presence that always left us calm; my mother was the rock of our family.

"San, let's go home. Calm down, don't go after him," Mom asked calmly.

"I'm going to my house and I'll wait for the moment when I get my wife back. If I find out that Cinzia was induced to take the morning-after pill," I grunted, evading my father's hold, "they're dead."

"I believe that you probably didn't achieve this so quickly because Cinzia, like her mother, might have difficulty getting pregnant," Aldo looked at me with a smug smile.

"I'm a Vacchiano, and everything I touch comes to pass. Inside your daughter, a child of mine will grow, and he will be conceived and come into the world. For that reason, I don't care what you say. Cinzia is mine!"

"You should take better care of what you consider to be yours." Before I could move toward the *consigliere,* my father pulled me by the arm.

"Let's go. The other man has already left. I'll make it very clear that I don't want him here anymore. Aldo, I want you in my office with Enrico. We'll talk and sort things out as we always have," my father concluded, taking me out of the residence.

I could hear my mother apologizing to Cinzia's mother as she followed us.

This wasn't over yet, and I wasn't going to give up on what I wanted so easily.

CHAPTER THIRTY-SEVEN

Cinzia

I descended the last step of the stairs, and my parents quickly rose from their breakfast chairs when they noticed I wasn't heading toward them.

"Where are you going, daughter?" Mom asked quickly.

"I'm going to Pietra's house," I declared promptly.

After spending a nearly sleepless night staring at the white ceiling of my room, thinking about the mess I had gotten myself into and the way Santino lied when he knew who my intended was going to be. He wanted to take my virginity with a purpose, his wounded ego knowing that I would marry another man, and that man was Marco.

Marco, my friend, the man who understood me.

"I'd prefer you not visit her house for now," Dad said.

"But I am going, Dad. Pietra is my only friend, and I'm not going to stop visiting her house because her brother is a jerk," I said, not breaking eye contact.

"I had a conversation after the incident yesterday; your marriage to Santino will be reinstated. It was a consensus decision." Dad crossed his arms.

"Your definition of consensus isn't quite right, because as far as I know, consensus should include my decision too, and no one asked me anything. I'm not marrying Santino, not when I wasn't consulted. I'm exhausted by this. Cinzia gets married, Cinzia annulled her marriage, Cinzia finds another suitor, Cinzia is back to marrying the Vacchiano.

Have you noticed, Dad? All of this could have been avoided if, just once in your life, you had asked for my opinion. It's always about you, never about me. Just because your marriage to Mom works that way doesn't mean my future can be the same."

I turned my back, and luckily I was close to the door, opening it and leaving in a hurry. They weren't going to stop me; no one was going to stop me. Santino had his chance, we were married, and I wasn't going to face the humiliation of marrying a man twice because of a decision made by our parents a second time.

My hurried steps led me to Pietra's house. It was mid-morning; she must be having breakfast with her son. I didn't even have my phone after receiving messages from Marco. The way he was insisting on that marriage intrigued me, for a man who didn't love me. Was there something behind it?

He even said he would take on a child that wasn't his, but that the best thing would be for me to take the morning-after pill to avoid getting pregnant. But I wasn't going to do that because I was almost sure I wasn't pregnant. My mother took a long time to get pregnant with me, besides the miscarriage she had with her first child. Even though we had had unprotected sex three times, I still believed I wasn't pregnant.

I could still feel his traces, as if every time I walked, I felt the slight burn from where he took me. It was three times, three times for someone who was a virgin, and I liked it, but I wanted more. Santino made me want more of him, but I hated him, hated him even more for that slight burn in my intimacy from our intense first time.

I approached Pietra's house, crossed the street, walked up the driveway, and stopped in front of the door, noticing it was open.

"Friend?" I called out a little loudly so she could hear me.

"I'm in the dining room, come in!" she called back.

I followed the sound of her voice, finding her seated in a chair next to little Tommaso, who looked up with his green eyes in my direction.

"Hello, godmother." He smiled slightly while continuing to eat.

"Sit down, friend. Have you eaten?" Pietra pointed to an empty chair across from her.

"I haven't eaten," I said, hearing my stomach growl. "Your brother is going to drive me crazy," I grumbled, heading toward the chair, pulling it out, and sitting down across from my friend.

"Enrico told me. What a madness, friend, did you lose your virginity to Santino? I think he's crazy, but he's not crazy alone; you're just as crazy as he is." Pietra shook her head with a mocking smile.

"I don't know, he tied me up, and before I knew it, I was completely surrendered. Did you know about your brother's fetishes?" I raised an eyebrow.

"Yes, he and Valentino are part of a secret club. They think no one knows, but it's impossible to hide something from this family. I've never been interested in it, but from what I know, Santino isn't much into it, but Valentino frequents it a lot." Pietra shrugged. "Tommie, eat more..."

The boy huffed, taking a bite of his cake.

I grabbed a cup, filled it with steaming coffee, savoring the freshness of the caffeine as it entered my nose, and placed a toast on my plate.

"How was it?" My friend wanted to know.

"Good?" I raised an eyebrow, looking at Tommie, who was distracted, fiddling with his phone while eating.

"Just good? Nothing special?" I heard the door open and the sound of male voices entering the dining room.

"Yeah." I shrugged, not going to admit it was so good I repeated it twice.

I lifted my eyes to see the twins entering the dining room together, along with Enrico. The three of them were wearing typical dress pants and black shirts with the top buttons open, which made it easy for me to spot that damn Santino.

"Has your father spoken to you, Cinzia?" Santino said immediately.

I pretended not to hear him, taking a bite of my toast, not even looking at him, keeping my eyes fixed on my friend.

"I believe you heard me..."

"Sorry, Pietra, is someone talking to me? I heard a grunt, more like the growl of an angry dog. Did I just hear that?" My friend struggled to keep from laughing, covering her mouth with her hand.

Footsteps approached, and soon a shadow appeared beside me, the strong masculine scent reaching my nose.

"I'm talking to you, damn it!" he roared beside me, his mentholated breath hitting my face.

I turned my face at that moment, our eyes meeting, his nose close to mine, his hand gripping the edge of the table.

"I don't talk to liars," I said calmly, "and you are one!"

"You're going to marry me again!" he snarled through clenched teeth.

"I'm not! I want you to go to hell if necessary, but I'm not marrying you! From now on, I'll be the one deciding my future," I roared, rising from the chair and pushing it back. We were only a step away from each other.

"And what will your future be?"

"Anywhere far from a bastard like you." Santino took a step toward me.

"It's mine, and I decide what I do with your future." I widened my eyes as his hand touched my neck, as he always did when he was angry.

"I'm not yours, I'm no one's. I will disappear, relinquish everything if necessary, even be disowned by my parents, but I will not allow men to decide my future anymore!"

I declared, bringing my face close to his, knowing that to leave the mafia, I would have to be disowned and never have contact with anyone who belonged to Cosa Nostra. It was a crazy decision, but it was one that would require the best for me.

"Not if you're carrying my child..."

"Your child? My child! Only mine! You lost all rights when you omitted who my intended would be. As long as it's inside me, it's mine! And don't dream about it, because I might not even be pregnant, and if that happens, you can say goodbye to the idea of being a father, because I'll make that child disappear," I declared with fire in my eyes.

His hand tightened on my neck, even preventing me from swallowing saliva.

"Not over my dead body..."

"That's what we'll see, Santino Vacchiano," I declared defiantly, even with my throat constricted.

Santino abruptly released me, his eyes half-closed in my direction, turning his body and storming out, stomping his feet.

Damn bastard!

CHAPTER THIRTY-EIGHT

Santino

"Hell," I growled as I left my sister's house.
"Damn it, Santino, you need to control yourself." I heard Valentino's voice behind me, holding back his usual irony.

"Control myself? Remind me of that when it's your turn..." I grunted, heading toward my house.

"I intend to be practical, not divorcing my wife just out of my own whims." I turned my face to glare at my double, as if looking in a mirror.

"I'd pay to see that. You're more of an idiot than I am; we know how sadistic you can be," I said, shaking my head as a smile formed at the corner of his lips.

"That's why I'm going to keep my wife in captivity, use her until I'm bored, or until she gets pregnant, after all, I need an heir." My brother shrugged briefly.

"You know mom will never allow that, right?" I crossed my arms, resuming walking with him by my side.

"I know, that's why I'm thinking of having a honeymoon, man. I'm going to fulfill my biggest dream, having that sharp-tongued Colombian tied up and delivered to me. She'd better watch out."

Valentino spoke in his sadistic way, knowing his brother, he knew they'd be going through something.

"Actually, what happened at that fraternity when you went after the girl?" I asked, knowing Valentino didn't want to delve too much into it.

"The girl snubbed me, saying she'd only be with me after marriage when I gave her the chance to take my virginity at that moment. To get back at her, I went to a fraternity party and participated in a group sex session. Those freshmen were crazy; I lost count of how many mouths sucked my dick, not to mention the pussies I fucked..."

"When I say you're the craziest of us two, no one believes me," I mocked, shaking my head.

"Brother, no one says no to my face and gets away with it. Now she'll have to live with it for the remaining two years of her course. I even made sure to threaten all the men who passed by me, making it clear that Yulia Aragón is the fiancée of a heavy hitter. Anyone who gets involved with her risks being killed. I'm eager to see who will be brave enough to approach her." I entered my house, Valentino following me.

Since Cinzia left that house, it has never been the same. Without her presence, her scent, the smile full of irony or anger, that house felt like a calm day without my hurricane.

"I foresee strong emotions," I mocked, heading straight to the bar.

"I'm going to fuck that Colombian's pussy so much that she'll never say no to me again," Valentino declared, determined.

"Good luck then, because you just asked me to stay calm when it comes to my hurricane." I grabbed a glass and filled it with amber-colored liquid.

"Your hurricane is impossible to tame, brother. You're so screwed. Put some soldiers on her trail because Cinzia wasn't bluffing; the girl will run away even if she's pregnant." I brought the glass to my mouth, listening to Valentino's words.

We had an appointment; we went with Enrico to his house to pick up some documents for the distribution center. The problem was that here I was, drinking whiskey, seething with rage, thinking about my damn girl.

Damn it, I made a mistake in annulling the marriage, and I was reaping every fruit of my error, a mishap that could have been avoided if I had only lowered my guard a bit from the beginning to have Cinzia.

One thing I realized, if I hadn't lowered my guard, she wouldn't have done it. I had spent too many years admitting that Cinzia Bianchi, the little girl I saw grow up, the girl who ran around the pool in a bikini playing with my sister, always smiling, would become my wife. At first, I didn't want her, but either I or my brother would have to choose who she would be with, and Valentino wanted to lead the mafia, unlike me. He was the one who chose. I didn't want the burden of carrying a clan like ours on my back, so Valentino chose the Colombian, and I ended up with Cinzia.

I had no choice. It was her, it always was her, my hurricane. A few years ago, I wouldn't have cared if she went with someone else, but at that moment, I did. I worked so hard to have that woman, and I was going through hell since I annulled the damn marriage. Damn it, I wanted her.

I thought it would be easy, but it wasn't, especially after I took her virginity. It was like feeling every part of my sweet and spicy girl.

I felt my phone vibrating in my pocket. I took it out and saw my detective's name flashing on the screen and promptly answered:

"Got something good to tell me, Alex?"

"Marco Lombardo is actually Marco Lombardo Giancarlo. Does that surname ring a bell?" Alex said on the other end of the line.

I fell silent, trying to recall who the hell that man was. The surname Giancarlo wasn't unfamiliar, but there were so many surnames of enemies who hated me that I couldn't even remember that one.

"Just spill it, Alex," I asked, a bit impatient.

"Marco is the brother of Liara Lombardo Giancarlo, a girl who killed herself five years ago. No one knew the reason for her death, but Marco told some close to him that he would avenge his sister's death.

Liara got involved with you, Mr. Santino. From what I found out, she took her life after you told her you'd never be with a girl like her..."

"Damn it! Now everything makes sense," I declared, running my hand furiously through my hair. "Send me the full dossier. I've told you how fast you are, Alex."

My detective laughed before saying goodbye. I placed the phone on the mahogany bar and let out a long sigh. I didn't remember that Liara woman; maybe if Alex had a photo, I could recognize her.

I had been involved with so many women throughout my life, how could I remember one who meant nothing to me?

Alex was a good detective; he always worked with speed.

"San? Any news?" Valentino asked, a bit worried.

"I'm screwed. And when Cinzia finds out about this, she'll hate me even more because there's another girl involved, supposedly a girl who killed herself after I rejected her. Now this Marco guy, her brother, wants to avenge his sister's death. And what's the best way to do that but to want my girl? Marco has been working on this for a long time; he gained Cinzia's trust and possibly her love. How do I tell her this story without her hating me even more?" I let out a long sigh, seeing the email notification with the information Alex was sending me.

CHAPTER THIRTY-NINE

Cinzia

Santino hadn't returned to Pietra's house. Her husband had gone out to handle Cosa Nostra matters with the twins, which gave me some relief, knowing he wouldn't be coming back to bother me.

It was late afternoon. I was lying on the chaise longue at my friend's house while Pietra came in with the little one, who was already drooping from spending too much time in the pool.

My eyes were closed, concentrating on the distant sound of the sea. It was soft and far away. Even though I had talked to my friend and told her everything, I still felt confused. Santino's summons felt like he wanted me only because someone else did. And if that other person weren't there? Would he want me anyway?

Frustration took hold of me. The anger at having lost my virginity without even being married irritated me, and worse, I liked it. I liked it so much that we repeated it three times. I could still feel his touch, my pussy slightly sore, pulsing for him with the same intensity that I wanted to punch that bastard.

The touches made me shiver, as if it were real, as if Santino's presence was right there.

"What are you thinking about, *ragazza mia?*"

I quickly opened my eyes, startled by the soft breath in my ear.

"What are you doing here?" I asked, wide-eyed, seeing the bastard kneeling beside me. How crazy, how could I have thought it was just a daydream?

"What are you thinking about, Cinzia?" He didn't answer, just squinting his eyes at me in that typical Vacchiano way.

"Anything but you," I retorted, turning my body, about to get up from the opposite side. "Ouch!"

I let out a little scream when he grabbed my wrist, pulling me back onto the chaise longue, his hand lifting my wrist above my head, his face close to mine, his intense green eyes locked on mine.

"Cinzia Vacchiano, answer my question," he growled in his possessive way.

"Go to hell, Santino. I'm no longer a Vacchiano. I stopped being one when you annulled our marriage. By the way, that was the only right decision you ever made in your life," I declared, my face close to his, not intimidated by his presence but almost vibrating inside from the firm touch of his hand on my wrist.

"If it were right, I wouldn't be going crazy looking for you," he roared.

"You're doing this out of wounded pride because you saw that you might lose me to someone else..."

"Where did you get that conclusion from?" His head tilted slightly to the side, his eyebrow arched just a little, his lips straightening in understanding.

"Stop pretending to be the regretful man, as if you were like this after my father wanted to marry me off to someone else. Or have you forgotten that you always said you didn't want this marriage? You were doing it for the honor of your clan, so honorable that you annulled the marriage..."

"I annulled it because all we do when we're together is fight!" he grunted.

"For the first time, I have to agree with you. By the way, that's what we're doing right now, fighting. Now, if you could let me go..." I tried to pull my arm, but he prevented me by placing a bent leg over the chaise longue, his face getting even closer to mine, his lips almost touching mine.

"You're going to marry me again, Cinzia. I'll fuck your pussy as many times as I want, I'll make you beg me to stop, and I won't. Do you know why?"

"*Huum?*" Instinctively, I wanted to know what he was going to do.

"Because my cock enjoyed your pussy, it was an immediate addiction. Your dirty mouth made me want you even more, and I'm going to mold you to be my little slut..."

"Bastard!" I grabbed his shirt tightly, trying to push him away.

Santino didn't even flinch at my force, which didn't even compare to his. His other hand held mine, which was trying to push him, guiding it towards my head, keeping both there, his eyes fixed on mine.

"I tried. Well, actually, I'm flawed because my attempt was short. I have no patience, and I'm going to claim what is mine, and you are mine, Cinzia Vacchiano. You've been mine from the beginning, mine when I kissed you for the first time. You were meant to be my redemption, and I'm going to take advantage of every piece, *amore mio*..."

"Take me by force, marry me by force, because I'll resist as much as I can..."

"You can resist, do whatever you want, but we both know how much you want this, how much you crave my hand touching your body. Otherwise, you wouldn't shiver every time I touch you..."

"You're being too presumptuous, Vacchiano," I retorted.

"I'm being realistic, my *little hurricane*. I'm going to have you tied up, gagged in my bed. Your body will shine from all the sweat, and I'll fuck you, Cinzia, fuck you the way you deserve to be fucked. I'll beat you as you deserve to be punished, and I'll make you forget there's another man besides me." Santino moved his face away slightly.

There couldn't be another man when Santino had everything I wanted. He was incredibly handsome and sexy. His touches always gave me shivers, not to mention that I loved facing that man.

It's crazy because I always loathed him, and even if it was indirect, I wanted him.

"You'll never achieve that because I'll always think of another man." I smiled, lying with the boldest face.

Santino tightened his grip on my hand, his eyes narrowing, a growl escaping from his lips.

"We'll see, *ragazza mia,* you'll beg, and nothing will make me stop." Santino pulled away.

I felt the loss of his touch. He stood up quickly, my eyes scanning his body—the shirt with the top buttons undone, the dress pants tightly fitting his legs, shaping the semi-erect member, making me salivate inside.

My eyes met his, a half-smile of self-assurance on his lips.

"You can say whatever you want, but deep down, your body desires mine, just as I desire you..."

Santino didn't even finish his sentence, turning his back and leaving, leaving me there alone, making me crave more of that madness, more of him, more of everything. I wanted Santino Vacchiano, but no one needed to know.

CHAPTER FORTY

Cinzia

"Come on, please," Pietra pleaded, clasping her hands in a supplicating gesture.

"I'm not sure if I want to. Your arrogant brother will be there," I said, pouting.

"My arrogant brother, whom you light up every time you look at him." Pietra shook her head in her typical smug way.

"*Okay, okay*, I must admit that Santino is starting to grow on me, all this persistence of his," I declared, recalling my troublesome twin.

"Girl, he's a Vacchiano. We never give up." My friend shrugged. "So, are you coming? I don't want to go to this event just with Enrico, and Mom won't be going because Valentino will be representing Dad."

Valentino had not yet taken over the Cosa Nostra; his initiation was due to happen soon. Mrs. Verena was trying to convince her husband not to do everything required by law, but from what it seemed, it would be done. I wasn't sure how it worked, but from what was said, it was intense. Valentino would undergo an intense training for a few days.

"I need to go home, see how things are there, and check if my father will find any excuse not to go." I rolled my eyes.

"Aldo is a bore," Pietra pouted.

"I'll text you," I said, saying goodbye. It was already late, and if I was going to that event, I needed to get ready quickly.

STRANGELY, MY FATHER accepted that I go to the event without questioning me. In fact, I wished he would find an excuse, knowing that Santino would be there. I was desperately trying to avoid that man who was messing with my head.

The car pulled up in front of a massive mansion. I wasn't sure whose it was; I was only told it belonged to a Cosa Nostra associate, a very influential family. Enrico was accompanying the future Don of the mafia, and of course, Santino would be by his brother's side, as the loyal right-hand man he was.

My door was opened, and I gave a polite smile to the soldier assigned as my security. I knew Santino had something to do with it; after all, he was crazy enough to put a soldier entirely at my disposal. My father thought it was absurd, considering we had no remaining ties. It was madness; arguing with a madman was pointless.

My long dress dragged on the floor as I walked, with a slit on the right side exposing my leg as I moved. The heels were high, and the neckline dropped to the middle of my breasts, making them quite visible and emphasized. I chose to style my hair in loose curls.

I felt beautiful, as always. I must admit that I wanted to come across as sensual to provoke a certain twin. He was in my mind when I chose that dress. I shouldn't, but I enjoyed provoking him, which made me briefly forget my escape plan. Did I really want to stay away from the madness of being near Santino?

Yes, I wanted my independence, but I also craved that damn man's touch. *Hell!*

I gave my name at the entrance and was allowed in. I stepped into the enormous ballroom, scanning for my friend who had texted me she was already there.

I held a glass of champagne in my hand as the waiter passed by offering it.

"Cinzia?" I recognized Marco's voice behind me, and a smile formed on my lips as I turned to face my friend.

"Marco?" I was genuinely surprised, and it made sense why my father had let me come to the event—he knew Marco would be there. Aldo hadn't given up on his plan yet.

"My uncle is around, and I thought I could accompany him, with a rather explicit reason." He winked at me. That wasn't the Marco I knew; it was as if he was hitting on me.

"Oh, it's good you came. After that madness, I thought I'd be far away from Sicily," I said with a half-smile.

"I don't give up easily on what I want," Marco said, taking my hand, making me jump slightly at his touch. It was a normal touch, like touching anyone else.

I searched for that electric sensation, the tingles that ran through me when Santino touched me.

"Marco, I'm not sure it was a good idea for you to come to this event," I whispered, trying to pull my hand away, but his grip tightened, his eyes hardening.

"There's something you don't know, Cinzia..."

"Oh? And can you share it with me too?" I jumped slightly at the imposing tone he took.

Santino looked incredibly handsome in that suit. Damn, I shouldn't get wet every time I looked at him, but there I was, drooling over the bastard.

Shamelessly, Santino yanked my hand away from Marco's, taking the champagne glass from my other hand.

"Get the hell out of here, you piece of shit. If I see you circling my woman again, I'll kill you." He wasn't bluffing, and I knew that better than anyone.

"Not before telling her something," Marco replied.

Santino growled like a caveman, positioning himself in front of me in his black suit, but I could audibly hear what the Vacchiano declared:

"I know what you want, Lombardo. I've researched everything about the piece of shit you are. You won't lay a finger on my girl. Your revenge plan won't work on me because I'm always one step ahead."

What was Santino talking about? What was happening? What plan was that?

"We'll see about that. Death doesn't scare me when you've already taken the best I had," Marco declared, stepping away.

I looked down at Santino's clenched fist, veins bulging. He turned, his eyes lowering to mine.

"You'll stay away from that bastard, got it?" His fingers lifted to touch my chin, his warm touch sending shivers through me.

"What was he talking about?" Of course, I wasn't going to remain passive about that.

"Answer my question, *ragazza* stubborn!"

"I won't promise anything, not after this strange business."

Santino growled, his eyes dropping to my chest, lingering too long on my breasts, which was the result I wanted—the Italian's lustful gaze on me.

"If you wanted to provoke me with that dress, you succeeded." I shrugged, trying to take the champagne glass from his hand. "No!"

"Why not?" I crossed my arms, indignant.

"You might be carrying my child..."

"We don't even know if I'm pregnant." Before I could grab the glass from his hand, he took it all.

"Bastard," I muttered.

I turned away from the incredibly arrogant and delicious Italian, finally locating my friend.

CHAPTER FORTY-ONE

Santino

"Fuck!" I growled as I approached Valentino.

"I see everything is calm in your paradise," my brother mocked.

"You're lucky you don't have to get married now," I grumbled, searching for the damn girl.

"Man, you're in love with Cinzia Bianchi. It's so obvious, screaming in neon letters on your forehead." I turned my face to look at my clone.

"Fuck off!" I yelled at the craziness he just spouted.

"Yeah? Then tell me, what was the last girl you fucked? Not counting Cinzia." Valentino put his hand in his pocket. I stayed silent, trying to remember the last one, but no one came to mind. It had been so long I couldn't even remember. Since my marriage to Cinzia, I hadn't thought of another woman. "See? You just answered my question."

"Shit!" I muttered, running my hand through my hair, roughly pulling at the strands.

How could I think of another woman when my Sicilian hurricane was destroying everything in her path? That bitch rented a penthouse in my mind. I wanted her, and I would have her just as I desired—on top, underneath, chained, handcuffed, gagged. Damn hellcat!

We both turned, looking at my girl. She was next to Pietra, smiling at something my sister said. Her lips glistened with gloss, her blue eyes crinkled with her smile, a necklace with a small diamond pendant around her neck, her blonde hair falling in curls over her shoulders.

"Marco is here," I told my brother.

"We could deal with him…"

"No, we can't. The bastard is the son of influential doctors in Sicily. We can't stir up trouble, but if he doesn't stop circling my girl, I'll give the bastard a scare."

"Well, one member of that family has already killed himself. What's one more?" Valentino said nonchalantly.

"Sometimes I forget how insensitive you are," I declared with a mocking smile.

"I couldn't care less about that family. I don't know them. If it were me, I would have already gotten rid of that idiot."

"What are the girls planning?" We turned our eyes to see Enrico approaching.

He always spoke to us like that. When we were kids, we didn't like it, but arguing with Enrico Ferrari was a waste of time. The bastard was like an uncle to us, and at that moment, a brother-in-law, since he married our sister.

"Ways to solve San's problem," Valentino answered.

"There's always the way to hide a body, like a corpse floating in some river," Enrico shrugged.

"You're pushing my urge to go after that bastard," I declared, watching Enrico growl.

I followed his gaze, seeing my sister smile at a couple who approached her, bringing with them a young man.

"Why did I even marry a stubborn child? I've told that little one a million times to stop spreading those innocent smiles," Enrico made me laugh along with Valentino. The Cosa Nostra underboss sighed in frustration as he headed towards his wife.

We followed him, approaching the couple, recognizing the party's hosts, attorneys of the Cosa Nostra. The man with them was the son following in his father's footsteps.

"Salvatore." My brother immediately recognized the man.

"It's an honor to have the future of the Cosa Nostra here." The older man took my brother's hand and touched his forehead, as everyone did in respect to my father.

It was as if they were already seeing Valentino as the new Don. If the Don extended his hand, it was a sign of approval, and the person would touch their hand to their forehead, bowing their head.

Valentino was born for this. He was good at everything he did—sharp, thought before acting, made the best decisions, didn't act on impulse, mostly insensible, but had the iron fist a Don needed. Unlike me, who was extremely impulsive, didn't think before acting, and didn't want the burden of carrying a clan like ours on my shoulders.

"This is my son, Alex Salvatore," the man introduced the young man.

Valentino just nodded, didn't extend his hand, waiting for the introductions. As the good forgetful person he was, I hadn't remembered the names of the people we were meeting. They were insignificant to me. Anyone was insignificant if they didn't have an obvious purpose.

Enrico greeted the man, calling him Adam, which reminded me of his name. But my eyes were on the bastard's son, who was looking at my girl, at that damned indecent neckline, the fucking breasts I'd already fucked with my cock.

I walked behind my sister, my steps silent as I approached Cinzia, sliding my hand down her back, feeling the curve of her ass.

Cinzia raised her eyes to meet mine.

"Marking your territory, Vacchiano?" Her voice was pure provocation.

"I want to tear that damned dress with my teeth," I growled, lowering my face close to her ear.

"There's no more contradictory man than you," Cinzia whispered.

"Amore mio, in this life, I'm sure of only one thing: I want to fuck you every way, every day, until I get tired," I declared near her ear, feeling her shiver.

"And if you never get tired?" Her words came out with a sigh.

"I'll never stop." Cinzia turned her face, her nose brushing against mine.

She didn't expect me to be so close. I moved my hand from the curve of her ass, feeling her rear under my hand, so round, perfect for my spankings.

"Raise your hand, Vacchiano, I didn't give you that freedom." The bitch didn't even turn her face, even as her body surrendered to my touch. Cinzia wasn't frightened.

Our brief confrontation was interrupted when someone addressed me. I didn't leave the blonde's side, my hand constantly on her back. Cinzia didn't remove my hand, didn't stop my touch, as if she was enjoying the defiance. That was my girl.

CHAPTER FORTY-TWO

Cinzia

I moved away from Santino and went to the bathroom. Being next to him for too long was driving me crazy, as if I didn't answer for myself anymore. I wanted his touches, those tingling sensations, his possessive hand, even when he gripped my neck with ownership.

I didn't even want to go to the bathroom, but I needed to distance myself from him for a moment.

I entered the powder room, which had only three stalls, all unoccupied. I stopped in front of the mirror, noticing my flushed cheeks. I wasn't even wearing blush; it was the effect of that damned Italian bastard.

Through the mirror's reflection, I saw Marco closing the door.

"Marco?" I raised an eyebrow, confused.

"Shall we run away?" He was direct, catching me by surprise.

"What?" The word came out automatically.

"Let's do what we wanted to do from the beginning..."

"I can't put you in danger," I murmured, starting to feel my hand sweating cold.

"And why would you do it before? Are you scared? I'm not afraid..."

"No, Marco, that was before, before I got close to Santino. I thought he wouldn't care if I ran away, but if I do, I know he'll come after me. I know I'll put you in danger, putting myself in danger. I can't be a coward to that extent," I whispered, watching his hurried steps towards me.

I took steps back, feeling my back hit the sink.

"Marco, no..." My plea was muffled when he grabbed my face tightly.

His aggressive lips touched mine. I spread my hand on his chest, wanting him to back off, his teeth against my mouth. I didn't even move mine; I didn't want that.

"No!" I begged through clenched teeth, but nothing made him stop.

"What does that fucking mobster have?" His muffled voice on my mouth roared in a terrifying way.

"Marco, stop..." I began hitting his chest, lifting my leg to strike his groin.

At that moment, the bathroom door opened. Marco released me, bringing his hand to his groin where I had hit him.

"Fuck, do I need to get rid of the evil at its root?" I widened my eyes when Santino drew a gun from his waistband, pointing it at Marco.

The scene happened in a split second. When I saw Santino, he had the gun pressed to Marco's head.

"No! Santino, no!" I cried, running toward the scene.

"I can't leave the person who touched what's mine alive!" Santino pressed the gun harder.

"Go ahead, you bastard, pull the trigger, do what you did..." Marco's sentence died when Santino struck him on the head with the gun.

Santino's eyes met mine. He was visibly angry, and I knew it was only a matter of time before he pulled that trigger, but he wouldn't do it—not for me.

"Get out of here, Marco, please..."

"You need to know, Cinzia, that..."

"Get the fuck out!" Santino roared like I'd never heard him before. His voice was deep, clearly controlling himself not to use his gun.

Marco took one last look at me before leaving the bathroom, the door closing behind him.

"Fuck! I want to go back there and kill that bastard," Santino growled, pacing back and forth, holding his gun in his hand.

"Thank you for not going after him," I murmured fearfully.

He stopped pacing, looking in my direction, his expression hardened, eyes narrowed.

"It's taking everything in me not to go after him. I want this, I want to take the life of the bastard who touched my wife! Understand one thing, Cinzia Bianchi, you're my fucking wife, and he touched my fucking wife." Santino turned toward the door, heading after Marco. I knew he was going after him.

I ran towards him, grabbing the same wrist that held the gun. I don't know where I found the strength, pushing him against the wall. He turned, our eyes meeting.

"Don't, don't do this," I pleaded calmly for the first time, unsure if I wanted to see Santino take a man's life.

Santino closed his eyes tightly, all his muscles tensed. He wasn't even touching me, as if I were dirty.

"Sammy, erase the traces of that kiss with yours?" I asked calmly. He opened his eyes slowly, dropping his gun to the floor, grabbing my neck, shifting his position, pressing me against the wall.

"Then answer me, who is your master?" he asked with that mixture of possessiveness.

I let out a small, sly smile, responding in a whisper:

"You..."

"Then you'll let me use something on you," he growled with a voice full of desire.

"Yes..."

"Are you answering without knowing what it's about?" His head tilted to the side.

"Then no," I murmured, feeling the atmosphere around us change.

"Too late, you already said yes. But before that, I need to deal with your issue." His face moved closer to mine.

His lips covered mine, starting a slow kiss, his tongue touching mine. Without releasing my neck, I lifted my hand to his hair, dragging my nails along his neck.

With his other hand, he found the slit in my dress, lifting it, his fingers touching my skin, stopping over my panties.

"Spread your legs," he instructed, and I obeyed. "This way I'll judge you're submissive..."

"Far from it, darling," I whispered provocatively.

"Stay still, I'm going to insert two little balls inside you..."

"No," I cut him off suddenly.

"You said yes. Or are you scared?"

"I'm not afraid of anything," I declared, feeling his tongue circling my lip.

As if he were a stormy sea pulling me into the chaos that he was.

"Then spread your legs, *amore mio*," he said. I did as he commanded, fearing the madness we were indulging in.

His fingers moved my panties aside, circling my pussy.

"Ah, what a wet little pussy, and mine." I felt him inserting two objects inside me. "Stay calm, they can be removed, but only I can remove them..."

"Ah!" I let out a squeal when that thing vibrated inside me.

"That's right, you'll keep them in if you don't want me to take the life of your little friend, and you'll spend the rest of the night by my side." Santino adjusted my panties back in place.

"It vibrates," I muttered, discomfort and excitement mingling.

"You don't want anyone to find out you're wearing vibrating plugs in your pussy, do you? Every time you move, they'll vibrate. By the end of the night, you'll be so turned on you'll beg for my cock..."

"We'll see about that." I smiled confidently, though it was somewhat forced, as just the vibration had already aroused me.

Maybe I wasn't doing it just to prevent him from killing Marco; maybe I really wanted to know what it was like to be Santino Vacchiano's woman.

Santino followed me out of the bathroom, picking up his gun from the floor and putting it away.

CHAPTER FORTY-THREE

Santino

I lowered my face, feeling the new pinch on my palm. I bit the corner of my lip, suppressing my laughter. The girl was losing control; the more Cinzia moved, the worse it got.

"Are you okay, friend?" Pietra asked, genuinely concerned.

"I'm fine, why wouldn't I be?" A bead of sweat formed on my girl's forehead.

"You're tense, sweating, and it's not even hot in here." My sister looked at me.

"Santino?"

"What?" I raised an eyebrow.

"What did you do to my friend?"

"Why would I do anything?" I asked casually.

"Those who don't know you should buy you." Her eyes narrowed at me, but she didn't say anything more.

I kept my eye on the bastard who had touched her lips. I hadn't done what I wanted to do to him yet. Who did that bastard think he was touching my girl? Cinzia didn't even let me protect her; when I arrived, she kicked him in the balls so hard it hurt my own. That was my girl.

It made me think that Cinzia didn't love him. But why did she ask me not to kill him? I could have ended that bastard right then and there; I didn't give a damn about what others would think. What mattered was her safety. The damn kiss wouldn't leave my mind.

"Shall we go?" Cinzia whispered to me.

"Do you want me to come with you?" I played dumb.

"Bastard!" she whispered back.

I turned my face, knowing Valentino had already done everything he needed to do.

"Brother, I'm leaving," I announced, placing my hand on Cinzia's back.

"Already?" my sister asked.

"Yes, Cinzia isn't feeling well. I'm going to accompany her," I said, holding back laughter at Cinzia's forced smile as she took a step.

"If you prefer, I can take you, friend. We're leaving soon anyway," Pietra offered.

"No need, Santino is leaving too," Cinzia let slip.

"Is something bothering you?" Pietra asked again.

"Just a discomfort in my shoe." Cinzia quickly made up an excuse.

We said our goodbyes. These events were important for strengthening our bonds with the associates, especially since we were going to take over. My presence would always be by Valentino's side.

"I want to kill you!" she growled as we moved away from them.

We passed by the guests, with Cinzia staying a little ahead of me, as if she wanted to get to the car as soon as possible.

"Darling?" I was intercepted by a woman.

"Get lost, I'm in a hurry," I grunted, but the woman took it as a positive affront, sliding her hand across my chest.

"We could repeat what we did last time..."

"You're mistaken," I growled. I hadn't been with that crazy woman; it must have been Valentino.

"Damn it!" Cinzia appeared, intertwining her hand with mine. "Look, there's a copy of this one around. Go after the other; that one is free, this one is claimed."

My hurricane pulled me along, making me laugh. I followed her steps, easily matching her pace, releasing her hand and placing it over her shoulder, walking beside her and savoring the sweet, delicious scent that filled my senses.

"So, this copy is yours?" I asked playfully.

"Of course, it's only fair. If I'm yours, you're mine." We left the mansion. "And I don't need you to keep emphasizing it. I just take it as mine."

It was impossible not to laugh at her words and her urgency to get to the car, which was luckily already parked. Cinzia got in first.

"We're going home," she told the driver, closing the partition of the car.

I sat down beside her, closing the door.

"Take that out of me now, and let's fuck..."

"Are you sure?" I asked just to tease, because I would have fucked that woman anywhere.

"Now, Santino, now!" she ordered with a hoarse voice.

I pulled my woman onto my lap, sliding my hands up her legs and lifting the fabric of her dress. Cinzia removed the sleeves from her arms, exposing her full, swollen breasts to me.

I placed my hand on her breast and squeezed it tightly.

"I always get what I want, Cinzia," I whispered with a rough voice.

"You bastard, you did this to make me go crazy with desire! I still hate you, but I can hate you and want your hand on me too..." She closed her eyes, tilting her head back.

"Hate me, *amore mio*, but don't deprive me of your delicious curves," I begged, enjoying the glamorous view of Cinzia's sweaty body.

I pressed my hand against the side of her panties, pulling forcefully, tearing them and tossing them aside. My hand grazed her intimacy, which was so wet it was dripping onto my fingers. I pulled out the two balls, which I had in my pocket because I always wanted to do this with my dirty-mouthed wife.

Her nervous fingers tried to lower my pants, but she couldn't even unbutton them. I did it myself, pulling them down along with my underwear, just enough to free my cock, which was aching with desire for my hot little blonde.

"Sit on my cock and grind that sexy ass *like* hell," I asked, holding the base of my penis.

Cinzia didn't even question it. She sat on my cock, slowly sliding her pussy over it, her fingers digging into my shoulder. I lowered my hand, palming her big, sexy ass, and gave it a hard smack.

"Bastard!" I smiled at her curse.

"Admit it, deep down you enjoy being fucked by me," I declared confidently.

"Liking being *fucked* by you doesn't mean I like you," she declared as she lifted her ass, making me deliver another smack, this time harder.

I took the two balls beside me and brought them to her mouth.

"Open your mouth," I ordered, and she did, sliding the ball that was in her pussy into her mouth. "Do you taste yourself? Even your taste is bold, like your dirty mouth..."

"Santino Vacchiano..., I'm too perfect even for you," she said provocatively, sliding her tongue over the ball I had taken from her mouth.

"*Amore mio,* you are perfect for any man, but I'm selfish enough not to share my hurricane, so everything about you belongs to me."

I started thrusting my cock harder inside her, burying my entire member, listening to her moan loudly. Her sweaty body, even with my thrusts, didn't stop grinding. What a hot woman!

Cinzia slid her hand through my hair, hugging me tightly as I felt her walls convulsing in relief. That was the climax that led me to come hard, deeply, my jets going all the way.

"Point *for* me," I murmured as I came inside her.

"Damn Italian," she grumbled with her head resting on my chest, making it clear she was exhausted.

CHAPTER FORTY-FOUR

Cinzia

The car was still moving, my head lazily resting on Santino's neck, his masculine scent mixed with nicotine and post-sex aroma filling my nostrils, making me sigh.

He could be everything but not a man who didn't smell good; I didn't even care about his nicotine-scented aroma.

"Sammy," I murmured lazily.

"You know I hate being called that, right?" His hand slid over my ass, caressing it tenderly.

"That's exactly why I'm going to call you that," I declared with a smile. His member, which was between us, began to harden again, touching the tip of his stomach. "No use getting happy like that," I murmured, looking at his erect penis.

"It's impossible for me to remain indifferent to this delicious body, this ass that makes me hard every time I touch it. You're my ideal number, little blonde." I turned my face, and in the dim light of the car, I found his eyes on mine. "Marry me again, Cinzia."

He didn't ask; he just stated it, as if he were commanding.

"No," I declared, not breaking eye contact with him.

"What do I need to do for you to agree to marry me?"

"A proposal? Stop being an asshole? Well, the asshole part is welcome now and then because it makes me smile," I said, watching his hand rise to touch my face.

"I want you, I truly want you, *amore mio*," he declared, bringing his lips close to mine, sucking on my lower lip.

His tongue brushed against mine, a sigh escaping my mouth.

"Is there something behind Marco's desire for my marriage to him? I felt like there's something I don't know," I asked when his lips moved away from mine, our eyes meeting.

"There is," he simply replied.

"Aren't you going to tell me what it is?" I asked, suddenly pulling away, gripping his shoulder.

"What's the point in saying no?" Santino raised an eyebrow.

"I want to know; if I'm involved in this, I need to know," I insisted, watching him sigh heavily.

"Fine, I'll tell you, but with one condition," he declared.

"And what's that condition?" I asked, seeing he wasn't going to say anything.

"Sleep with me tonight, and I'll tell you in our bed," he asked, sliding his hand over my ass again, his touch causing those delicious tingles.

"I'll get into trouble with my father all because I don't want to hear any more lectures about how a woman should behave." I rolled my eyes.

"Well, my wife needs to behave deliciously well on my cock, sliding over it," Santino pushed my ass against his erect penis.

"Like this? Like that?" I provocatively teased, rubbing even more against his cock that was still pulsing from the last orgasm.

"Ah, *amore mio,* don't provoke me..."

"You have no idea how much I love to provoke you," I whispered softly.

"And I love being provoked by that daring mouth." Santino pulled me close, biting my lip and pulling it back.

"Don't change the subject, Vacchiano, I want to know," I emphasized.

"I already said I'd tell you, only if you sleep with me, *ragazza mia*.

"You like seeing me in trouble with my father, don't you? Not that I care about his opinion, but Aldo knows how to be annoying," I grumbled, getting off his lap and adjusting my dress as I saw we had passed the gate of the condominium.

Santino quickly adjusted himself, putting the two balls in his pocket, followed by my torn panties. The car door was opened, and we both got out. I saw his house, or rather, the house that was supposed to be ours.

His fingers intertwined with mine, giving a brief gesture to go with him. I looked far off, at the beginning of the street where my parents' house was with the lights off. I knew I was already a 23-year-old woman, but all I was trying to avoid at that moment was unleashing Aldo's fury, proving to him that I could be a good daughter and then escape. But the truth was that the plan was getting more distant with the desire to be with Santino.

"Cinzia?" Santino called me, and I followed him down the short path of cobblestones to the entrance of the house.

He entered the password slowly in front of me for the first time, letting me see the sequence of numbers.

"Wait, the password is our wedding date?" I asked, somewhat perplexed.

"Yes." He shrugged, pushing the door open for me to enter.

"This has to be a joke, right?" I asked, still a bit irritated.

"It's not." I watched him take off his jacket, unbutton the first few buttons of his shirt, and head towards his bar, where he grabbed a bottle of amber-colored liquid.

I entered the kitchen, looking around and thinking about how everything could have been different if we hadn't attacked each other from the start, if we hadn't lived in constant war. I wanted Santino, and I knew he wanted me with the same intensity. But for the first time in my life, I wanted to make a decision on my own, not have others decide for me. I wanted to marry Santino again, but I wanted a proposal, a proposal made with feeling, with his desire.

"What's the problem?" Santino asked, coming closer.

"Why don't we work?" I turned to look into his eyes.

"Because we're too alike in many ways—impulsive, dominant, unyielding..."

"And you still want me back?" I asked, confused.

"Yes, I want you because I've never found a woman who challenges me, who tells me what I need to hear, not what I want to hear. We're so different and yet so alike. I want you, Cinzia, you were like a hurricane that swept through my life, making me realize that I can surrender to this marriage," Santino placed his glass on the table. "But there is something that might make you hate me a little more..."

"I don't think there's anything left that could make me hate you. After all, you've done everything bad to me. Does it have something to do with Marco?" I asked, raising an eyebrow.

"Yes, but I'll only tell you in our room. That way, if you want to run, the door will be locked..."

"Vacchiano..." I cut him off, scolding him.

"Come on, *amore mio*." His hand intertwined with mine, pulling me towards the stairs.

"I might get used to you calling me that way."

"There are many ways I can make you get used to it, and one of them is letting me take care of you," he declared, and I fell silent. That version of Santino Vacchiano left me weak in the knees.

CHAPTER FORTY-FIVE

Cinzia

I entered the room, hearing the door close behind me as Santino locked it.

"Is this all because you're afraid I might run away from you?" I turned my body to see him putting the key in his pants pocket, his eyes meeting mine.

"I'm a cautious man." He shrugged, pointing to the bed.

I turned to the bed, remembering it was where it all started—the loss of my virginity, when he tied me to that very bed, the room that was supposed to be ours, the closet meant to hold both our clothes.

I walked towards the bed, sitting on the edge. Santino moved around, undoing the last few buttons of his shirt and taking it off.

"Is there any need to be shirtless?" I asked, looking at his defined chest. Even when he sat, his muscles were well-defined.

"It's hot, isn't it?" He raised an eyebrow, leaning against the headboard of the bed. He was barefoot, his feet resting on the mattress.

"At this moment? It's getting hot." I declared, bending down to remove my heels.

"Come here." Before I had a chance to sit back on the bed, he leaned over and pulled me down, making me lie on the bed.

Santino covered my body with his, the tips of his fingers sliding down the side of my face. I closed my eyes, feeling the caress as his fingers moved to my neck, brushing against the side of my breast through the neckline of my dress.

"Vacchiano, I still want to hate you," I murmured, opening my eyes to find his green ones gazing at mine, a faint smile on his lips.

"If hating me means having you here with me, hate me as much as you want." His face moved closer to mine, brushing our lips together.

"It makes me extremely angry," I declared, raising my hand to touch the back of his neck and sliding down his back, feeling every inch of his skin.

"I gave up on our marriage too easily. The blame is all mine. I know that my indignation comes from the fact that the first time we almost killed each other, and I could have lowered my guard, but being as spoiled as I am, I wanted to confront you and not come out as the loser. But if there's one thing I want to be, it's the loser and lower my guard for you." His nose brushed against mine, his face moving to my neck, leaving kisses. "Maybe now I understand what my father goes through with my mother..."

My weak laugh made him lift his face, interrupting his words.

"Your beard is tickling me," I said as he rubbed his beard against my neck.

"How so?" he asked, brushing against my neck again.

"Stop!" I tried to push his chest away due to the tickling, a laugh escaping from my mouth.

"Who gets tickled by a beard brushing their neck?" Santino stopped, raising his eyes to mine.

"I never said I was normal," I declared, looking down at his bare chest, examining his tattoos.

"You're perfect and unique." My eyes returned to his.

"Are you trying to soften me up to tell me what you're hiding?" I asked, seeing him get off me.

He sat down next to me, and I did the same, adjusting my dress to sit over my legs. Santino focused his eyes on mine.

"Understand that what I'm about to tell you happened before you, something that occurred without me even knowing, a situation that spiraled out of control." He began to speak, making me even more nervous.

"You're starting to make me anxious," I said, somewhat apprehensive.

"Marco Lombardo wants to take something important from me, just like I took from him," he declared, leaving me confused.

"I don't understand." I instinctively shook my head.

"A few years ago, I had a relationship with a girl. I don't even remember her features clearly; she was just another woman among the many I've been with. I always knew my marriage would be arranged, which is why I never opened my heart to anyone. In fact, love was never an option for me. When I met Lombardo at his parents' house, I had my detective find out everything about him, and I discovered that he was Liara's brother, a girl who committed suicide years ago. My detective contacted people close to him and found out that Marco wants to avenge his sister's death because she killed herself over unrequited love. This was reported in the newspapers at the time. I didn't see it myself; my detective obtained the news reports, which include many statements from Marco about his sister's death."

Santino stopped speaking, and I remained silent, trying to process the madness of it all. How could this be? In the end, I was just a pawn in a revenge scheme I had nothing to do with. He didn't look away from me as if he wanted to see my reaction. But I had none. I was confused. There was a person who had died, who had died because at some point Santino had been involved with her. I didn't judge Marco, as he lost his sister in a cruel way.

"Say something, *amore mio*," Santino asked, calling me that way which made me melt little by little.

"There's nothing to say, someone committed suicide, Santino," I murmured, confused.

"You wanted the truth, and this is the truth," he stated succinctly.

"But why me? After all, Marco has known me for at least a year," I asked, trying to make sense of the madness.

"Simple. He knew you were my fiancée. He would make you run away with him, marry him, and thus, he would hit me somehow."

"But I've never had any importance in your life. How would that affect you?"

"Cinzia, you've always been significant to me. At first, it was a matter of honor to my clan, but now it's much more than that. I can't lose you; I need my Sicilian hurricane." Santino leaned forward, pulling me by the wrist and making me sit on his lap.

The dress rode up, making it easier for me to place my legs on either side of him.

"Even if we hated each other at first, it's that hatred I want to live with, that madness of living with the woman who has me. Now I understand, it was meant to be you, it has always been you." His hand lifted, tucking my hair behind my shoulders.

"This is madness, too much madness," I declared, realizing it was all part of Marco's plan, a plan in which I was caught in the middle.

"Understand now, *ragazza mia*, I can't lose you. I've been mad enough to annul the wedding once; now I'll do things differently. Even if I have to force you to marry me, I won't let you leave my side. Understand, you might want to run away, but there will always be one of my men on your tail. I'm crazy enough to make sure what's mine stays by my side."

"You're crazy, Vacchiano," I declared, holding onto his shoulder.

"A crazy man totally in love with you," he said without thinking, his eyes widening. But to keep the spell from breaking, I leaned my lips towards his, pulling him into a kiss, needing his touch.

CHAPTER FORTY-SIX

Santino

I grabbed her hair, laying her back on the bed, my body covering hers, her blue eyes fixed on mine, her red lips pleading for my kisses. The word "passion" echoed in my mind.

I loved her, I loved Cinzia Bianchi and I wanted her in that house, to wake up with her, see her wake up every day by my side, her provocations, even when she called me Sammy.

I held her hands above her head, a half-smile forming on her lips.

"What do you plan to do, Vacchiano?" she asked in her most provocative tone.

"Fuck those red lips with my cock," I declared, not taking my eyes off her mouth, feeling my cock begging for attention inside my underwear.

"I think in this position I'm at a disadvantage."

"In this position, you can suck my cock until it hits the back of your throat." I grinned perversely.

"I hate your need to always be in control." A pout formed on her lips.

"Amore mio, you might have control over my heart, but in bed, I always want to dominate you." I lowered my face, licking her lip, hearing her sigh.

"Sammy..." Her voice was weak.

"Tell me, ragazza mia," I asked, lifting my face, letting go of her hand as it moved to my pants, easily unbuttoning them. I planted my feet on the floor, getting off her to remove my pants, leaving me completely naked.

"I want you, you bastard," she declared, sitting up on the bed, moving closer to me.

I ran my hand along the strap of her dress, sliding down her arms, moving over her ass, until I reached her knee, and with her help, I removed the dress entirely, leaving my girl naked.

"How do you want me?" I asked, smiling.

"In every way..."

"Be more specific," I interrupted, lowering my eyes over her full breasts. I lifted my hand, pinching her hardened nipple, bringing my mouth close, grazing my tongue around her pink areola.

"I need you, Santino Vacchiano," she pleaded, dragging her nails across my neck as I began to suck on her nipple.

"In what way do you need me?" I needed specific answers from her.

"You fucking bastard!" Again, she didn't answer, making me stop licking her breast.

I pushed her, making her lay her head on the pillow. Her eyes widened briefly at my sudden move. I crawled over her, lifting her hands above her head, stopping on top of her breasts. My cock touched her chin.

"Tell me, Cinzia, how do you need me?" I grunted, holding her wrists with one hand, using the other to stroke her neck, tilting her head slightly, which made my cock brush her lip.

The damned woman smiled, opening her mouth and swirling her tongue around the head of my cock. She knew what she was doing, and damn the man she had done this with before, because I wanted to kill that bastard.

"I need you in every way." She stopped speaking, opening her lips, making me thrust into her mouth, my cock being encircled by her velvety lips, sliding in and out slowly. "I need our constant fights, I need what exists between us, I even need your possessive nature..."

I grunted, interrupting her and going deep into her throat. Cinzia choked but didn't stop; her eyes watered. I released her hands, which moved to my waist, her touches causing a wonderful tingling sensation.

My cock reached the back of her throat again; she moved one hand to the base of my cock, giving her more control over what she was doing. I pulled my cock from her mouth, saliva dripping from the side of her lips. A sly smile appeared on her face, and her makeup started to smudge from the sweat.

"Tell me, amore mio, who is your master?" I asked, tracing her lip with the head of my cock.

"You, Santino Vacchiano, always you, even when I didn't want it to be."

"Have you loved another man?" I asked, hoping she would say no.

"No, there's no way to love anyone when I had a piece of the wrong path like this." I felt her hand scratching my chest.

"But why would you run away with another man?" I asked curiously, still brushing her lip with my cock.

"I would do that because you always made it clear you didn't want me. Why would I stay with someone who didn't want me? I wanted a marriage with love. It's hard to want anything less when I see the devotion of all the couples I know. Even my parents, in their twisted way, love each other." I resumed thrusting into her mouth slowly, feeling every corner of her mouth.

"I put you on such a high pedestal because I knew you could destroy me. I didn't want to surrender to the feeling that makes a man vulnerable, and you made me vulnerable. Giving up on our marriage was my biggest mistake, and I regret the decision I made, giving up the only woman who touched my heart." My speech was interrupted by her lips, which started to suck me forcefully.

Cinzia said nothing more. I began to fuck her mouth hard, her eyes filled with tears streaming down her face, her mouth slightly swollen but still sucking me, saliva dripping from the corner of her mouth.

"Fuck! I'm about to come," I grunted, and she didn't stop.

Gripping my waist with one hand and holding the base of my cock deliciously with the other, I splayed my hand in her hair, gripping it tightly.

Cinzia was the storm that pulled me into it, destroying my entire life, as if out of nowhere she was the spark I needed, the fiery woman who had me in her hands.

Fixing my eyes on the hot girl with the seductive gaze was the trigger for coming deep in her throat. She choked, but I kept my cock deep, holding her chin with my free hand, making Cinzia swallow all my cum, which made me smile perversely, and she gave a little punch to my abdomen.

"Damn it!" That was the first thing she said when I pulled my cock from her mouth.

"Amore mio, get used to it, because you're going to get a lot of my cum..."

"Keep dreaming, Vacchiano."

"I've already told you that every challenge you give me makes everything more enjoyable." I smiled, getting off her.

"Maybe I love this crazy side of yours..., maybe," I laughed at her words, gripping her hair tightly, pulling with such force that Cinzia let out a little scream, hitting my chest.

CHAPTER FORTY-SEVEN

Cinzia

I ran my hand over Santino's abdomen, feeling his muscles, my eyes lifting to meet his.

"I'm still not tired of you, my *little hurricane*." His fingers traced along my back; we were both naked on the bed, the bed that should have been ours from the start.

"Vacchiano, you do realize I need to get back home, right? There's still hope my father won't find out I'm here and spare me his lectures." I moved, placing a leg on each side of his waist, looking down at him.

His fingers spread over my thigh, one tattooed hand contrasting with my skin, his eyes half-closed as he slid his hand over my ass.

"Will you give me everything?" he asked in a rough tone.

"Is giving you my virginity not enough?" I raised an eyebrow.

"I want your little ass, *ragazza mia*."

I shouldn't have reacted like that, but his words made me wet.

"I don't think you deserve that, Vacchiano..." I smiled as his finger traced my opening.

"Oh, I deserve everything that includes you."

Santino moved, effortlessly laying me on the bed and getting up.

"Hey, where are you going?" I asked, biting the corner of my mouth as I admired his round ass.

"Calm down, *amore mio*, I'll be back for you..." he mocked, going into his closet. It took him only a few seconds before he returned.

Santino held a silver object in his hand, and my eyes widened as I recognized it.

"No!" I shook my head vigorously, leaning back against the bed.

"I promise you'll like it." His smile grew even wider.

"Like having an anal plug inside me? You must be crazy." I was incredulous.

Santino knelt on the bed, holding my legs apart, positioning himself between them as his hand slid along my legs.

"*Amore mio,* just try it first, and then make your judgment." His fingers touched my fully exposed pussy.

"I can make a judgment in advance about this." My voice came out nervous yet curious.

I felt the metal of the plug touch my intimate area, sliding over my folds.

"Get on all fours for me, *amore mio.* " My eyes met his.

"Vacchiano, no!"

"Am I going to have to force you?" He raised an eyebrow.

"Force me, then. Let's have a battle." His face moved closer to mine.

"Why do you always have to contradict me? If I say you'll like it, it's because I'm not lying!"

I sighed deeply, and Santino smiled to himself, knowing that deep down I was curious about the experience.

"I hate having to lower myself to you." I rolled my eyes.

Santino moved from between my legs, and I turned, still apprehensive. Being in that position left me completely at his mercy. I lifted my ass, resting my head on my arms, feeling his hand caress my butt.

"You know you're extremely hot, don't you?" he whispered, squeezing my ass. "I could fuck you every day of my existence."

"Lucky for you, you don't have that capability." I murmured. "Ouch!"

I let out a little yelp when he smacked my ass, the sound echoing in the room.

"When you're mine again, you'll sleep in my bed every night, and I'll only close my eyes when my cock slides into your tight little pussy and is completely mine..." His sentence trailed off as a moan escaped my lips, caught off guard by his mouth burying itself between my ass cheeks.

"Vacchiano..." I whined as his tongue circled my opening.

"Your little ass will still be mine, but today you'll know what it's like to be fucked with the plug in it."

"Bastard," I whispered as the tip of the plug touched my opening.

Santino pressed it in, using his other hand to slide over my pussy, circling his fingers and pushing the small crystal-tipped plug into my opening, making me moan loudly as I bit my lip hard.

It hurt, but it was a strange pain, a pleasurable pain.

"Ah, your little ass gleaming from the plug's crystal makes me so hard, *amore mio*..." he whispered, kneeling and pressing his incredibly hard member against my pussy.

I closed my eyes as his member entered me, sliding over the walls of my pussy, the delicious pressure of the anal plug making me sigh as his cock moved in and out slowly.

His hand went underneath me, touching my pussy, his cock pressing against my ass.

"Touch yourself, Cinzia," he whispered, pulling his hand away and squeezing my ass.

I reached down, my fingers caressing my folds, feeling them wet and sticky from the honey dripping from my pussy.

"What a fucking tasty ass," he grunted, delivering a slap to my skin, running his finger around the plug.

"Bastard," I whined, enjoying it, enjoying being fucked this way.

"A bastard you want to fuck you all night long..."

"Oh, I'd beg for mercy all night." I closed my eyes, listening to his rough, delicious laughter.

"*Amore mio,* such a tasty ass deserves to be eaten in many ways, but there's only one exception: it will only be fucked by one cock, mine."

Santino fucked me harder, his pelvis crashing into my ass, moans escaping from my mouth as I gripped the pillow tightly, pulling my fingers from my pussy because I was at such a high peak of pleasure, like being at the top of a mountain ready to leap.

"Sammy," I lamented his name, rolling my eyes and writhing on his cock.

The combination of the anal plug and his cock brought me to a level of pleasure I never thought possible; I surrendered, I leaped.

Santino came with me, roaring as he thrust one last time inside me. His aggressive fingers squeezed my ass.

I collapsed, exhausted, on the bed, his body coming down with mine, and we stayed like that for long seconds.

"Vacchiano, you're suffocating me," I whispered with his weight on top of me.

He smiled, getting off me, his fluid dripping down my legs. He removed the plug and placed it beside the bed. He pulled my body, making my hand slide over his sweaty chest.

"So? Are you going to tell me that orgasm was forced?" His tone was laced with irony.

"I don't want to admit defeat." I pouted, lifting my face to meet the sly smile of the man I had fallen for.

"*Amore mio,* admit that I master the art of sex, just accept that I can give you the best orgasms..."

"But this Italian is so full of himself. What confuses me more is who leaves the house with those little balls, has anal plugs at home... what else do you have?"

"Everything is extremely planned, all because I wanted to see my future wife sweating in front of everyone and then see her desperate for my cock." His smile was enormous.

"So you brought that with you with a purpose in mind?"

"Yes, everything I have here is new, and I'm going to use it with you..."

"Vacchiano!" I cut him off.

"*Ragazza mia,* in the end, you'll like it." His long fingers touched the side of my face.

"You don't exist. Why do we take the longest paths?"

"If life came with an instruction manual, everything would be easier," he mocked. "Come on, let's take a shower so I can clean this tasty little pussy..."

"I need to go home." I moved my body, sitting up on the bed.

"No, you're staying with me tonight. Don't forget what we agreed on!"

"But you've already had your sex," I declared, still confused.

"But I want your scent, your body pressed against mine. I want you here with me, Cinzia, understand? It's not about the sex; it's about you, my Sicilian hurricane." He got up from the bed, extending his hand.

"We might be heading in a different direction..."

"Or I might be surrendering to you," he cut me off, making me let out a squeal as he picked me up and sat me on his lap.

CHAPTER FORTY-EIGHT

Cinzia

My phone kept vibrating non-stop, the sound of multiple messages coming through. I opened my eyes; despite the blackout on the curtains, I could see that the day had already dawned through the gaps.

I stretched my arms, grimacing as I reached for my phone on the nightstand. Santino's strong arms were wrapped around my waist as if he wanted to protect me from something.

Among the numerous messages was one from my father. The phone had come out of "Do Not Disturb" mode, receiving all notifications. I read my father's message, where he seemed to have thrown in the towel:

"*Cinzia Bianchi, know that if you don't show up at this house tonight, you need never come again!*"

Great, Aldo Bianchi was treating me coldly. At least I didn't have to witness a live, colorful show at Santino's house; he must have assumed I was there.

I just wanted to be a normal 23-year-old, but they didn't even allow me that.

One fact reminded me that the next day would be my birthday. I would be turning 24, and it didn't seem like I would be celebrating another year of life in this catastrophic situation.

But what caught my attention the most was the number of messages from Marco, some of them recent, asking me to meet him at the beach because he needed to talk to me. How did he get into the condominium? How did he get to the beach? There was only one way to get to that part of the beach, and that was by crossing the rocks from the sea.

"Sammy?" I whispered, feeling indebted to Marco. We had always been friends, and despite the disagreement, I couldn't believe he would do me any harm. "Santino..."

"Hmm..." he murmured, removing his hand from me and turning his body as if nothing had happened, going back to his deep sleep.

I got out of bed and headed to the closet. I found a change of clothes Pietra had brought secretly the night before. My friend might be crazy, but she was a great partner.

I put on the shorts and shirt, tied my hair into a bun, slipped on some sandals, and returned to the bedroom where Santino was still sound asleep. I walked over to him, placing my hand on the corner of his eyes. He gave a half-smile without opening them.

"I'm going to the beach. Marco is there. I need to talk to him and ask him not to contact me again," I whispered.

"Hmm..." I had no idea if he had heard or if he just accepted it without knowing exactly what it was about, as he accepted it very easily.

I left the room and headed to the back door, not wanting to pass by the front so no one would see me. I walked across the lawn, following the path with stones that led me to the beach. I saw the sea; it was rough, and the noise of the waves crashing made me flinch slightly.

I love the sea, but I appreciate it from a distance. I didn't know how to swim, so I preferred to stay away.

I took off my shoes as my feet touched the sand. In the distance, I saw a man sitting and quickly recognized Marco; his hair seemed damp. I walked toward him, my feet sinking into the sand. As I got closer, he noticed me and got up from the ground.

His expression was stern, his eyes cold—a Marco I had never seen before.

"Marco, what are you doing here?" was the first thing I asked.

"Isn't it obvious?" He gave a forced, sideways smile.

"Sorry?" I raised an eyebrow, not understanding what he was talking about.

"I came to take you away. I figured out how to get across the sea..." At that moment, I noticed his clothes were all wet.

His face had deep dark circles, as if he hadn't been sleeping well—a troubled man.

"No, Marco, I'm not going to put you in danger. Santino has many men watching me," I said, watching him look around.

"Where are these men? I don't see any," he mocked in a way I didn't like. "This man did something you need to know..."

"I know, Marco," I cut him off, seeing him narrow his eyes at me.

"If you know, why don't you run away from him? If you know, why do you seem to be supporting the fact that someone was killed by him?"

"He didn't kill her..."

"Yes, he did!" Marco suddenly became agitated. "That bastard didn't return her love. My sister took her own life out of neglect, an unrequited love!"

"Marco..." My sentence died as he gripped my wrist tightly, pulling me abruptly.

"You're going to run away with me. I'm going to take from that bastard what he took from me," he growled, revealing a side of himself I truly didn't know.

"Marco, no! I'm afraid of the sea." I tried to pull my hand away, seeing him look at me with a wicked smile.

"So be it. If dying in this sea does no harm, then that bastard will know what it's like to feel the pain of death." I started to panic.

"No, Marco!" For the first time in my life, I felt fear.

I looked around and saw no one, the houses in the distance, the sea breaking in angry waves, his fingers tightening around my wrist.

"How could you, Marco? What about our friendship?" I asked, my voice beginning to break.

"Friendship? There was never any friendship. In fact, I always found you too annoying. It was all a plan, but in the end, everything went wrong, or rather, right! Because if you die in that sea, the bastard will know what it's like to lose someone he loves." I began to pull my arm.

I struggled. How could I have thought he just wanted to talk? That we could understand each other as friends? *Damn, how was I so stupid!*

"Stop, you bitch!" he growled, pulling me towards the sea.

I didn't stop struggling until, in a moment of his slip, I broke free, turning and starting to run. My blurry vision guided me towards the path back to Santino's house.

Running on the sand is difficult, especially with a man much larger than me on my tail.

A scream escaped my throat as I felt his hand grip my wrist again, pulling me back.

"Fuck! You're not escaping me," he roared, this time with a firmer grip.

"Marco, no! Please, I have nothing to do with this," I begged in a plea.

"You do. That man loves you, and I'm going to take from him what he loves, just like he took my sister from me..."

"He doesn't love me," I declared, resisting his steps, but it was in vain; we were getting closer and closer to the sea.

"Yes, he does. I saw the way he looks at you," Marco said, pulling me without even looking in my direction.

He didn't want to escape with me. On that side, we were far from the rocks that separated us from the other side of the sea. Marco wanted my death.

The water began to touch my feet. I couldn't die, not on the eve of my birthday. How could I, who considered myself a smart person, fall into such a mistake?

"Marco, I beg you!" I cried in desperation.

"I have no pity for you. I want revenge, even if it means both of us have to die," he said, his eyes briefly meeting mine before turning forward.

A wave crashed against my knees, causing me to lose my balance and almost fall, salty water touching my face. No, I didn't want to die; I kept struggling, but my body was growing tired. Marco kept pulling me, and I was becoming more desperate.

A wave crashed over us as the water reached my neck. The strong wave caught Marco off guard. By that point, I had swallowed a lot of water. His hand let go of mine, and I tried to swim, to surface, but another wave collided with the first, dragging me down again. I could no longer see anything; I didn't know where Marco had gone.

There, many waves were crashing, and I couldn't surface anymore, everything dragging me further down. My eyes were closing, my body becoming light, going wherever the turbulent sea took me. If this was death, let it take me quickly, for I didn't want to feel...

CHAPTER FORTY-NINE

Santino

When Cinzia spoke to me, I thought I was dreaming, until I woke up and questioned whether she really said what I heard.

Had Cinzia gone to meet that bastard? That woman must have lost her mind. I quickly put on a pair of shorts, leaving my room, hoping that what she said was just a dream, or rather, a nightmare; I didn't even put on any shoes.

The back door of the house was open.

"Cinzia!" I muttered in a reproachful tone when I saw the open door.

I started running, knowing at that moment it hadn't been a delusion; she had really gone to that damned beach. I didn't even take the longer route, climbing over the huge rocks, looking out at the vast sea, seeing in the distance my girl struggling as the man pushed her away.

Damn!

I climbed over the huge rocks, jumped onto the sand, running as if my soul were escaping from me, the image of the waves crashing over them. My girl struggling to get out of there.

A sense of desperation overtook me, the fear of losing her, the fear of losing that little whirlwind. I approached where they were. At that moment, a wave crashed over them, making my Cinzia disappear, then coming back up, but with the new wave, she was gone again. *Fuck*!

My feet automatically stepped into the churning sea, my eyes fixed on the spot where she had disappeared, my body engulfed by the amount of water covering it. I knew how to swim, but at that moment I was acting out of desperation, the pain of loss.

No, I couldn't lose the only woman I had!

Cinzia didn't come back to the surface, which made me even more worried, just like the bastard didn't come back either. Noticing that a wave was about to crash over me, I stretched my arms and dove, my eyes wide open, guiding me towards my girl.

I came back up, my feet no longer touching the ground. I knew I was close to her, knew she had to be around. I dove again, the incessant noise of the waves crashing in the sea making me believe I might be too late. But that wouldn't make me stop.

I dove, my eyes scanning everything in the murky water until I spotted her arms raised, her body being guided by the turbulent sea.

I kicked my feet, propelling myself towards her. If this was fear, if having the sensation that you could lose someone is fear, then I was terrified.

With ease, I embraced her waist, my breath starting to fail. I needed to get back to the surface. Cinzia's body was heavy, she didn't even respond to my touch. FUCK!

I kicked my feet, trying to bring us both up when I felt something grabbing my ankle. I looked down and saw an arm circling my ankle, the bastard's face right below.

Hell! With my free leg, I allowed him to pull me down until I was close to his head, kicking his head with force. I felt his hands release my ankle. I had been holding my breath for too long, going up to the surface and finally finding air.

I pulled him forcefully, feeling the air fill my lungs. I had to release one of my arms around my girl, holding her with just one, moving, kicking my feet, being pushed by the waves that guided me closer to the sand. I still couldn't touch the ground; my arm was starting to go numb from the strain of pulling Cinzia's body. The desperation returned, as she wasn't reacting. I needed to get out of there.

I looked up and saw a man entering the sea, or rather, two men—my father and my brother—coming towards me.

I felt my feet finally touching the sand, walking, wrapping my girl in both arms. The waves that crashed over me guided us aggressively towards the shore.

"Son, what happened? We heard her scream from up there..." Dad said immediately.

Scream? What scream?

My ears seemed deaf in the face of the fear that overwhelmed me, as if I couldn't hear, only react.

Valentino took the other side of Cinzia, and my father lifted her from my arms. The two of them carried her to the sand, and I followed alongside them, my feet trembling. Once on the sand, Cinzia's lifeless body was laid down. I knelt beside her, my girl's hard features, her full lips slightly parted.

"No, she can't die," I whispered in desperation.

My father began pressing on her chest, but Cinzia didn't even respond. I ran my fingers over her cheek, which had always been rosy but was now pale.

"Don't stop, Dad," I pleaded.

I held her chin, bringing my mouth close to hers, drawing her air with mine. I tried once, and nothing; twice, and still nothing.

"Cinzia Bianchi, you're not leaving me like this," I growled in my desperation.

"Brother..." Valentino's voice carried that tone of regret.

"No!" I roared, pressing my mouth back to hers.

No, I wasn't going to lose her, not lose her enchanting smiles, the provocations that made me mad with desire. As if I gave everything of myself to that woman who had me, filling her with my air.

That was when she took a deep breath, turning her face, water escaping from her mouth, an incessant cough making her blue eyes finally open. I fell to my knees, my body becoming light. She was alive. My Cinzia was alive.

I moved closer to her, her eyes focusing on me. My father, who was performing chest compressions, moved away. Cinzia raised her arm, and I took that as a request for a hug. I pulled her into my arms, her body finally feeling light compared to how heavy it had been before. I drew her to my chest, a moan escaping her mouth, my eyes becoming blurred.

"Sammy..." Her voice came out in a hoarse whisper *"I... I..."* thought I was going to die...

"My love, I will never let you go. You're mine, and no one has the right to take what is mine." My fingers pressed into her wet hair.

Her hand gripped my chest, feeling her chest rise and fall, knowing she was alive, breathing in my arms. There was no price for that. Going through all that and knowing I could have lost my girl, I didn't want it anymore, even if it meant putting a tracking chip on her. I wasn't going to lose Cinzia. I wasn't going to lose the only woman who had me.

CHAPTER FIFTY

Cinzia

I clung to Santino's chest as he carried me in his arms. The smell of him made me breathe a sigh of relief. Just when I thought nothing of me would be left, he was there, he showed up to save me.

I don't remember anything, only waking up with his lips on mine. We were heading to his parents' house, which was closer. As we went through the back, we heard footsteps approaching us.

"What happened?" I managed to distinguish my father's voice.

Santino growled as he passed by my father, hearing Mr. Tommaso say:

"That man you wanted as your daughter's husband almost killed her," he said, echoing what Santino had told him before we came to their house.

Don had ordered all his men to stay close to the sea to make sure Marco either returned or drowned. They wanted him not to come back. At that moment, all I wanted was the warmth of my home, the security I felt when I was in Santino's arms.

"How did this happen?" Dad spoke again as we entered the house.

"Simple, that man wanted to marry Cinzia just to get revenge on Santino!" Tommaso said.

"Come on, son," I heard Mrs. Verena asking us to go upstairs.

"I don't want to talk about it right now," Santino declared, heading towards the stairs. "Just leave us alone for a few minutes."

He climbed a step at a time, entering a room.

"I left a change of clothes on the bed for her. I'll prepare breakfast for you," Verena said, leaving us alone in the room.

I looked around, recognizing Santino's old room. I had been there when he was a child; I knew he used to sleep there. After all, even though Valentino and Santino were alike, they had different personalities.

Santino set me down on the floor, his hand gently cupping my cheek, his eyes locked on mine.

"*My love,* I was so scared," he whispered, holding onto the hem of my shirt, pulling it over my head.

"You scared?" I tried to smile as he undressed me.

"I can't lose the woman who was my redemption. My *little whirlwind*, I love you." His fingers undid the button of my shorts, letting them fall to my feet.

He knelt down, pulling down my underwear, and as he continued to kneel, he hugged my waist tightly, as if he was still frozen in his thoughts until I heard him sniffle.

He was crying, not lifting his face. I ran my hand through his hair, kneeling in front of him, our eyes meeting—his red with tears. Santino was crying, many tears streaming down his face. I raised my hand, sliding along his cheeks, touching the tears.

"I was so scared. I thought I was going to lose you..." His voice was interrupted by a sniffle.

I pulled his face against my chest, his hand encircling my waist. His grip was tight, as if he wanted to ensure that I was truly alive, here with him.

"You saved me, darling. I'm here because you saved me," I whispered, feeling my eyes become misty.

I loved Santino Vacchiano so much it hurt. I didn't know what I would have done if he hadn't shown up at that moment.

"You shouldn't have been there, you shouldn't have gone through that. I should have done something when he first appeared. I shouldn't have left you defenseless; it's my fault..." Santino's tears bathed my chest. "Damn it! I don't know what I would have done if I had lost you."

"You haven't lost me, you won't lose me. It wasn't your fault. I went to that beach..."

We stayed like that for long seconds, tears starting to fall silently on my face. Santino didn't let go of me, his sobs mixing with his uncontrolled crying, the explicit fear in the way he held me.

"Sammy, my love." I ran my hand over his chin, his red eyes meeting mine.

"I won't let anything separate us. I won't allow anyone to take away the reason for my happiness. Cinzia, I'll only stop when I'm sure you're mine again, when you agree to marry me once more..."

"*Schii*..." I touched his lips. "I've never stopped being yours, you fool. I'm yours, I've always been yours, since I was little. You are mine, I am yours. I love you, my crazy Vacchiano..."

"Please, say it again!" he asked, smiling slightly, his tears finally stopping.

"I love you, Santino Vacchiano," I declared, watching his smile grow.

"Damn it! Let's get married tomorrow, I need to be sure you're officially mine..."

"You silly, I'm yours. A civil *status* isn't going to change that," I declared as he got up.

"To me, it makes all the difference." Santino removed his shorts and underwear, lifting me onto his lap. "I'll take care of you, *my love*, make sure every part of your body is washed, never let you go again, keep you by my side forever. Nothing and no one will ever take you away from me."

"Sammy," I whispered as he entered the suite, opening the shower, and carefully setting me down on the floor.

He turned on the shower. I stood beside him as his hand intertwined with mine, the water falling on my back. My hand rose, touching his firm chest, our eyes locked on each other.

His body pressed against mine, I brushed my hand over his shoulder, caressing his neck, feeling his erection starting to touch me. He smiled to the side, gently squeezing my ass.

"It's impossible to stay indifferent to these curves," he whispered with a sensual voice.

"Don't be indifferent. Take me as yours, Sammy. Make sure this isn't a dream, that I'm alive, that I'm here with you," I pleaded.

He didn't even question it, picking me up in his arms, pressing me against the cold wall, his penis brushing against my cunt, entering slowly.

"No one will ever take me away from you. I'll go to hell if necessary to have you. I love you, insanely. I love you, my *little whirlwind*," he declared in his ragged voice.

I embraced his body, feeling his penis move in and out, my body pressed against the wall. I had no doubts; he was the owner of my heart, the man who had the power to irritate me just as much as he made me love him.

CHAPTER FIFTY-ONE

Cinzia

Santino intertwined his fingers with mine as we descended the stairs. My eyes lifted towards the living room where everyone was gathered—my parents, my friend Pietra with her son and husband, Santino's parents, and his brother. Upon seeing me, my mother rushed over, and I released Santino's hand to embrace her.

"My daughter." She sniffled amid the hug.

Mom was never an overly affectionate mother, but she was always there for whatever I needed. I felt her body pressing against mine, her scent filling my senses.

"I would never forgive myself if something happened to you," she said as she pulled away.

"I'm fine, Mom. Nothing will happen to me," I declared, holding her hand and listening to Santino's footsteps as he joined his family.

"Cinzia." I lifted my eyes to meet my father's.

"Dad..." I whispered, bracing myself for the lecture that was about to come.

"I'm so sorry," he said suddenly, catching me off guard. I opened my mouth several times without a reaction. "I should have protected you. I should have listened to my Don when he said he didn't approve of your relationship with that man. I acted recklessly, thoughtlessly, out of control, as if I hated when things went beyond my control. I'm so sorry; I should have protected you. You're my daughter, my only daughter, and I failed to do that for you..."

"Dad, I'm fine," I whispered, repeating what I had said to my mother.

"But you almost weren't. If it weren't for Santino, you wouldn't be here. Damn it!" Dad ran his hands through his hair, desperate. "Here I am, the one who's always been the sensible one, acting without thinking..."

"There's a first time for everything in life; that's why you should retire," Santino appeared in his mocking tone, placing his hand on my father's shoulder. My father looked at him with narrowed eyes.

"I'm grateful for you saving my daughter's life, but I'll only have a civilized conversation with you when you make my daughter your wife..."

"Dad!" I grumbled in reprimand, rolling my eyes.

Santino winked at me before turning back to his family. My mother didn't let go of my hand, my father stood by my side, and my friend had tears in her eyes as she looked at me. She smiled broadly, as if living in a parallel reality.

"I asked them to have breakfast ready. We'll all eat together after this scare," Mrs. Verena said.

"First, I want to know if they found the bastard," Santino asked his father.

"Nothing. We're sure he didn't leave the sea; by now, he's probably drowned," Tommaso declared nonchalantly.

I didn't want Marco to die, but at that moment, I sighed in relief, as if a weight had been lifted from me. He had wanted to kill me, to kill me for something I wasn't guilty of, as if I were the cause of his sister's death.

My eyes met Santino's. He was searching for any sign of regret in me but found none. If Marco had wanted my death, I also wanted his.

"Before we have breakfast, I want to do something," Santino said suddenly. He was nervous, his unsteady steps coming towards me.

I was puzzled, raising an eyebrow as he stood in front of me.

"Vacchiano..." I said in a reprimanding tone.

The jerk gave a crooked smile, pulling a small velvet box from his pocket, making me step back, astonished and surprised. He knelt in front of me, opening the little box to reveal a small diamond ring. It wasn't the same ring from our first wedding; it was a different one.

"Cinzia Bianchi, this may seem quite cheesy, in fact, it's ridiculous even for me, but I fell in love with you. I didn't want to believe that a crazy girl like you could touch my heart. I believe that only a crazy girl could fall in love with a crazy guy like me. I love you, and for years, men have dictated what you should do, which is why I'm making this proposal to you, not to your father, not to my father, but to the woman I love, the only woman who has me in the palm of her hand, in front of all our family, risking being mocked for the rest of my life. But I don't give a damn because your happiness is what matters to me. The fact that I have you alive is what keeps me going. Will you marry me? Will you be my Mrs. Vacchiano? This time for real, this time because we both want it, be mine, *amore mio*?

I put my hand to my mouth; I really didn't expect this, didn't expect such a display of love in front of all our family. The shock left me silent, the *yes* on the tip of my tongue, but it wouldn't come out.

"Damn it, Cinzia, if you say no, I'll make you say yes. No is not an option here," he said nervously, impatiently, causing everyone around us to laugh.

"Shut up, Vacchiano, of course it's yes," I replied quickly, seeing his smile grow wider.

"Of course, the proposal had to come like this," Valentino teased.

Santino took my hand, sliding the beautiful ring with a diamond onto my finger, and then kissed my finger.

He stood up, holding both sides of my face, caressing my skin with his thumb, making me smile.

"We're getting married tomorrow," he announced loudly for everyone to hear.

"You must be crazy," I said, finding it all a bit insane.

"We've been married once; we're just going to formalize what we already had. I'm not taking the risk of you changing your mind. We're getting married tomorrow, just our family." His tone made it clear he wasn't joking.

"But you know I love you. I'm not going to change my mind..."

"No, Cinzia, we're getting married tomorrow. You're as crazy as I am; what if you wake up deciding not to get married? I've already made up my mind." He shrugged, making everyone look at us.

"You're impossible, Vacchiano, wanting everything your way." I crossed my arms, pouting.

"Well, I think I can arrange something just for us and call Father Miguel to bless the wedding," Mrs. Verena said, trying to diffuse our argument.

"See, my mom has a solution," Santino declared, winning that round of discussion.

"This time, yes, but know that there will be many more battles." I shrugged, watching his laughter echo.

"If this is love, I refuse to feel it," Valentino said as he passed by us, making a face and heading towards the breakfast room.

"If you're really getting married tomorrow, we need to at least prepare a dress, a family dinner..."

"And the cake for the birthday girl," Santino cut off his sister's enthusiastic wedding talk.

"You know tomorrow is my birthday?" I asked, amazed.

"Of course, *amore mio.*" He winked flirtatiously.

"Just because of that, I'll forgive you for planning a wedding at the last minute." Santino put his hand on my shoulder, whispering as we all went to the breakfast table.

"*Ragazza mia,* in the end, you'll always forgive me..."

CHAPTER FIFTY-TWO

Santino

"His body was found," Valentino said as I buttoned the last button of my shirt.

"Should I be worried?" I turned my body, analyzing Valentino's calm features.

"No, because they found the body far from here, and it was ruled a suicide." Valen shrugged, unconcerned.

"Great, one less bastard in the world." I took the jacket my brother extended to me.

"I can't believe you're actually getting married of your own free will." He shook his head, trying not to laugh.

"I love that woman." I slipped my arms into the jacket, the final piece to complete my outfit.

"I wonder which of you two will kill each other first. Together, you're like fire and gasoline. If you're not fighting, you're having sex." Valentino made a face.

"Don't forget that you're getting married too," I teased.

"Yes, I am, but that Latina will dance to my tune. My brother started walking toward my bedroom door.

"I can't wait to see you fall in love..."

"I'm not going to fall in love. I'm going to have heirs, that's all, and luckily, my fiancée is a fiery, beautiful, and hot Latina who will give me good children..."

"What are you two talking about, children?" Mom appeared at that moment.

"Valentino is talking about your marriage to the Latina. He thinks it will only be about heirs." Mom crossed her arms, giving my brother a stern look.

"It's a good thing you're going to live here in this house because I won't allow you to mistreat that poor girl," Verena scolded him.

"Fortunately, I'm thinking about a honeymoon, maybe in Greece, having my child in paradise, using everything I dreamed for that girl..."

"Damn it, Valentino," I cut him off with my laughter, "you're a sadistic lunatic."

"Is it too hard for you to be like your brother?" Mom crossed her arms at Valentino.

"You know that Santino and Cinzia almost kill each other, right? Besides, Cinzia is just as crazy as he is. In a weird way, they complete each other. If I had a wife like Cinzia, I'd be dead by the honeymoon. Luckily, she's yours." My brother moved out of Mom's way, stepping aside.

My eyes met my mother's blue ones. She was short, with blonde hair pinned in a hairstyle. Years might pass, but she remained a woman with delicate features, always calm.

"What to do with your brother?" Mom sighed.

"Just leave him, Mom. Valen has never been good at following rules. The more you pressure him, the more he'll rebel. He's less volatile than I am, which makes him act without being noticed, while I'm the one who's flashy." I shrugged, extending my arm to Verena. "Shall we?"

"Yes. Let's go. I have a son to marry off." She smiled sweetly.

"For the second time..." I teased, letting my words hang in the air.

I descended the stairs without letting go of my mother's hand, and we passed through the living room, finding our family gathered in the garden. It was late afternoon.

I spent the morning with Cinzia. She thought we'd be apart that day, but I didn't let her leave the bed until I felt relieved and sure she would come to our wedding. I loved that woman, loved everything about her, even our arguments.

That day was her 24th birthday, but I was the one receiving a gift—the gift of having her by my side, bringing excitement to my days.

It might sound crazy, but it was just love, an unconditional love, a feeling of possession, a sense of belonging to her and her to me. I might be crazy, but I was a passionate crazy.

We walked down the red carpet. I lowered my face when I heard a sniffle, smiling at the sight of my mother's tearful eyes.

"Shut up, you little rascal. I'm emotional; my son is getting married," she said, even though I hadn't mentioned anything.

"Mom, you know I didn't say anything, right?" I whispered back.

"But you were thinking it."

"Besides, it's not like I'm getting married for the first time." I made a face.

"Yes, the first time for love..." We stopped in front of the priest, who held a rosary in his hand.

I cupped my mother's face in my hands, bringing my lips to her forehead, and gave her a kiss, whispering:

"You're the best mother anyone could have, Verena Vacchiano."

"Just trying to make me cry more, huh?" Mom pulled away, smiling awkwardly, making me hold back a laugh.

She went to my father, who put his arm around her shoulders, pulling her to his chest and kissing the top of her head. I finally understood him, understood why he would do anything for her, move worlds for his wife, because I shared the same feeling for my future wife. I knew what it was like to feel the desperation, the almost-loss of your girl.

I loved Cinzia, and I knew I'd do anything for her, even face hell.

I raised my eyes and saw the woman in the white dress approaching, her father by her side, her face illuminated by her blue eyes. Damn, what a beautiful woman and mine.

They walked towards me, the dress subtly trailing on the floor, both stopping in front of me. Aldo took his daughter's hand, placing it on mine.

"I hope this time it's for real," he whispered.

"Your daughter will be the happiest woman of all, in my own way." I shrugged, seeing Cinzia's sly smile.

Aldo stepped back, Cinzia stood by my side, the ceremony was brief, the priest blessed our union, and in the end, said the phrase I had been waiting for:

"I now declare you husband and wife. The groom may kiss the bride." We stood facing each other.

I slid my hand over her cheeks, feeling the softness of her skin against mine.

"My Mrs. Vacchiano, officially mine, you might want to run from me, but your fate has been sealed and claimed to be mine. I love you, my Sicilian hurricane," I whispered, bringing my lips close to hers.

"It's always been you, my first in everything, my first kiss, my first man, I love you Sammy." Her smile made me press my lips to hers.

Cinzia came into my life like a hurricane, making me surrender to this feeling. I, who had always been selfish with everything, who never wanted to be the loser. But if it meant having her smile in my life forever, I was a winner by losing.

She was my redemption, and in return, I gained her love.

CHAPTER FIFTY-THREE

Cinzia

A Few Months Later...

The pain cut through me intensely, the contraction causing me to squeeze my husband's hand, who was beside me trying to stay composed, but grimacing at the pain I was causing him.

"I'll never again say you're weak," he declared, making me glance at him with my eyes half-closed.

"Shut up, Vacchiano," I grunted, as he used his other hand to wipe the sweat from my forehead.

My legs were spread apart, with a midwife positioned between them.

Why on earth did I decide to have this baby at home? Why didn't I go to a maternity hospital and opt for a cesarean? At that moment, there was no choice left; the baby was already coming into the world. I didn't want to know the sex, all to tease my husband, leaving him anxious about whether it was a boy or a girl.

I loved teasing him, loved how well we always got along when we talked. Deep down, we were more alike than it seemed. He was the best husband I could have asked for. In those months of marriage, he did everything for me, even conceded in our arguments when he was clearly right.

My pregnancy was a surprise to me, as I had thought it would take time to get pregnant, but it became hard to delay when you have a husband who's extremely addicted to sex.

"Just a bit more, ma'am, you're almost there..." the midwife said.

My eyes met Santino's green eyes, his face somewhat hardened, trying to remain unaffected by the pain he was feeling. He gave a lopsided smile, the smile that I knew was the one that brightened my days, the man I looked forward to coming home to after he went out to handle something with the mafia.

"I love you, *amore mio*," he whispered.

I squeezed his hand tightly, a loud moan escaping my mouth, closing my eyes amidst that immense pain until suddenly a small cry filled the room.

"Oh, God..." escaped my mouth as a relieved smile formed on my face.

"Would you like to cut the umbilical cord, Daddy?" the midwife asked.

Santino released my hand, first checking the sex of our baby. He took the cord, smiling as a tear rolled down his face.

"Let me be the first to hold my little girl," he said, and I knew at that moment it was a girl.

They wrapped the tiny bundle in a cloth, handing it to my husband, who brought her to me effortlessly. My eyes fixed on the little baby. My husband sat beside the bed, lowering our daughter.

"It's a girl, our little Bella." He smiled, saying the name we had agreed upon if it was a girl.

My eyes filled with tears as I looked at that tiny being, with golden strands on her little head, contrasting with a light brown tone, her tiny hand outstretched, fingers open.

A calm, gentle cry. With the help of a nurse who was present, they placed her on my chest, feeling that tiny baby.

"She's beautiful, the most beautiful thing we've ever created." Santino's eyes were fixed on the two of us.

It was impossible not to love our Bella. She was beautiful, a completely helpless little girl, needing both of us for everything, the little girl that came from our love.

I SLOWLY OPENED MY eyes; after the delivery, it was as if someone had pressed a power-off button, and I simply shut down.

I lazily raised my eyes, seeing my husband with our little one in his arms. I smiled at the sight of Santino with that tiny bundle on his chest, whispering a lullaby to her, as if he were born for that role. His eyes met mine.

"Mommy's awake," he said tenderly.

"I hope I didn't sleep too long." I gasped, propping myself up on my arms, leaning my back against the headboard.

"Not long, just two days." He gave me that sly smile.

"You fool." I rolled my eyes as he came closer, bringing our daughter.

"Just two hours. We had a nurse here in case we needed any help." Santino sat on the bed.

The little one was sleeping in his lap.

"Not to brag, but her mouth is mine," my husband said proudly.

"Are you going to insist on that too?" I whispered, meeting his sparkling eyes.

"I won't, because she should have taken after her mother; I'm just a better version for the male version," he joked casually.

"Crazy, she's perfect," I whispered, running my thumb over her delicate cheek.

"The best gift a man could receive," Santino declared, doting on our daughter once more.

There was a knock on the door. I lifted my eyes to see my mother-in-law and father-in-law enter. Verena had a radiant smile in her eyes.

"It's a girl?" she asked, holding back tears.

"They say every man needs a daughter to appreciate life," Tommaso teased, standing beside his son and placing a hand on his shoulder.

"She's so beautiful," my mother-in-law said, standing next to her husband.

"Now I have two granddaughters; it reminds me that I'm really getting old," the Don of the mafia said casually.

"It's time for us to enjoy our grandchildren and pass on the baton to our children," Verena declared with affection.

"Yes, we've delayed too long; it's time for my children to take care of our legacy." Tommaso and Santino exchanged a long look, knowing that my husband would be the right hand of the new Don, my brother-in-law Valentino.

"You know I was born ready to sit in the chair next to my brother." My husband always said he wanted to be there.

Mr. Tommaso and Verena doted on their granddaughter for long minutes. My husband stayed by my side the entire time.

In the end, I knew I made the right decision. It was always Santino, even though he didn't want to admit it at first. He was the man who had me like no other, who made me feel revitalized. We completed each other. Waking up and going to sleep every day beside him made any difficulty we faced in life worth it.

And with our little Bella, I was even more certain that he was the man of my life, the same man who had the power to push me to my limits and back a million times. But without him, none of this would be as meaningful.

EPILOGUE

Santino

5 Years Later...

I felt around the edge of the bed, searching for my wife's presence, but I didn't find her, feeling her side of the bed empty. Where the hell did that crazy woman go? On this day? On her birthday, on our six-year wedding anniversary.

I swung one leg out of bed, dragging my feet as I left the room, heading towards our daughters' room. I noticed the door slightly ajar, gently pushed it open, and found my wife lying on Giulia's bed, our youngest. My little girl's blonde hair spread across her mother's chest, as her arms held her tightly.

I approached them, stroking my wife's hair. I noticed her eyelids fluttering, slowly opening and meeting my gaze. She smiled in that way she always did when waking up.

"She had a nightmare," she whispered, running her hand through Giulia's curly blonde hair, settling her on the pillow. Our little one grumbled but went back to sleep.

I reached out, intertwining my hand with hers and leaving the room. Cinzia pushed her hair back.

"Did Tommaso scare them again?" I asked about my sister's son, that little terrorist when he teamed up with Raffaele, Valentino's son. They only knew how to scare my girls.

"No, this time it was just Raffa. I still think that mini-Vacchiano is worse than Tommaso." My wife rolled her eyes.

"I don't know if talking to Valentino will help," I murmured.

"Your brother is as crazy as his son. I'll teach my daughters to kick those boys. — Cinzia shrugged, entering our room.

I watched my wife, the satin nightgown riding up her thigh. She stopped at her side of the bed, smiling at the small box I had left there, which she hadn't noticed. She picked it up and opened it.

"Sorry about last night?" I raised an eyebrow at her sly smile.

"Is this for the apology or for my birthday? I need to know so I can demand more presents." She pouted.

"It's for the apology; after all, I went overboard...

"Good that you know, Vacchiano. That man wasn't even looking at me." She rolled her eyes.

I walked around the bed, stopping in front of her.

"Yes, he was. I'm not blind. I saw him looking at every part of your body. She's my damn wife, and I lose it—" I grumbled, taking the necklace she held out to me.

We had gone out the night before for a Cosa Nostra event. Since my brother couldn't make it, I represented him, and I saw that damned bastard staring at my wife's legs, those filthy eyes fixed on her cleavage—a cleavage that only I should be allowed to admire for too long.

Everyone knew I was known for being the most impatient man in the Cosa Nostra. I wasn't crazy; crazy was the one who looked at my wife.

"Vacchiano, years may pass, and you're still as possessive as ever," Cinzia grumbled.

I pushed her hair to the side, kissing her neck.

"Amore mio, if I don't take care of you, who will? You're mine, plain and simple." I closed the small diamond necklace that sparkled. "Happy birthday, my little tornado..."

She turned to me, her blue eyes meeting mine. We had been married for six years, the craziest six years so far. Everything with that woman was intense; there were no bad times, just some summer storms, but they were quick.

Cinzia came to show me that even a jerk like me could surrender to love.

"Daddy!" I looked up to see our eldest daughter enter our room.

Bella had dark brown hair, unlike our youngest. Bella was my spitting image, with bronzed skin, green eyes, and always messy hair. She loved running on the sand; I always had to control my adventurous daughter's spirit. She might be adventurous, but she was more affectionate than her three-year-old sister.

It was as if Bella was the softness missing in me and her mother.

"What is it, *bambina mia?*" I watched her settle onto our bed, looking up with her sparkling little eyes.

"Can I invite my friends from class to my birthday?" she asked, pouting.

"Can we think about it?" I asked, knowing that most of her friends were from outside the mafia, which made everything more complicated.

"Okay, *papá*..." she grumbled, sitting on the bed. "Today is Mommy's birthday. Will there be cake?"

"Any excuse for cake is a good one, right, sweetheart?" Cinzia smiled, tapping the tip of our five-year-old daughter's nose.

"Happy birthday, Mommy!" Giulia bounced into the room, running toward her mother and throwing herself into her lap.

Giulia was a perfect replica of Cinzia, even inheriting her wild streak.

Cinzia picked up our three-year-old daughter and hugged her. Bella got off the bed, and I lifted my eldest into my arms.

"Of course, Daddy couldn't let a family cake go unnoticed," I declared, leading my girls along. "And tonight, we'll take advantage of having your grandparents at home and have a family dinner."

I mentioned this knowing that soon my parents would travel again, along with Aldo and my mother-in-law. The four of them were enjoying their retirements. The only one left behind was Enrico, as Pietra said it was an old people's activity. My sister only went with them occasionally but often traveled with her husband to other places, and Enrico didn't seem to mind. It was as if Pietra was everything he needed.

The Cosa Nostra had become Valentino's responsibility, and I was right by his side. I never thought being the underboss would be such a demanding task, but I enjoyed what I did.

Deep down, I always knew my life would be like this—a home full of affection, a place where I found the reasons for my existence, the women who took my breath away. Cinzia didn't just change me; she changed everything about me. She made me see life through different eyes. I remained the same impulsive man, but it was all out of love for my wife. She was mine, and I took care of what was mine, just as I would forever take care of my two girls.

Cinzia gave me her love, and I surrendered to her body and soul.

THE END.

Did you love *Bound by Honor*? Then you should read *Bound by Shadows* by Amara Holt!

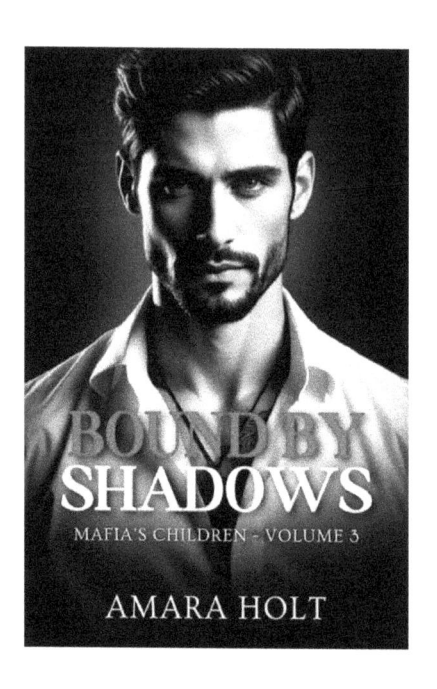

Bound by Shadows

In the world of **power** and **deception**, Valentino has always lived in the **shadows**. As the heir to the most feared Don of the Cosa Nostra, perfection is not just expected—it's demanded. Now, as the newly crowned Don of the most powerful Italian mafia, Valentino must embrace the **darkness** that has defined his life. But with this power comes an unexpected responsibility: an arranged marriage to the **enigmatic** Yulia.

Yulia was living the life every woman dreams of—until her future husband shattered it. A spirited **fashion designer** with a heart of gold and a **razor-sharp tongue**, Yulia never imagined her path would cross with the ruthless mafia world. But when Valentino tore her world apart, she vowed to return the favor.

As these two unlikely souls are forced to share the same house and the same bed, the line between **love** and **hate** blurs. Valentino hides **demons** no one has ever seen, but Yulia is determined to break through his iron-clad defenses. In a game of **passion, secrets**, and **power**, will they destroy each other, or will their hearts be forever **Bound by Shadows?**

This intense mafia romance explores the battle between **love and duty, secrets** and **truth,** and the dark allure of a forbidden connection. Perfect for fans of **enemies-to-lovers** stories, **Bound by Shadows** will keep you on the edge of your seat, wondering if the Don will surrender to his chosen bride—or if their **pasts** will consume them both. Discover a world where **love** is a dangerous game, and only the strongest hearts survive.

About the Author

Amara Holt is a storyteller whose novels immerse readers in a whirlwind of suspense, action, romance and adventure. With a keen eye for detail and a talent for crafting intricate plots, Amara captivates her audience with every twist and turn. Her compelling characters and atmospheric settings transport readers to thrilling worlds where danger lurks around every corner.